FIREBIRD OF GLASS

ZOE CHANT

For the hound-keepers and hidden heroes.

FAE SHIFTER KNIGHTS

Four shifter knights from a faery world are trapped in glass ornament avatars and find themselves in a strange world of vacuum cleaners, BigMarts, and ham sandwiches, bound to human keys who can unlock the power in their hearts.

Fae Shifter Knights is a sizzling portal fantasy paranormal romance series with side-splitting humor, thrilling adventure, and heart. Each stand-alone novel features noble heroes and brave, resourceful heroines, adorable pets, and one bad-tempered, non-binary fae.

Although this novel, *Firebird of Glass*, stands alone, this is the final book in the series, and it will make the most sense to read the books in order:

Dragon of Glass (book 1)
Unicorn of Glass (book 2)
Gryphon of Glass (book 3)

CHAPTER 1

$\mathcal{A}$nsel wasn't sure when he'd gotten used to having a big house full of people and pets and a foul-tempered fable.

The quiet was weird now, with most of them gone.

"I can hold," he said patiently into his phone. He stood up and paced to the kitchen.

Fabio, a golden-haired afghan hound, feared this meant further abandonment and followed him from the living room anxiously, pressing close to Ansel's knees. Tiny Vesta, a miniature Italian greyhound, startled from sleep, barked in a moment of alarm and then scampered down off the couch to follow them, making nervous, trembling circles.

"Would you guys relax?" Ansel said in gentle disgust. "I'm just going into the next room." When there was an expression of confusion at the other end of the phone, he hastily added, "No, not you, sorry, just the dogs! I'm calling to follow up on an email regarding the repair of a glass ornament…"

He was braced for the disappointing reply by now, thanked the artist for her time, and hung up.

"Superglue," he said in disbelief. This was the fourth glass crafter with the same answer: they couldn't repair broken glass. They could make a new ornament, or he could put the pieces together with superglue.

"Superglue!" he repeated in outrage, rummaging through one of the kitchen drawers to see if he even had any. They were suggesting that he superglue the pieces of a magical firebird ornament that housed a faery knight from another world together and just...hope that it worked.

And the worst part was that he didn't have a better idea.

The pieces in question were laid out on the counter, about a dozen chunks of red glass that had been spread wings, a long, swan-like neck, and a flaming tail. They were big pieces, at least, not a hopeless mess of shards, and the largest piece of all was the unbroken ring of white.

Henrik, Rez, and Trey had all puzzled mournfully over the parts of their shieldmate, Tadra, and tried all the tricks in their enchanted arsenal before declaring that there was no magic that they knew that could put her back together.

"Perhaps her key can magic her back together?" Ansel had suggested. "Or Robin?"

"I do not believe that either of them could call her from a broken vessel," Henrik said, frowning. A gryphon shifter, he was the knight most skilled at magic. "The ornament must be repaired in mundane fashion before magic could be worked on it."

"It is possible even her key could only bring her back in pieces if her avatar was not whole," Rez said mournfully. "I do not know if I could mend her human body." He was a unicorn shifter, with a specialty for healing.

"Robin was not able to free us from our glass prisons at all," Trey added. "But they may know what to do next."

Robin, their fable mentor, had been missing for more than a month now, hunting for Tadra's key in Ecuador. The knights from the faery world and their paired human keys had decided to try to find Robin shortly after the package with Tadra's broken avatar arrived in the mail, fearing the worst from their long absence.

Ansel was given the task of repairing the firebird...and taking care of the pets.

"It falls to you, landlord of light, to try to repair our shieldmate," Rez said solemnly. "Your world has wondrous crafters and miracles of technology. We trust you with the sister of our heart."

"You have fixed many things for us," Henrik added, looking sheepish and probably thinking about the garage door mechanism that he'd broken throwing an axe in frustration.

"You are an admirable hound-keeper," Trey said, ruffling Fabio's ears.

Ansel tried to feel honored by their trust, instead of just sidelined by his own mundanity.

He had to shove Fabio to one side now to try another drawer in his hunt for the right glue. White school glue wasn't going to cut it.

"Well," he said out loud, "you wanted to play *some* role in this grand fantasy adventure."

It was a lot of pressure being the only mortal man in a house full of fae shifter knights from another world. They could turn into a magnificent dragon, unicorn, and gryphon respectively, and with the assistance of their human keys, Daniella, Heather, and Gwen, could work actual magic.

Ansel? Ansel could pay the utilities and provide the house and put things back together when the knights were foiled by modern appliances.

With a battle to forestall the end of the world from galloping down on them, it didn't feel like his role was all that important.

Ansel was still bending over the junk drawer when he heard Vesta's telltale whine of greeting and there was a soft *thunk* at the end of the counter. "No, Socks, hssst!" he warned, and he stood up just in time to stop the Siamese from stalking right into the broken glass with a feline's disregard for anything fragile. Socks crouched down and glared at Ansel, not quite daring to walk past him on the counter. Unfortunately, Vesta thought that Socks had established a free-for-all for all pets on the counter, took a running start, and flung herself upwards.

"Nope!" Ansel intercepted the tiny Italian Greyhound mid-air and placed her back on the floor, whining in protest and dancing on her clacking claws.

Socks took his moment of distraction as an invitation and continued her march along the counter. One of the glass pieces chimed warningly against another and Ansel swept in to pluck her up and deposit her on the floor.

She hissed, swiping claws at Ansel. Vesta could not resist such temptation, barking and mock-charging, but she kept her distance; she'd been at the receiving end of those claws often enough to learn caution. Fabio whined and leaned against Ansel beseechingly.

Ansel carefully folded the glass shards back into the bubble wrap and tucked them into the box they'd come in, then waded with it through the tense standoff to return to his second-floor bedroom and shut the door on the dogs, who were not interested in letting him—the last human of the house!—out of their sight. Vesta yelped for a time and he could hear Fabio's heartbroken sighs as the afghan leaned against the door in defeat. Socks was undoubtedly back on the counter licking the faucet at the kitchen sink, just to be contrary.

Ansel found a tube of superglue in the back of his desk drawer and carefully unpacked Tadra's ornament once more, spreading each part out in order.

As puzzles went, it wasn't that difficult to figure out how everything fit together. The white ring was miraculously whole, and there were only sixteen pieces of the phoenix.

The first two shards, a clawed foot and a sheared leg, were the hardest—more because Ansel was still appalled by the idea of using superglue on a magical vessel than that it was an actual challenge to his dexterity. He stopped breathing altogether as he was applying the glue and then held the pieces together much longer than the instructions said, peeling his fingers off slowly and holding it up to the light.

It was a good seal and at some angles, he couldn't even see the break. Maybe this *was* going to work. He cautiously tested the bond and the joint didn't flex in the slightest.

The worst of it after that was the waiting between each joint, holding the parts carefully together until his hands cramped, meticulous about not letting it shift in his grip and spoil the seal. He tried not to think too hard about failing, about somehow making things worse with his efforts, and wished he'd thought of turning on music or television. On the other hand, he didn't want to be distracted from what was probably the most important, meticulous task he'd ever attempted.

Vesta finally quieted, which was probably an indication

that she'd found something to destroy to punish Ansel for abandoning her. Fabio occasionally turned over noisily just outside the door and gave a great mournful huff of breath. Socks yowled from downstairs at one point, undoubtedly lodging a complaint about her water dish or litter box.

Ansel only glued himself to the glass once, peeling the skin off his fingertips after the joint had finally cured. The joint looked clean after he rubbed off the excess glue, so hopefully, a little flesh in the glue wouldn't harm anything.

The firebird slowly took form from the pieces and Ansel felt a swell of satisfaction in his chest. It was delicate work, exacting and demanding, and the beautiful result was worth the time and patience. He held the final parts together and tried not to fidget.

Socks had stepped up the volume and frequency of her grievances, Vesta was yipping again, and Fabio was sniveling. Ansel's shoulders ached from hunching over the work so long. It was late and the dogs probably needed to go out, but he was so close to the end.

The red glass reflected like blood on his palms as Ansel cupped the firebird, focusing on keeping his grip steady. The superglue bottle said to hold for only a minute, but not to disturb the parts for at least ten minutes, and he was taking no chances. He watched the computer clock to make sure that nothing, including putting down the ornament, disrupted the cure.

Ten minutes had never seemed so long and his fingers were cramped from holding so long and hard, having to be so careful not to slip on the smooth glass.

If only…

Ansel tried not to let himself be jealous; he had plenty to be grateful for.

But watching the knights bond with their keys woke a longing in his soul that he never expected. To have a love like they had, a perfect partner like that...Ansel would have given anything for such a connection. He felt like an afterthought in their story, the sidekick, or the stranger at the crossroads. He was the sage advice, not the hero of the saga.

And he'd never win the princess...or in this case, the knight.

After all, Robin had cast a spell dowsing—searching—for Tadra's true key, and it had led them unerringly to South America.

The clock on the computer ticked past the allotted minute and Ansel released his fingers and let the firebird rest loosely in his hands. Tipping it into the light of the desk lamp betrayed the seams in turn, a slash of light in every place it had broken, but he could barely feel them when he ran fingers over each one.

The ornament was whole again, as whole as it would ever be, and there was no urgent desire or whispered words the way the keys had described their first encounters with their captive knights. There had been no call when Ansel first found all four of the ornaments, almost two years ago.

No matter how much he wanted to be, Ansel wasn't her key.

He nestled the firebird back down into the bubble wrap and stood up, rolling his protesting shoulders back.

The dogs heard him through the closed door and went ballistic, circling and whimpering in a near-frenzy. When he opened the door, he found the remains of one of the uglier couch cushions, torn into pieces across the hall.

"Who did this?" he demanded, looking at Vesta knowingly.

It was Fabio who looked most guilty, of course, but the smaller hound was the one with stuffing hanging from her mouth.

"I hope you didn't eat enough of it to make you sick," Ansel scolded her. "Heather would never forgive me."

Vesta's ears went flat back against her head and her eyes, already bulging in the fashion of her breed, went wild. Did she recognize her mistress's name? Ansel wasn't sure how smart the creature was—sometimes she seemed very clever, but she also ran repeatedly into walls and was scared of Christmas lights and crinkly bags.

"C'mon, you guys probably need to go out."

After he'd brought the dogs back inside, fed them, and rearranged the food in Socks's bowl to make it look full again, he climbed back up the stairs to his room, rubbing his sore fingers. Probably the fingerprints he'd rubbed off with glue would grow back.

He left the door open and Fabio and Vesta, after investigating the entire house in case their real people had quietly returned while they were eating, came in to compete for sleeping space on his big bed. Vesta took up a shocking amount of space for her tiny size and Fabio was not a small dog. Eventually, Socks would creep up and claim a spot at Ansel's feet—once it was late enough that she didn't look needy.

Ansel pulled off his shoes and socks, wiggling his toes in the plush carpet. Fabio was groaning and rolling around on his back with his paws in the air while Vesta burrowed down into the blankets, scratching with her claws.

Ansel was drawn back to the desk; a chance red reflection from the desk lamp shining on the ornament made the box look like it was on fire. He picked it up, his touch hopeful, but there was only his own yearning for something more, no immediate magical connection, no call to his soul.

He wasn't Tadra's key.

And his kiss wouldn't unlock her.

Later, he wasn't sure what it was that prompted him to brush his lips against it anyway. Did he think he'd regret not trying? Was there some shred of hope at the bottom of his empty heart? He certainly didn't *expect* it to work...and he nearly dropped the ornament when it did.

CHAPTER 2

The first thing Tadra knew again was pain.

She was shattered, the flame of her firebird soul fractured and burning its way through her human body. She tried to scream and failed, as memory flooded back like a landslide: battle, her shieldmates at her side, spells colliding in wild chaos, confused and unending imprisonment, and now this...

There was a strange, handsome man standing before her, his skin warm brown and his hair bleached golden-yellow, and Tadra struck out before she could think or make sense of the bizarre, dim-lit room.

She had no weapons, not even clothing, but she still caught him by surprise, realizing too late that he was holding the glass ornament that had been her prison for so long. They both watched in horror as it slipped from his grasp as she hit him. It fell—undamaged!—to a floor that seemed made of a dry fiber moss.

He scrambled after it. "It's okay. It's not broken," he exclaimed, standing with it cradled again in his hands. "I'm not going to hurt you!"

Tadra opened her mouth to protest that she was a knight of the broken crown and had no fear of him and found that the words burned in her throat and made no sound. He had enspelled her voice? Who was this upstart witch in his fancy trousers and curious workroom?

Tadra tried again to speak, to demand to know what he was doing with her glass firebird vessel and where this place was. Even if it did not hurt quite so much the second time, she was still quite incapable of making even a single strangled noise.

She turned in a circle, taking in the incomprehensible room. A dark, framed mirror—for scrying perhaps?— shelves of books, and a wide bed draped in rich blankets. There were wild creatures on it, rising to defend their master—a half-hound, half-horse with a floating golden mane, she thought, and the other seemed to be a hairless rat. There were no weapons at hand to take up, so she shifted to fight them back.

At first, she thought the world had expanded around her. She ought to fill the room with her firebird glory, but the walls stretched out in all directions and she realized in horror that she was impossibly tiny, barely the size of a songbird. The hound-things were excited by her shift and rose, baying and jumping. The witch flung himself between them, hollering an enchantment that involved words of power—*vesta* and *fabio* and *dammitdumbmutts!*—as he tried to keep the ornament safely out of their reach and prevent them from jumping at her all at once.

She made a circuit of the room and even her brightness was dimmed, not only her size. When she opened her beak to cry out in protest, she was still silent in this form. She fell on the man, swiping with claws, snapping with her beak at his unprotected face.

He flinched away, flinging up an arm, and cried,

"Tadra! Stop, please! I'm not going to harm you! Vesta, Fabio, *down!*"

The creatures ignored their master and Tadra paused in her attack. How did he know her name? He was still trying to protect her ornament; did it give him some power over her? She swooped down on him again, trying to make any sound and failing.

When she pivoted and flew away at the last moment, he lowered his arm trustingly—foolishly, Tadra thought. She was a firebird knight of the fallen crown and even in this size and strange world should be able to bring him down with ease. She alighted on a rod near the ceiling that held draperies and stared across the room at him.

To her surprise, he put the ornament gently down in a box filled with some kind of captured bubbles near an unflickering lamp with no smoke.

"Tadra," he said, turning back to her, and he put out both his hands.

It took Tadra a moment to realize that he intended her to land there. The idea of landing on someone at her usual size was absurd! She opened her beak to squawk a protest that wouldn't sound and clacked it instead. The hounds were still milling around him, leaping on and off the tousled bed as they barked and ignored his commands.

"If you can't mind your manners, get *out*," he commanded at last, and he caught the small one in his hands and herded the other with his knees to the door, forcing them both out and then latching the smooth-hinged door behind.

"Tadra," he said again, turning back and offering his hands. "My name is Ansel. I am a friend to your shield-mates, Trey, Henrik, and Rez, and your mentor, Robin. I am sorry they are not here to greet you themselves. I know this is really confusing, and I'm not sure what to say to convince you."

Tadra hopped along the drapery rod but did not offer to fly to him. When she reached for magic to renew her strength, she could not sense it anywhere nearby. Were they in some kind of ward that dampened her power? Had this man cast a spell on her?

Ansel was continuing to speak, slowly and gently. "You're in a place called Wimberlette; it's a little town in Michigan, which will mean exactly nothing to you. Uh, okay, Henrik said that you would like chocolate, but oh, you don't know what that is yet. Robin said you were the bravest of their knights, and the most foolish. Which seemed like it was saying a lot, given how foolish and brave your shieldmates are."

Robin. Robin was here somewhere. And if they were here, and if they truly trusted Ansel, Tadra might too. Then, it could be a ploy of some kind. Did he mean to trick her?

The only exit was the door behind him, a door where she could still hear the half-hounds howling and scratching. She wasn't going to let her guard down, but the witch's—Ansel's—goal did not appear to be her immediate destruction. She would accept his truce and watch and wait for his true nature to show.

CHAPTER 3

*A*nsel felt a thrill of triumph when Tadra flew to land in his hands, followed swiftly by alarm. She weighed almost nothing, but appeared to be on fire, her tail and wings shedding sparks like a blacksmith's grindstone. She didn't feel hot to the touch and his skin didn't burn any more than his curtains had. He relaxed, gazing down at her tiny form in rapt wonder. As small as she was, she was shaped more like a swan than a songbird, and her tail was almost serpentine, feathered in flickering embers. Gleaming black eyes blinked at him, and then she was shifting in his hands.

Cupping her firebird form translated to cradling her face when she was standing before him in her human form, and Ansel was struck absolutely dumb by the feel of her skin against his palms. She had been attractive enough striking out at him, her flame-red hair wild around her pale, bare shoulders, but now, standing still and gazing up at him with quiet patience, Ansel thought he'd never seen anything in the world so beautiful and breath-taking.

She was smaller than Ansel had anticipated from the

other knights' descriptions of her fighting prowess; he had somehow expected her to be of Amazon height and build, but she was very close to his own height and slight, if clearly strong and fit.

She was also *completely* naked, and that was disturbing Ansel's ability to form words or think straight.

They'd made up a room for her and there were clothes in the room, but Ansel wasn't sure if he'd be able to make it that far. Robe. He could lend her a robe.

"Here...let me...I can...you should..."

Ansel had to let go of her first, and no part of him wanted to. It wasn't magic, he didn't think, it was just that she was a whole lot of gorgeous naked woman and it been a really long time since he had one of those in close proximity. And despite all those tantalizing, curvy parts below her neck, it was her face that Ansel wanted to gaze at most.

He could fall straight into those golden-brown eyes...and he wasn't sure he'd make it back out in one piece.

She tried to speak again. Ansel could see her mouth move, feel her jaw in his hands, and she was puzzled and frustrated, lifting one hand to run her fingers over her lips. The question on her face was obvious.

"I don't know why you can't talk," he said, finally able to pry his hands away from her. This, unfortunately, gave him a much clearer view of the rest of her and, for a moment, he was as speechless as she was. "Your ornament," he managed, after a few attempts. "It broke. Maybe that's why?"

He wrenched himself away and went to his closet. He could think more clearly with his back to her and when he brought the bathrobe back to her, he kept his eyes averted to the side.

She took the garment and Ansel saw her mouth words

that must have been polite gratitude out of the corner of his vision. Not looking at her made communication even more complicated; he was glad when she drew the sleeves over her arms and tied the belt around her waist.

It was only a little big on her, the seams just off her shoulders, but it made her look smaller and more lost than ever. She was asking something, her mouth working and her hands fluttering, and Ansel had to guess what it might be.

"Are you wondering where your shieldmates are?" he hazarded. If he'd suddenly woken up in a weird world, he'd want to know where *his* friends were.

She nodded rapidly and added something anxious.

"They're fine, great. Probably." Even clothed, she made it hard for Ansel to think straight. "Robin cast a spell and found your key, but when they went to get him, they didn't come back. So the team—your knights and their keys—went to find them. I don't know when they'll return."

Tadra's face scrunched in confusion. She mouthed words, then made a fist with her hand, her thumb on top, and twisted it. A key, Ansel thought. She shrugged and spread her hands.

"Oh, keys, of course, you wouldn't know." Ansel knew he was making a mess of explaining things. He hadn't expected to accidentally release Tadra, and he hadn't prepared for this in the slightest. "The spell that sent each of you here was supposed to help you find the person in this world who could help you unlock your power. Your magic works differently here, and you need a local to help you tap it. Daniella is the key for Trey, Heather for Rez, Gwen for Henrik." But not Ansel for Tadra, he remembered, and his disappointment was like a splinter under a fingernail.

She looked down at her hands and nodded slowly, then made a small shape with her hands and expanded it with a broad, spread-fingered wave. Her small firebird size, compared to the size she'd expected, perhaps? She gave a soundless sigh and her shoulders slumped inside the robe.

"Are you hungry?" he asked, casting for something to offer her to cheer her up. "I have food."

She bobbed her head without enthusiasm and Ansel opened the door for her, momentarily forgetting about the dogs waiting on the other side. They swarmed in, more of a pack than two dogs ought to be, particularly since one of them was smaller than a loaf of bread. "Vesta, Fabio, behave now."

Tadra knelt fearlessly before them as Ansel introduced them. "Fabio's the sweetheart with the buttery hair and Vesta is the little nervous one."

They greeted her with wagging tails and whines, Fabio trying to lick her face as Vesta danced on her hind feet and quivered in excitement. Tadra smiled and Ansel guessed she was giggling by the shake to her shoulders. She was deft about keeping Fabio's tongue from her face, and after a moment of petting each of them, she stood again.

"How about some food?" Ansel offered. He should be chivalrous; the knights were always painfully polite. He offered his arm, hoping he didn't look too foolish.

She lifted her chin and slipped her hand into his elbow.

"This is Gwen and Henrik's room, this one is yours," he said, as they passed the doors, pausing to look briefly in.

She drew her fingers along the railing as they went down the stairs, touching things curiously. Ansel tried to explain as they went, "That's a television, that's a thermostat." He knew it must be meaningless.

Tadra drew to a stop at a framed photograph of Daniella, Heather, Trey, Rez, and Gwen. Fabio was resting his head on Daniella's knee and Vesta was in Heather's arms. Robin sat on the back of the couch behind the rest with their arms crossed; a casual viewer might wonder why a lifelike doll had been posed in the picture.

Her mouth in a soundless little O, Tadra touched the glass and glanced at Ansel. She mouthed something, but Ansel had no context for what she was asking. Maybe she was wondering why Henrik wasn't in the photo? "That was taken before we found Henrik's ornament," he explained. Tadra didn't look satisfied with the answer.

"I worried about putting this out where someone might see it," he confessed. "This world doesn't have fables, but we do have stories about fairies. I was surprised that Robin's wings don't show in the photo, but I guess it makes sense, since they say we only see an aspect of the magic."

Tadra was still looking at him expectantly, so Ansel tried to explain further. "I guess, for you, in your world, magic is something you can see and understand and control, but we don't have magic here, at least not that we know about. Robin says that our minds interpret it in some way that makes sense for each of us. We all see a different style of wing on the fable, and each of the keys has a different way of channeling magic for their knight."

Tadra's brow furrowed skeptically.

"Daniella sings," Ansel said. "She hears magic as music. Heather sees the magic as glowing fibers and can weave and knit them. Gwen sees it like a video game interface, with options that she can control." He pointed out each of the keys in the photo.

That, of course, only confused Tadra further and Ansel flailed trying to explain video games as he led her into the kitchen.

What did you feed a mute knight from a faery world? It occurred to Ansel to wonder if her throat had been damaged and if she'd be able to eat at all. "You can sit here," he offered, pointing at one of the stools on the far side of the kitchen island.

The fact that it could spin caught Tadra by surprise, and she was first alarmed and then delighted, testing its range of motion with interest and spinning in slow circles.

Ansel poured her a glass of water first, and she carefully turned it to look at the bar logo, mouthing the name. Of course she could read, Ansel realized. All the knights were literate, and Trey had already charmed the local librarian into letting him use Daniella's library card whenever he visited. A story about losing his own identification while he was traveling had been unconvincing, but librarians were the kind of people who recognized a story when they were in one, and they rarely impeded reading.

Ansel realized that if she could read, she could write, and he found the notepad that he kept by the house phone, as well as a pen, then showed her how to click it open to expose the tip and show her how it wrote. "You probably have a lot of questions, and I'll answer anything I can."

She was thrilled by the device and clicked it several times before settling down to write while Ansel went to the other side of the island and loaded a plate with everything he thought she might like: chocolate chip cookies, a handful of potato chips, a slice of cheese, a pickle, some strawberries, a few nuts… His own stomach grumbled and he made up a second plate for himself. "How hungry are you?" he asked. "Should I turn on the oven for a pizza or dinner pockets?"

Tadra wiggled her fingers in what Ansel guessed was a "medium" or "so-so" answer. "We can start with this," he decided, and Tadra nodded agreeably as she bent and wrote another line on her paper.

She put the pen down and set the notepad aside when

he brought her the heaped plate. "Does your…throat hurt? Will you be able to eat?"

Tadra started to mime something, then reached for the pen and wrote "Did hurt. Doesn't now."

Ansel glanced at the lines above it.

> *Where are we?*
> *Was Cerad brought to justice?*
> *Were my shieldmates hurt? Are we all mute?*
> *What is your title?*
> *How do I get back home?*

Her handwriting was tidy, like a scholar's, with a slight cant to it and the very barest of flourishes.

She didn't need words to express how pleased she was with the food, tasting a little of everything first, and savoring every bite with amazement and interest. Ansel took more pleasure in watching her eat than he did in his own plate, even though his long labor over the ornament had left him hungry.

Vesta and Fabio begged at their feet.

"Let me try to explain as much as I can," he said when he realized he couldn't just gaze besottedly at her. "You were caught in a battle."

Her face went still and full of sorrow. She nodded.

"There was a spell…no, I guess there were a couple of spells. Cerad tried to make you fragile, and Robin tried to save you. And I think that Henrik was doing something, too, and maybe there was more. You would probably know how it worked better than I do, since you were actually there, and you understand how magic works. But the end of it is that the four of you and Robin were sent here, to our world, and you were imprisoned in glass, from which you could…only be released by your keys."

Except that he wasn't her key. "Well, at least, I thought…"

She licked her fingers and wrote, then tipped the pad to him. "You can do magic?"

Ansel shook his head. "No. Aside from what the keys can do with the knights, magic is just a myth here. Though, we do have a lot of technology that looks like magic at first."

She tapped the second question.

Ansel dreaded giving her the answer, but reluctantly did. "He won. Your world has fallen. Robin described a land washed in darkness and despair, beyond saving."

Tadra bowed her head over her food and chased a macadamia nut around her plate, then straightened bravely and tapped the next question.

"Your shieldmates were fine just a few days ago," Ansel could promise. "They can speak, and are in good health. They're really happy here. Their keys are their perfect partners in every way, and they've adapted to our society quite well. We've only had a few minor house fires."

She gave a silent sigh of relief and gave Ansel a very thoughtful look as she touched the next line.

"Just Ansel," he said apologetically.

Tadra's eyebrows knit in confusion. She wrote, "Justice? As in law?"

"No," Ansel said. "*Only* Ansel. I don't have a title. I'm not a knight of a realm or a prince or a wizard. Just…me. Keeper of hounds, I guess. But…"

He didn't want to tell her the rest. He wanted to leave her thinking that this world was safe for them, that she would be happily reunited with her shieldmates and her greatest hurdle would be figuring out how to use a flush toilet and a microwave.

She tapped him with her pen and glared at him. She

didn't need to write out that she knew he was keeping something from her.

"The veil between our worlds weakens with the year," Ansel said reluctantly. "And Cerad has designs on adding this one to his conquests. Last year, we—well, *they*, not me." He wasn't a warrior; she'd learn that soon enough and stop looking at him with appraising respect. "Trey and Daniella and Robin and Henrik's key Gwen fought bleaks and dours to keep them from opening portals and letting a great army through. It was everything that they could do to win the day, and Robin fears we'll need all four of you, with all the magic we can muster to fend them off again this year."

Tadra swallowed. She was watching his face carefully, and he could not help but look at her just as closely, using the excuse of her silence as a reason to watch her for clues. Her face looked sadder now, drawn and tired. She clicked the pen and dropped her gaze at last, crossing off her final question.

CHAPTER 4

The hound-keeper, Ansel, was patient with Tadra's questions, and with the time it took her to write words out when expressing things with her hands failed.

"I can teach you some sign language," Ansel said as he collected their plates and took them back into the gleaming food workshop.

Tadra cocked her head at him, waiting for him to explain, and he gestured for her to follow him. She gathered up the fine paper he'd given her, along with the dipless pen. He led her down a hallway, not touching her in a curious, careful way that suggested he wanted to but wasn't sure how to, until they came to a room where smokeless lights sprang to life at his command. She didn't understand how that could be possible without magic. She didn't understand any of this.

He noticed her awe and showed her a switch on the wall that he'd used and turned the lights off and back on to demonstrate, then let her try it. That didn't really diminish the wonder of it.

They sat together on a wide couch facing a black painting and Ansel took what looked like a plate of print-setting type into his lap. Vesta and Fabio both leapt up beside them, Vesta trembling on Ansel's far side and Fabio taking as much space as he could and putting his head trustingly in Tadra's lap.

With a few of Ansel's touches on that board of letters —Tadra tried to memorize the ritual as he did it—the dark painting on the wall came to life and proved to be a portal or perhaps a scrying surface.

Ansel spoke as he worked. "We have something called the Internet, a vast network of information, like a library, but interactive and virtual."

Virtual? It was...*almost* a library? Not quite?

"What's a word you'd like to be able to say?" Ansel asked.

Tadra pondered. What words were important to her? She circled the word shieldmate on her list.

"That's not a thing we have here," Ansel said apologetically. "Pretty sure there's not a sign for that. We might have to make one up."

Tadra felt slow and stupid. She was caught in a world where she knew so little that she couldn't think of what to ask.

"What kind of things would you need to tell us?" Ansel suggested kindly. "Like, *hungry*, or *I have to use the bathroom?*"

Tadra nodded agreeably and Ansel pressed letters that appeared on the scrying surface. She gazed in wonder as he did something with his hands she couldn't even follow and it turned into a portal of a woman making motions with her hands. But it wasn't magic?

"Hungry!" Ansel said, and they followed the teacher's example of making a C with their right hands and moving it from neck to stomach. "Okay, I can see how they came up with this. It makes some sense."

Bathroom—apparently what they called the necessity in this world—proved to be a thumb through the next two fingers, held palm forward and twisted side-to-side. The teacher—a different one, standing in a different scrying surface—explained a way to remember it as the letter T for toilet, and this led them to practice the alphabet together for a while, though spelling words out by sign proved time-consuming and even more frustrating than writing things down.

They chased words through conversation, Tadra half-writing, half-pointing: *dog, chair, couch, computer*—though she wasn't sure when she'd use that in casual talk. *Yes, no, thank you, good, bad. Sorry, you're welcome. Tell me, show you.* The more abstract words were harder to remember, and they quizzed back and forth as Tadra tried desperately to hold them all in her head.

Danger, fight, help, fly, friend, right, wrong… her paper grew crowded with words and she wrote smaller and smaller, not wanting to waste another precious page.

Key, she wrote at last.

Her earlier guess for the word has been surprisingly close; many of the signs made a certain amount of logical sense, which made them easier to remember. They signed it to each other, and Tadra caught herself looking at Ansel's face in wonder.

He was her...key. He had freed her from her prison, and he would be her conduit to what magic this world had.

Tell me key, she signed at him, coaxing with her hands for more.

Ansel looked flustered, though no flush showed on his brown cheeks and he didn't drop his gaze; he blinked more quickly, and his mouth tightened. He didn't even bother trying to limit his explanation to the few signs they knew, but spoke in words. "It's magic, which I couldn't start to explain, but Robin says that each of your keys here is...a person here who is your other half, your perfect match, someone you have a deep connection with at once. A...soulmate."

He did turn his eyes aside then, looking conflicted. Did he not wish to be her key? Was there some burden to the task, such that he didn't want to bear it?

He went on quietly, not looking at her. "The closer you get with your key, the more you...love each other...the more powerful you will be."

Love, she wrote, and to her surprise, Ansel didn't have to use his scrying computer for this one. He put up his smallest and pointer fingers, thumb extended outwards. "It's...shorthand for I love you," he said, pointing out how the I and L and Y combined. "Some signs are commonly used among the hearing, too."

She *could* love this man, Tadra decided, forming the sign with her hand. She already trusted him and could tell that he had a true heart and a clever mind. He was kind to his ill-trained hounds, and patient with her whenever she grew frustrated with her puzzling inability to speak. He had fixed her broken glass prison, a testament to his patience and skill. And he was courteous, assuming no liberties with her person from his bond with her.

Tadra almost wished he'd take those liberties.

He was so handsome and strong, with his shocking bright hair and his sepia skin. There was the barest stubble at his finely shaped chin. She found herself tracing the lines of his neck with her gaze, and the breadth of his shoulders, wondering what it would be like to feel it with her fingers. It stirred something inside of her, making her keenly aware of her own skin against the silky fabric of the robe that was all she was wearing.

He was within arm's reach; all she had to do was extend her hand and touch him, and she craved that touch in a way she had never craved it of her shieldmates, more than merely for comfort and comradery.

"Are you okay?" Ansel asked in concern, and Tadra abruptly realized she wasn't. All the energy in her body felt as if it had suddenly been sucked out of her.

Tired, she wrote briefly, and Ansel didn't think for a moment that she meant it as the next word they should learn.

"You've been through a lot," he said, banishing the scrying screen with a few swift movements. "I can show you to your room and you can rest."

The hounds recognized the cues at once. The tiny dog bolted off the couch and began to make laps of the room and Fabio groaned in her lap, not wanting to move.

Tadra was alarmed to find that she had trouble pushing him off. She was never the strongest of her shield-mates, with her smaller frame and slighter build, but she had always outlasted the other knights, tough and dogged at any task. Now, it seemed that even breathing was a labor. Her arms ached, and she was finding it difficult to concentrate. Exhaustion made her want to simply lie down in Ansel's lap where she would be safe and could sleep again at last; the weight of a hound's head seemed insurmountable.

CHAPTER 5

*A*nsel hadn't been oblivious to Tadra's swiftly draining energy. Her graceful hand motions grew abruptly clumsier and she was slower to react. Had something happened? Was she sick? It was sudden and alarming.

"Fabio, off!" he commanded, getting to his own feet.

Fabio heaved a great sigh and rolled reluctantly off the couch. Tadra looked at her legs in consternation, as if she was expecting them to do something they couldn't.

"Here…" Ansel offered her an arm, and she clasped him by the forearm and flowed back up to her feet.

Sorry, she signed with her free hand.

"No," Ansel said swiftly. "No, don't be sorry. Everything is really strange, and it's a lot to take in, and it's no wonder if you need some time to recover. You've been stuck in your ornament much longer than your shield-mates, and it was *broken*. You probably need time to heal." He cast about for something comforting. "Maybe tomorrow, you'll be able to speak again. There's so much we don't know." Maybe Robin would have some fix for her when they came back with the rest of the team.

Back...with Tadra's key.

She smiled wanly at him and tucked her arm into his. She leaned much more heavily on him returning up the stairs than she had coming down them; Ansel was not sure if she would have remained standing without his support, and their progress was slow.

"This is the bathroom," he said, stopping there first. "I'm afraid you'll have to share it with Gwen and Henrik. They have the next room after yours."

He demonstrated the faucets and Tadra looked amply impressed, trailing her fingers through the warm water. He signed *toilet* at her and lifted the lid. "You sit here, do what you need to. Close the lid when you're done because the dogs are disgusting and will drink out of it if you don't and Vesta might drown in it because she's not that bright. This handle flushes it, like so..."

Tadra startled back at the noisy flush and watched the water swirl away in wonder, clinging to the counter.

"I can give you privacy, if you need to..."

Tadra shook her head wearily and mimed putting her head on a pillow.

"This way." Ansel skipped the shower and bathroom appliances and helped her to the room they had prepared, opening the door to the closet to show her the clothing that had been set out for her and pointing out the electrical sockets. "Don't put anything in those little holes," he cautioned. "This is the light switch, here."

Tadra absorbed it all, not offering to touch anything, her hands clasped before her and Ansel turned back from closing the curtains and caught her swaying in place.

"Here," he said quickly, throwing back her blankets.

"Lie down, before you fall down. You can sleep as long as you need."

Tadra staggered to the bed and laid down, and when she seemed incapable of arranging her limbs, Ansel cautiously straightened her legs and tucked her arms in, trying not to linger over the feel of her limbs under his fingers under the thin robe. He pulled the fabric smooth and with every scrap of self-control that he had, flipped the blanket back over her. One of her hands caught his and she gave him a quick, grateful squeeze.

"Sleep," he murmured, but when he tried to take his hand back, Tadra held on, so he sank down on the mattress to sit beside her.

She gave a sigh of contentment—the air made some sound, even if it was a poor echo of the noisy, throaty sighs that Fabio was capable of vocalizing—and closed her eyes.

Ansel stared at her, like she was a subject he wanted to memorize to draw later.

There were not enough freckles on her pale skin to call her freckled, but too many to entirely discount. She was so pale that he could see the blue veins of her blood at her temples, and there was a slight diagonal scar at the bridge of her nose. Her hair was a bold shade of red—dark, but too true of hue to be auburn; it looked as dyed as Ansel's, but he suspected that it was natural on her. As natural as a magical firebird shifter from a faery kingdom could be.

Her hand in his felt like a home he'd never known to yearn for, and he held it long after her breathing went steady and even with sleep.

Finally, he slipped his hand slowly from hers and tucked the blanket up around her chin. For a guilty moment, he wanted to lean over and kiss her, even just a chaste brush on the forehead, but he'd already caused enough trouble with ill-planned kisses.

Instead, he stood and turned off the light. He left the door open, wanting to be able to hear if she—oh, but she wouldn't be able to call for him. Maybe he should get a bell for her to ring if she needed anything. There was a Christmas bell in the decorations that Daniella had put out, he could put it on her bedside table for her.

Walking quietly through the house with the dogs anxiously following so close that they stepped on his heels more than once, Ansel found the bell and returned to Tadra's room with it. Would she figure out what it was for? Should he leave a note explaining it? He realized that he was gazing down at her again and shook himself impatiently.

He tripped over Fabio trying to leave her room, cursed quietly, and went back to his own room to get his phone. There were no missed calls.

He shut the door and called Daniella's cellphone. It went straight to voicemail, and he left a brief, urgent message. "I know you guys just left, but Tadra is here, in *person*, and I think you should get back here right away. I hope you've had good luck finding Robin and..." Tadra's key, Ansel told himself firmly, but he couldn't bring himself to say it out loud. "Hope to see you really soon."

He left the same message on Heather's line. Gwen had left her own phone behind, as he found out when he called her and it started ringing in her room.

He hung up and put the phone facedown on his desk, carefully picking the glass firebird up from its nest of bubble wrap.

"C'mon guys," he said to the back of his phone. "Get back here before I do something dumb like fall in love with this woman."

He wondered if it wasn't already too late.

CHAPTER 6

*T*adra woke up feeling a lot more like herself and blinked up at a curious white plaster ceiling in a perfectly rectangular grid. There was light coming in around the curtains, but she had no idea what time of day it might be.

She tried to move and had a moment of dismay, thinking that her legs were still heavy with exhaustion. There was a sleepy little *mrrrt* of protest and she realized that there was a cat sleeping on top of them. When she sat upright, the cat made an irritated noise, stretched, and began to groom itself. It was a pale, cream-colored feline with dark points and accusing pale blue eyes.

Tadra opened her mouth to greet it and didn't remember that she couldn't speak until she had tried. She touched her lips with a hand and frowned. She had hoped that her voice would return with rest, but as hard as she tried, she could not make any sounds that were not air in her mouth.

She threw the blankets aside, startling the cat. It puffed

into an arch of outrage and stalked away, just slowly enough to make its point as the superior creature. Cats were apparently exactly the same in this world as in Tadra's and she found that comforting.

Tadra swung her legs off and wiggled her toes in the strange, soft floor covering. She was wearing the robe that Ansel had given her the night before, and it still smelled faintly of him, which was pleasant and reassuring. She remembered the wardrobe-room that he had shown her, but when she looked at the choices, the selection was almost overwhelming.

After some consideration, she took a pair of soft breeches and a tunic of blue, with a sparkling butterfly on the front. There were socks and underthings laid out, the purpose of each of them clear. The fabric was impressively tightly woven, but surprisingly stretchy.

She was, by now, in considerable need of the necessity that Ansel had shown her the night before.

The flush was as alarming as it had been when Ansel demonstrated it, but Tadra found herself admiring the efficiency. She used the water pump that didn't require pumping and let the warm water pour over her hands for a decadent moment. She smelled the potions beside the sink, but didn't dare to use any of them, uncertain of their purpose.

What a world of riches and wonders.

The cat had vanished, but when Tadra came quietly down the long stairs, the dogs suddenly realized she was there and swarmed at her feet, their tails wagging. There was no sign of Ansel, but there was a bowl filled with tiny dry food on the counter of the kitchen-workshop with a note by it.

This is cereal. It's best with milk on it. Milk is in the fridge. I'll be back very soon. He had signed it *Ansel,* with a big round cursive A, and he had underlined the word very.

There was a spoon by the bowl.

Tadra looked around the kitchen. Fridge. What was a fridge? It had to be big enough to hold a milk pail, and she remembered the device of cold that Ansel had shown her.

A tug on the door revealed a lit chamber. There were two items within it labeled milk in fancy, decorated boxes. She chose one at random and returned to the counter. Was the spoon for dispensing the milk? Perhaps milk was very precious here; the boxes were not large. She unscrewed the tiny lid, measured out a spoonful and sprinkled it over the contents of the bowl.

The dogs watched her raptly as she did this, swirling around at her feet hopefully and she gave each of them one of the little irregular clumps. Fabio seemed to inhale his and nearly took Tadra's finger with it. Vesta chewed hers once and left it on the floor for Fabio to pounce on.

They both looked hopefully back up at her as if they had received nothing.

Tadra took the bowl back to the spinning stool where she'd eaten the night before. It was brighter outside and the room looked more welcoming. It helped that she felt considerably stronger. Her trembling enfeeblement of the night before had frightened her as much as the unaccustomed world.

She ate the dampened pieces of food with interest using her fingers—it seemed to be some kind of sweetened grain in clusters, and it was filling and pleasantly spiced.

The dogs didn't take their eyes off of her once while she ate, not even Vesta, who had rejected her previous offering.

When she had emptied the bowl, Tadra felt considerably better. Perhaps her fleeting frailty had only been caused by long hunger and a need for sleep.

She hopped down from the stool and tripped over Fabio, who stood up at exactly the wrong moment. Caught by surprise, Tadra shifted and flew rather than falling, and the dogs went mad at the sight of her firebird, barking and pinwheeling in place beneath her. She could not resist teasing them, staying just up out of their reach as she explored the house and gazed outside at the quaint little community of cottages, just visible through snow-covered brush.

She found the glass creatures that must have housed her shieldmates hanging over a window in the kitchen, shooting light through the room in green, blue, and gold; she had not noticed them against the dark window at night. Her own was not hung with them; Ansel must still have it in his private rooms.

There was a smaller bathroom on this floor, and a bedroom much like Ansel's, as well as a pantry, a modest dining hall, a gathering room with couches, and the room where they had learned signs from the portal-teachers. Tadra didn't move things, not sure what protections they might have, but she poked into corners and tried to make sense of the curious furniture and dark scrying portals, looking for clues that her shieldmates lived here and were truly happy.

She found many. There were tiny paintings everywhere, magically exacting in their accuracy. The downstairs room obviously belonged to Trey, and there were as many depictions of Fabio as there were of the knight and his key, including one where the hound was gleefully holding a curved yellow box labeled "I Can't Believe It's Not Butter! The Original."

The dogs followed her everywhere, excited whenever she shifted back and forth, as if she'd just returned from a long journey and she was their favorite person ever.

There was a larger door near the door to the house and it opened to a massive space that was clearly a place to spar, with thin mats down over a hard floor that seemed to be a single slab of rock full of inclusions. Weapons hung on the wall here, an axe as Henrik preferred, a sword of a design that Tadra had never seen, as well as more standard configurations, and a few battle staves.

She picked one up, testing her constitution with a few swings and turns. Fabio barked and fell to his elbows in an invitation to play. Tadra returned the weapon to the place she'd found it. She was certainly stronger than she'd been the night before; she would be able to fight in human form if her fate required it, even if her firebird was small and helpless.

Climbing back up the long stairs didn't wind her, and Tadra opened each door to investigate every room.

The suite to the left of the stairs was spacious, with its own bathroom and a wardrobe-room large enough for a dance hall. It was filled with beautiful dresses that might indicate a woman of rank and stacked bins of raw fiber and uncut cloth in all the colors that Tadra had ever seen. There were likenesses of Rez here, standing with the woman who must be Heather. They were smiling at each other, and Tadra was struck by his happiness and her obvious adoration.

She was not sure she had ever seen him look so content and joyful in all the years she'd known him.

The room beside her own was much more utilitarian, with a similar configuration and the same snowy view from the window. There were no pictures of Henrik, but Tadra recognized Gwen from the artwork downstairs, and there were others who looked like her in the frozen portals hung on the wall. Their wardrobe-room had a white uniform hanging in it, a woven black belt draped around the hanging hook.

She walked past her own door, and the final room on that floor was Ansel's.

It, like the kitchen workshop, looked much brighter and less frightful in the light of the day. Tadra sat down on the bed and the dogs leaped up beside her and made groaning noises of delight, rolling and playing on the smooth fabric spread. She patted Fabio absently and looked around, trying to absorb clues about the man who was her key in this world.

He was tidy, but not obsessive; there were a few items of clothing flung casually over the back of a chair, but the floor was clean. The surface of his desk was uncluttered, with just a few tools of his craft and Tadra's ornament was in a box in the center, nestled safely in a curious transparent fabric made of bubbles. There was also a ring of white glass in the box, a fine strand of golden thread dangling where the firebird should hang.

She stood up and lifted the central ornament carefully into her hands, mindful of the dogs wrestling good-naturedly on the bed behind her. It would be just her luck to break her avatar again, after Ansel had clearly put so much effort in putting her back together.

It was a cunning representation of her firebird, and close in size to her actual diminished form in this world. She turned it in the sunlight, watching the light play through it and reflect from the seams where it had been repaired. There was one at her firebird's throat, and she touched her neck as if she might feel it there on her flesh. Was that why she couldn't speak?

She returned it reverently to the box and traced the ring that framed it, feeling a distant shiver of magic.

Beside the box was a sketchbook with a hard black cover and metal wire binding. Tadra hesitated only a moment before opening it. She wanted to know everything she could about Ansel. He was her key.

CHAPTER 7

*A*nsel pulled the car eagerly up in front of the garage, his stomach a tangle of nerves and excitement.

He hated every moment that he'd been away, worried that Tadra would be awake and alone, but more worried that she wouldn't be awake, that she'd slipped into a terrible coma because he'd bungled her repair and ruined everything. Maybe he shouldn't have even tried. He should have just waited until Robin had returned with the others.

He opened the trunk and hooked bags over his arms, considered the logistics of the other things he'd bought, and left them there, awkwardly pulling the trunk lid down to keep snow from filling it.

He kept remembering Tadra's fluttering hands and her wild red hair, the way she'd looked naked—he had to jerk his thoughts away from that memory a lot. Her lively wit, her look of concentration as she memorized hand signs and absorbed all the wonders and technology he showed her.

The helpless sorrow in her face when she learned the fate of her world.

Even just thinking about that grief made Ansel desperate to fix it for her, but he knew that it was nothing he could repair with superglue and patience.

The dogs howled to greet him when he fumbled the keys in the door with one hand and he had to knee Fabio back as he came in, holding the groceries out of the way. "Yes, yes, I'm happy to see you, too," he scolded.

Vesta stood on the back of the couch so she'd be taller and barked until his ears were ringing.

Then Tadra was flitting down the stairs and Ansel didn't even notice the dogs.

She was dressed in a stretchy blue T-shirt, a sequin butterfly across her chest, and the knights had guessed her size well; the jeans looked like a good fit. Her hair was tousled from sleep and she was clutching something to her chest.

Ansel winced when he realized that she was holding his sketchbook. He never shared his work and was loath to sketch in public, preferring to keep his artwork hidden. He hadn't picked it up in months, because the house was hard to find privacy in when it was full of knights with a poor sense of personal space and a fable who went out of their way to be as annoying as possible.

She didn't offer to speak, so Ansel guessed that she still couldn't. She signed *hello* and Ansel nearly dropped his groceries trying to sign back before he remembered that he could say it out loud himself. "Hi."

She lifted the sketchbook with a curious look.

"I...ah…"

She put the sketchbook down on the counter and asked questions with her eyes about the grocery bags he was holding, crowding close as she touched the crinkly plastic in wonder and tried to peer into them.

"I got some more food," he said. "I hadn't stocked up on groceries because I wasn't sure when the rest of them would be back, and there were a few things I thought you might like." He almost tripped over Fabio taking the bags to the kitchen counter. "Fabio, out of the kitchen. Here, Tadra, I'll show you!"

Sharing his grocery store purchases with Tadra gave it all new meaning, and Ansel thought that no Christmas in the world could compare to watching her discover each mundane item.

The carton of eggs was opened and shut until he worried for the cardboard hinge, and she marveled over the grapes, eating a few with relish when he urged her to. She was as fascinated by the packaging as she was the contents, crinkling and un-crinkling one of the empty bags and laughing soundlessly as it sprang back to its original shape.

She was like a child...and so very not, Ansel thought, watching her turn the frozen pizza package over in her hands as if she suspected it was a threat. "I got you one with cheese," he explained. "All I had in the freezer was the cheese-free kind, and I've been told it's not very good. I thought you should have a better introduction to our earth food."

She rubbed her stomach, then pointed at a picture of cheese on the pizza box. They hadn't learned the word for *cheese* yet, but Ansel could guess what she meant.

"Oh, I got you something else," he remembered, when she found the package of markers. "Be right back…"

Fabio followed him outside and Vesta wasn't going to be left behind. She plowed directly into the few inches of snow, yelped in outrage, and jumped from footprint to footprint to tail Ansel to the car. "C'mon you guys," Ansel told them, but Fabio was sniffing urgently for a place to relieve himself and Vesta was whining to be picked up, thoroughly over the slushy snow covering the driveway.

"I can't carry you," Ansel protested, his arms full. "Fabio, hurry *up!*"

When he finally got them all herded back inside, Tadra had managed to draw on the tips of her fingers with the markers. She shrugged and grinned at Ansel, showing off the blue stains.

"That's what these are for," he explained, holding up the whiteboards. "I'll hang them up around the house and you can always have a place to write." He propped it up against the coffee maker and demonstrated with a bold red squiggle that he promptly erased with his thumb.

Tadra's eyes went wide, and she clapped her hands in glee. *Brilliant!* she wrote in tidy purple letters. Then she erased it with the side of her hand, to Ansel's vague disappointment.

"Make sure you put the caps back on the markers," he warned. "They'll dry out and be no good if you leave them open."

She nodded her earnest understanding.

She'd eaten the bowl of cereal he left her, but signed that she was still hungry. Ansel was relieved to see that she seemed completely recovered from her exhaustion the night before, flitting around with quick, eager movements. She all but danced around as Ansel put the last of the groceries away, peering into every cabinet he opened.

"I could make eggs and toast," Ansel suggested.

Tadra tapped the pizza box that was still out on the counter and rubbed her stomach hopefully.

"That's not something we usually eat for breakfast," he

said with a smile. When she looked faintly disappointed, he quickly added, "But there's no reason not to!"

He showed Tadra the oven and the freezer, explaining their purpose, and unwrapped two individual pizzas to bake. They looked up words on his phone as they needed them: *oven, hot, cheese, bake.* Her most used words were questions: *where, why, how, what?*

Ansel explained how his pizza was different. "Mine doesn't have regular cheese. I'm lactose intolerant," he said. "Milk and cheese don't agree with me."

That led to laughing until tears rolled out of their eyes over the sign for *fart.*

"I'm trying to spare you that," Ansel chuckled.

Tadra threw her arms around him and squeezed him, her silent giggle conveyed through her shaking.

Ansel reminded himself firmly that all the knights were just touchy like that, frequently embracing not only their keys, but each other, and anyone they considered a friend. He'd gotten used to the occasional surprise bear hug, and he'd had to explain more than once that the delivery driver did not want to be clasped in joy when he brought food.

But Tadra's embrace was more dangerous than that, by a lot, and it tested Ansel's resolve to do no more than pat her shoulder in return. She let go slowly, and Ansel thought her smile when she backed away was full of invitation.

Invitation he didn't dare accept, and was probably misreading anyway. Ansel closed his eyes, which was worse, because then he could remember more clearly how she'd looked standing naked before him.

He wrenched his eyes open and found that Tadra's expression had gone curious, probably because he was gritting his teeth like he was in pain. He'd have to be more careful with his expression.

The oven gave a cheerful tone to announce that it was

hot and he set the timer and slid the pizzas onto the stone. Tadra went back to where she had set his sketchbook down.

"I don't really show people that," Ansel said, fighting back his urge to snatch it away from her.

Why not? she shrugged at him with a pointed look.

"It's just..." Ansel wasn't sure how to explain. "It's private. I don't usually share it."

Tadra set the sketchbook back down on the counter, looking disappointed and guilty. Ansel wondered how much of it she'd already looked at.

Private? she wrote on the board.

Did they not have privacy? Ansel wondered. The knights certainly had a...*unique* understanding of it...an understanding that had led to many lectures about wearing clothing and closing doors. As Ansel was trying to figure out how to explain it, she shook her head and added *sign?* and pointed to his phone.

"Privacy is probably a useful word to know," Ansel agreed. "You're going to have to ask for it in this increasingly crowded house if you want any. Don't expect it from the dogs, though. Always latch the door when you go to the bathroom."

They looked up the word together and practiced it - their hands in an A formation tapping a thumb against the lips.

She pointed at herself, then drew fingers from her eyes to the sketchbook and added *sorry.* Her face, scrunched in guilt, said as much as her fingers.

Ansel felt his chest squeeze. "It's okay," he said quickly, because he didn't want her to feel bad. Then his thoughts caught up with him and he realized that it really *was* okay. "I don't mind," he said in surprise.

Her relieved smile was brilliant, then her brow furrowed. *Question,* she signed, pointing at the sketchbook.

"Sure," Ansel agreed. "You can look. I'm happy to answer any questions you have."

She opened the sketchbook and flipped a few pages to an elaborate sketch of a waterfall, the top lost in fog. There was a tree hung with lace at the bottom, and a fox drinking from the pool. Its reflection showed butterfly wings. She tapped the picture, then herself, then spread her fingers in all directions. When Ansel looked at her blankly, she reached for one of the markers and wrote on the flat whiteboard: *This is like my world.*

"Henrik described it," Ansel told her. "It sounded so beautiful. We have stories of faery. Old stories. I have some books I can lend you."

She turned a few pages. It was a still life, roughly sketched, of the three ornaments hanging in the kitchen window. "We hadn't found you yet," Ansel explained. When he looked at the sketch, he saw only the flaws, how Henrik's gryphon had too long a neck, how Trey's dragon wasn't quite posed correctly, a certain wrongness in the legs of Rez's unicorn.

But Tadra seemed genuinely delighted.

The next page was a study of only the rings, overlapping and falling off each corner, and in the center, a blank space.

"I was just playing with negative space," Ansel said apologetically.

She tilted her head at him, but Ansel couldn't guess what her expression meant and she didn't sign anything, flipping ahead to the final page that he'd sketched on.

This time, she did sign, moving her hand to point at her breastbone. *Me.*

It was a swift, spare sketch, just a few light lines, to

capture the way she had looked sleeping. Her eyes were closed, her hair splayed across the pillow. Ansel had sketched her freckles, the barest suggestion of her nose and parted mouth, the length of her neck, a hint of her collar-bone. He'd spent the most time on her hair, following the flow of it.

"I'm sorry," he said, feeling briefly like a creeper. "It was probably a violation of *your* privacy." He'd done it from memory, hoping that getting the image of her out on paper meant she would haunt his mind less.

Tadra shook her head vigorously and made the *I love you* symbol with her hand, pointing with the other to the picture.

Ansel was dismayed by how much even just the sign on her hands made him feel. "That's probably too strong a sentiment," he suggested. "How about a thumbs up?" He demonstrated. "That means, well done, or good. Two thumbs up for special occasions."

Tadra tapped the page and gave him two thumbs up. Then she scooped her hands toward her heart in an unmistakable instinctive sign. *It fills my heart.*

"I'm glad you like it," Ansel said gruffly.

They were sitting close together to look at the sketch-book, and Ansel's phone, right beside it, so he didn't have time to startle back when she leaned forward to kiss him. He'd half-expected her to press her forehead to his, the way the knights often expressed platonic affection, but he wasn't ready for the feel of her warm lips on his, the tickle of her hair against the edges of his face, or the touch of her hand on his face.

It took every shred of his self-control not to kiss her back, to claim her whole mouth, to clutch her gorgeous body close. For a moment, *not kissing her* was all he could manage, then finally, fighting for every inch, he took her by the shoulders and set her away from him. "What are you doing?" he growled.

Confusion clouded her face. She pointed at him, gestured to herself and signed *key* into her palm. *You're my key.*

Ansel felt his blood run cold, trying to remember what he'd said, and how he'd said it. Had he led her on? Had he longed so badly to be her key that he'd implied that he was?

He was no more capable of speaking than she was around the pain in his chest, and he could only sign back, shaking his head.

I'm not your key.

CHAPTER 8

*T*adra thought that she had finally figured things out, had finally made sense out of this mad world.

She was a firebird knight from a different land, and Ansel was her key. They would be a couple, the way Trey was with Daniella, and Rez with Heather, and Gwen with Henrik. Possibly, they would adopt a strange animal companion. Ansel would unlock her ability to draw power from the clouded leylines in this place so that they could protect the world, and he would look at her the way that her shieldmates' keys looked at them in their likenesses.

She wanted that more than she wanted her voice, or her firebird power.

She ached for that softness in his eyes, that stirring in her belly, the way his touch made her skin tingle with longing. Wasn't that what she was supposed to feel for her key? She didn't think she had mistaken the warmth in his face, or the way his breath caught in his throat when she touched him or stood close.

You're...my key? she signed again, her face the question mark at the end.

"No," he said, and his voice was gruff. "No. I didn't mean to imply it, I'm sorry. I'm just the guy who put you back together. I wasn't supposed to release you from your prison. Robin dowsed your key in another country—on another continent—really far away. I'm not him. I'm not supposed to be."

Tadra stared. She could see the grief in his face, the regret that he felt, and she couldn't make sense of what her instincts were telling her. Was this attraction misplaced? Could she not trust what she felt? She shaped the sign with her hand: *I love you.*

Ansel made a noise of dismay and caught her hand in his, gently folding down her fingers before he drew back. "You don't," he insisted. "Listen, I...feel things for you, on a lot of different levels, but your key is coming, and what you have in your heart now will be like a distant shadow of what you're going to feel. He will complete you in ways you've never known, in ways I never could. Don't confuse this—this *friendship*—with what you're *going* to have."

Tadra's imagination failed to supply the idea of anyone she would like more than Ansel. More kind? More generous? More handsome? She struggled with the limits of the language they had cobbled together. How did she explain the flutter in her chest and the yearning she felt, and the way that she trusted him? She'd thought that was all part of him being her key, and if it wasn't, what *was* it?

Not being able to speak only made it more obvious that she didn't know the words to describe what she was feeling. *Sorry,* she signed, because it was the only thing that came close to her emotions.

But Ansel knew what she meant, and he knew exactly what to say.

"Don't feel bad, we're even now! I wasn't supposed to kiss you, either, but here we are. And I can't blame you if I swept you off your feet," he teased her kindly. "I'm a good-looking guy, ask anyone! But when you meet your key, it's going to be electric—amazing! You'll *know*, and you'll be so glad I didn't let you settle for me. I'm sorry, if things were different—really different, like you weren't a stranger in my world and I wasn't the only person you'd ever met here, and you weren't destined for someone else, and the end of the world wasn't at stake...I mean, you're gorgeous, and you're smart, and you're funny and your key is the luckiest guy in the world."

He drew a breath at last. "I feel a lot of complicated things for you," he said with raw honesty, "but this can't be love. Don't think for a moment that I don't want it, or don't care for you. We're not meant for each other, but maybe we were meant to be friends."

Friends.

Tadra nodded, because she had nothing better to say. *Like*, she wrote on the whiteboard.

"Yes," Ansel agreed. "Like. Not love. Just like."

He looked up the sign on his phone—it was a motion like he was pulling a thread from his heart with his thumb and middle finger. *I like you*, he signed at her. Just a thread of affection, not the flame of passion that Tadra had confused it for.

She signed it back. He'd made everything safe again, after her terrible stumble.

"Here," Ansel said, offering his hand. "When we meet people, we greet them by shaking hands."

He demonstrated with a warm, firm single shake, then took his hand back.

Tadra suspected that he let go a little more quickly than he might have with someone else, but she knew how he felt, like if she touched him too long, she'd never get all the parts of herself back.

She still had the taste of him faintly on her lips, and it tasted like regret.

There was a sudden blast of shrill noise that had her startling back off of the stool, snatching up the whiteboard as the closest weapon-like item of any heft.

"It's just the timer," Ansel explained, getting off his own stool with far more decorum. "I have to check the pizza." He went around the counter to open the shining oven, the dogs hard on his heels with their hopes high.

Tadra slowly lowered the whiteboard. She had smudged the word *like*. It looked more like *live* now.

She wasn't hungry any more, though she felt more empty than ever. Ansel was wise, and he was gracious, and if he could put aside what he wanted for her own greater purpose, so could she. She just...needed a moment to get herself together, to remind herself that she was a firebird knight, not a lost girl pining over a man she couldn't have. A man she barely knew, anyway.

"It looks pretty good," he said, giving her a thumbs up. "I'm going to rotate them and put them in another few minutes."

Privacy, she signed, but Ansel was already bending back over the oven, and he didn't look up when she slipped out of the room.

She wandered through the living room for a few moments and found herself looking at the perfect painting of her shieldmates. Her key. Ansel wasn't her key. Her key would be someone else, someone she felt an immediate connection with. Someone she *recognized*.

Fabio came to the door to the outside and looked at it expectantly. Tadra patted his head and opened it, looking out on the alien terrain. There was a layer of slushy snow over a broad expanse of lawn and wide walkways and more was falling from the sky. A giant, awkwardly shaped conveyance, low for a carriage, but clearly on wheels, was dusted with more of the snow. A few trees and a tall hedge led away to a street where another similar vehicle suddenly barrelled by, drawn by some power other than horses.

Fabio went out a few steps and immediately turned around and went back in, but curiosity drew Tadra out. She closed the door behind her and wandered down to see if another of the things would pass. She wrapped her arms around herself; the wind here cut through the light fabric of her clothing and her feet swiftly became damp and cold.

Not far away, someone screamed, and Tadra was running towards it before she could give conscious direction to her feet. She was a firebird knight of the fallen crown, and it sounded like a child.

She had not run more than a few hundred feet down the empty road, following the twin tracks of the thing that had passed by through the snow, when there was a second scream. She slowed, realizing that it was not a scream of fear or pain, but of play, and came across the curious sight of a pair of cloth golems, riding down a side road on a bright, flat board. They came to the road and tumbled to the side into a snowbank, emerging to reveal that they were not at all golems, but children, thoroughly encased in padded suits.

They stared at Tadra.

Tadra forgot that she couldn't speak and tried to greet them, then settled for signing hello.

The girl shyly waved, and the other child snatched her hand back down. "We're not supposed to speak to strangers," he said hesitantly.

"Maybe she's lost," the other lisped. It sounded like lotht.

"Janice? Logan? Are you sledding into the road?!" a woman's voice demanded from out of view, followed by the sight of her hurrying down through the snow. "What did I tell you about that? Hello? Hello! Who are you?" She was wearing very tight breeches and a large sweater, her feet in hefty boots lined with fur, and she was carrying a shovel.

Tadra, she tried to tell them. *I am Tadra, defender of the broken crown, a fighter for light, a firebird knight.* But as hard as she tried, nothing came out. She used some of the signs she used with Ansel. *Hello. I thought danger.*

They all looked at her blankly and the woman moved to put herself in front of the children, her shovel held like a weapon.

"Are you hurt?" the woman asked, as suspiciously as her son. "Can I call someone for you?"

Could this woman summon people? Would she be able to bring Robin, her shieldmates, and her key directly to this place?

Tadra signed enthusiastically, cursing her limited vocabulary, but none of them showed any indication they understood a thing she said. Which of the signs had Ansel said were universal? *I love you* seemed wildly inappropriate here. She gave them a thumbs up, then a second one when they cautiously smiled at that.

The woman seemed to relax a little, but still kept herself protectively in front of the kids. "Honey, I'm just going to make a phone call and get you some help, okay?"

"Tadra!"

Ansel's voice made Tadra turn, and she told herself firmly that her heart should not leap like that at the sight of him and the sound of his voice. He was not her key.

CHAPTER 9

*A*nsel was glad for the interruption of the oven timer, and more glad when Tadra slipped out of the kitchen so he could curse in private over the pizzas. Neither was quite finished, and he frowned at his unattractive pie with frustration as he put it back in. The dairy-free cheese never melted quite right.

His pizza was something *like* real pizza, just like being Tadra's friend was something *like* being her key. He just had to accept that this was the way to less heartache and appreciate what he did have. At that moment, however, he hated Tadra's key with his entire being, and was made of nothing but jealousy and regret. His whole life was fake pizza.

When he reset the timer again, he turned to find Fabio and Vesta sitting at the edge of the kitchen staring at him avidly. "You're not getting pizza, guys," he scolded them. Two sets of tails pounded on the floor.

That was when he realized that Fabio had wet paws, puddles of melting snow around his feet, and that Tadra was not in the living room beyond them. "Tadra?" he called, and he stood a moment at the bottom of the stairs hoping she'd call back before he remembered that she couldn't. Fearing the worst, he ran for the front door and flung it open, causing a chaos of dogs. There was a trail of footprints out to the road that he saw before Fabio bounded out to destroy them. Ansel herded Fabio back into the house to shut him in and then sprinted out to the road.

"Tadra?"

She was standing halfway down the block, facing two children and Ansel's closest neighbor.

"Tadra!" He closed the distance between them at a sprint. "Oh, Mrs...ah...Kendall? This is Tadra, she's from...ah...Norway."

"Kensey," the woman corrected, looking more relaxed but no less confused as Ansel skidded to a stop at Tadra's side.

Ansel was pretty sure that the knights had given him a reputation for housing eccentric people. He sometimes wondered if the neighbors thought he was running some kind of hippy commune. A Norwegian hippy commune, maybe.

"It's Jenny Kensey. From Norway, you say? Is she...um…"

"Mute," Ansel said swiftly. "Genetic disorder. She's here to see...ah...a specialist."

He knew he was a terrible liar and wished he was a better actor, but Tadra nodded and shrugged and smiled winningly.

"Okay, sure," Jenny Kensey said dubiously. "Well, kids, it's time to come in."

The two gave wails of protest and she herded them back up the way they had all come as Ansel faced Tadra.

"You scared me," he scolded her. "You're not wearing any boots or a coat or a hat. Aren't you *freezing?*"

She was starting to shiver and Ansel wondered if he would regret putting his arms around her to keep her warm. It was something a friend might do, he assured himself, and he put his arm over her shoulders as they walked swiftly back up to his house. It was impossible for Tadra to converse with her arms wrapped around herself, and Ansel didn't try until they were back in the house, fighting their way through frantic dogs to get her to the couch and wrapped in an afghan. Her teeth were chattering.

One hand poked out and made a writing motion, and Ansel brought her a marker and the whiteboard, which was awkward and large on the couch beside her. She blew on her fingers and flexed them before writing in sloppy, tilted letters: *Never been so cold.*

"Doesn't it snow in faeryland?" Ansel asked lightly.

Had magic to keep me warm in cold places. She tried three times to cap the marker before Ansel did it for her and took the whiteboard off the couch to sit beside her.

"You'll be warm again when the others get back here with your key," he promised, putting a strictly friendly arm around her. That certainly explained why the other knights had to be nagged into wearing hats and gloves by their keys.

Tadra exhaled and sagged into him, still shivering, and Ansel rubbed her shoulder in vigorous just-friends fashion. Fabio flowed up onto the couch to warm her from the other side and put his long head in her lap. His tail wagged against the arm of the couch.

He could do this, Ansel told himself. He could be a comfort and companion to this curious, beautiful woman who wasn't his. He could warm her in his arms and keep himself from kissing the top of her head.

It was harder though, now that he realized there was a chance she might want him in return. The feel of her lips still burned on his mouth and he selfishly wished that he'd had a little less self-control so that he could have seen what it was like to really kiss her, to taste her, to have that one memory at least.

Other things were harder, too, and Ansel was afraid he was going to have complications standing up.

He was almost glad when the fire alarm went off.

Vesta went insane, barking and circling, and Fabio leaped from the couch to join her. Tadra, tangled in blankets, tried to rise to her feet and meet this new foe, snatching up the whiteboard like a shield.

"It's just the pizzas," Ansel shouted over the din of the dogs. "I forgot them in the oven. Hang on!"

He scrambled for the kitchen, snatching a dish towel from the rack to wave at the smoke detector over the island. "Shut up, shut up, I *know.*"

Smoke was seeping out of the oven and Ansel turned it off and flipped the fan on over the range before he opened it. A black cloud rolled out of it. Most of it was caught by the fan, but the room became noticeably smokier.

The pizzas were burned inedible, but not actively on fire, and frantically fanning the smoke detector finally silenced it.

Tiny firebird Tadra flew into the kitchen and circled it before landing on the counter. She clacked her beak and shifted into human Tadra, sitting with her legs dangling off the counter. She put her hands over her ears and glared up at the ceiling.

Sorry, Ansel signed at her. "It's a device that's supposed to wake people up if there's a fire while they are sleeping."

The charred pizza was too hot to throw into the trash, so he put the pan in the sink. "Why don't I make something else?"

Tadra looked at the oven and gestured with her hands like billowing smoke, then pointed two fingers at her eyes, then hesitated before spelling d-o-u-r and shrugging.

It took Ansel a moment to put it together. The black smoke from the oven had briefly looked like a creature of darkness. "It did look a little like a dour," he said. "But it was just bad cooking. This world didn't have dours before you guys came here, so there's not a sign for them. We should make one!"

After a few experiments, they settled on making a d with their finger and slashing it across the heart. "It seems appropriate," Ansel said. Dours were little wisps of warped magic, dark and not quite solid, able to twist their shapes into shadows and shade. They did not directly control a human, but with their evil grip, they could change their host into a violent and irrational agent of chaos, stealing away their compassion and rational thought.

"And we could maybe raise that into the air for a superdour?"

Tadra shrugged her question at him.

"Oh," Ansel realized. "You wouldn't know about those. They're...sort of a new wrinkle on the dours. See, the bleaks, the dark counterparts of the knights, they have a problem drawing power here just like you do. They can...choose a key, persuade a human to help them, but it's not like a true key, they don't draw power through them but *from* them, eventually leaving them a shadow husk of what they were. Like dours, this...not-a-key—"

The phrase from his own mouth startled him, poking the raw place in his chest where he wanted so badly to be a part of the grand adventure. He was a not-a-key, too. Not like that, of course, but not any more a true key than they were.

Ansel cleared his throat, aware of Tadra watching him closely. "This not-a-key is burned away into something *like* a dour, but they are able not only to infect a human, but to control them. There's a bleak here, at least one, who is making these."

Tadra shook her head in sympathy and dismay.

Neither of them tried to say anything for a long moment and the pan cooling in the sink creaked as the metal contracted. Ansel didn't want to leave the conversation on such a note and searched for something more cheerful as he scooped up the cooled burnt pizza and threw it out.

"Well, there aren't many bleaks on this side, so we just have to figure out how to stop them before their reinforcements get here at the end of the month."

Tadra rolled her eyes and shrugged. *That's all.*

"I've seen you guys in action," Ansel said reassuringly. "Or at least, lots of practice stunts and the aftermath of the damage you can cause, in *my* warehouse, I might add. No one will even insure it anymore!" He realized that he'd have to explain insurance and quickly added, "Don't worry! When your key gets here, you'll see what you can do. He'll probably fix your voice. And I have all the faith in the world that the eight of you—nine with Robin—you'll have no trouble saving us at all."

The nine of them.

While Ansel stayed home with the hounds.

But Ansel didn't have time to feel sorry for himself, because Tadra suddenly fell forward off the counter and collapsed into the reach of the dogs.

CHAPTER 10

*T*adra thought at first that it was just dismay and shock that made her feel like all of her energy had drained suddenly from her bones. She had been so relieved that all of her usual strength had returned in full after her long sleep. Her firebird form was stunted and she could touch no magic whatsoever, but her human body was still in fighting form.

But when she slipped down off the counter, her knees buckled beneath her and she was alarmed to find herself suddenly in tongue's reach of the dogs, who had been milling hopefully around in the kitchen, probably wondering why Ansel had thrown out perfectly good burnt food.

Vesta tried to climb into her arms, her whole body wiggling in joy and excitement, and Fabio licked everything he could reach as Ansel tried to haul them off and help Tadra back to her feet. "Back, Fabio! Vesta, stop jumping, leave it! Bad dogs, get back! Dammit!"

Then Ansel was lifting her back up out of the range of their tongues and carrying her out into the living room to the couch. "Are you okay?" he asked anxiously, tucking a stiff, square pillow under her head.

Even signing took too much energy, and Tadra only managed, *sorry*.

"Don't be sorry," Ansel scolded her. "I let you get chilled, and you haven't had enough food, probably. Maybe smoke inhalation? I'll air it out a little, make you a snack, some tea? Are you in pain?"

Tadra shook her head. She knew that whatever ailed her, it wasn't the cold, or the food, or the smoke, but she let Ansel fuss over her and tuck the afghan around her.

"Leave her alone," he threatened Fabio, "or I will lock you in the bathroom for the rest of the day."

Fabio sank down with his face on the floor and wagged his tail obediently, but as soon as Ansel had gone back into the kitchen, he crept across the room and crawled up onto the couch with Tadra, one limb at a time like he was sure he was going to be ordered off at any moment.

Vesta whined and paced nervously between the kitchen and the living room, not happy with having either of them out of her sight.

It was worse than the night before. Tadra wasn't sure if she hadn't quite recovered her full strength after all, or the sucking, draining sensation was more powerful this time. What was it? Why was she suddenly so incapacitated? Would her vitality ever return?

Even thinking was a chore, and she closed her eyes and drowsed for an indeterminate time.

~

"et off," Ansel was hissing when she woke again.

At first, Tadra was confused, wondering why Ansel wanted her off the couch that he'd so carefully helped her lie down on. Then she thought that he was talking to Fabio, who had taken his allotment of the furniture and then stretched further, crowding her legs almost off the cushions and resting his chin on her hip.

There was another weight at her shoulder, and this one gave a yowl of warning as Ansel pried the warmth of a cat off of her. Sharp claws briefly scratched her arm, and she gave a soundless hiss that was more surprise than pain.

"I'm so sorry," Ansel said. The cat he was lifting off of her growled in protest and twisted out of his grasp as Tadra opened her eyes. "You looked really uncomfortable."

The cat streaked out of the room, Vesta hot behind her. Fabio's tail thumped somewhere down below Tadra's knees.

Tadra didn't remember the sign for *better*, but she tried to nod reassuringly as she struggled to sit up.

Once Fabio's weight was off her legs, she felt fine again and she stood cautiously. No dizziness or weakness remained. She was a little tired, perhaps, but it was not the bone-deep exhaustion that had hit her so hard earlier.

"You slept for about an hour," Ansel said, answering the question that Tadra had been thinking. "Are you okay?"

Good, Tadra signed, and then she remembered the sign for better, because it was a progression. Three words had been taught in the same portal-lesson: *good, better, best*.

Better, she added. She tested her range of motion curiously and shrugged.

Whatever malady had afflicted her, it had passed quickly.

Ansel looked like he was trying to watch her without *watching* her, as guilty as Fabio eyeing food he knew he wasn't supposed to want. "I made you some tea, I can heat it back up."

Tadra nodded and resisted stretching again just to embarrass him for fun.

He chattered helpfully as she followed him into the kitchen, explaining the like-magic box that he used to warm the tea—a microwave—and a little that Tadra didn't follow involving a dangerous power called electricity. Was electricity this world's version of magic? Tadra didn't have the vocabulary to ask all the questions in her head.

One of the whiteboards had been secured to the refrigerator, but she wasn't even sure what to write. She doodled a little cloud in the corner and then a firebird.

"Your timing was really good," Ansel said, handing Tadra the cup of tea. "Christmas is in a few weeks."

The mug was surprisingly hot and Tadra had to dance it in her hand a little. She let her eyebrows ask what *Christmas* was as she sipped the tea cautiously.

"Christmas is probably our biggest holiday. It falls near the winter solstice, and we give each other gifts and celebrate love and family."

Tadra pointed at him with more questions in her eyes.

"My family?" Ansel guessed, and she nodded.

"I never knew my blood family," Ansel said slowly. "I grew up in a foster home—it was great, not like Oliver Twist or anything. Ah, I mean, that's too obscure a reference, sorry. I was close to my foster family. I never felt like I missed out on anything by not knowing my biological parents."

Tadra made a fist to her heart.

"You were like that with your shieldmates?"

She nodded.

"I'd normally be getting ready to travel and visit with them for the holidays, but of course, we've got the big destruction of the world coming up, and the heroes of the story needed someone to watch the dogs."

Tadra decided that the tone in his voice was regret and she thought she understood it. As a knight in her own world, facing an enemy of darkness and misery, she had a clear purpose, an unmistakable direction.

Here, stripped of her power, suffering some kind of intermittent weakness, in a place she didn't know or care for, her path was less clear. She felt sidelined, out of step from her destiny.

She put her tea down on the counter and took Ansel's face in her hands, surprising him.

"I can't—! What are you—?"

She didn't try to kiss him again, regretting her earlier attempt, but rested her forehead on his, trying to share her understanding and kinship through their touch without words.

After a moment, he took her face in his own hands and Tadra could feel the tension ease from him as well as from herself.

When she stepped back, they smiled at each other.

Hungry, she signed, and Ansel sprang into motion. "I've ruined the pizza, but I can still introduce you to something called sandwiches."

CHAPTER 11

*T*adra spent the next two days learning everything she could, furiously stuffing information into her brain from Ansel's not-magic portals, reading his books, and quizzing him. She wanted to be all caught up when her shieldmates returned, so that she could focus entirely on their pending battle and not be a liability because she could not operate a toaster.

(She only set it on fire once.)

He gave her a tiny phone of her own and showed her how to browse for answers to questions on her own.

"There is...ah...a lot of stuff you probably don't want to know on the Internet," he warned her, but when she pressed him, he only looked embarrassed and said something about *Rule Thirty-Four.*

Tadra preferred to ask Ansel her questions. The tiny screen was hard to focus on for long, it felt so fragile, and it frequently didn't make sense without his patient explanations, anyway. The scope of the world was vast and confusing, but everything was so *interesting.* She and Ansel added more and more words to their shared vocabulary, making up as many as they learned.

It was curious to find herself in the role of a scholar, she realized, reading one of Ansel's faery tale books for clues to how magic worked here. Trey had always been the one most interested in books, as Henrik was in magic and Rez was in healing. She had been the one who wanted to drill with the sword, or run, or fly.

She suddenly missed them, with a jolt of melancholy so deep and unexpected that she wasn't swift enough to dash her tears away before one fell onto a brilliantly illustrated page.

It didn't make a sound, but Ansel, reading across the coffee table from her, looked up and caught her wiping away a second betrayal.

He pushed Fabio, groaning, off his lap and moved to sit next to her.

Sorry, she signed, wiping the tear from the page.

Ansel didn't speak, only put a hand at her back and rubbed kindly as she pulled herself together. He sat just a little way apart, his thigh not quite touching hers.

Tadra didn't let herself cry any further—she was a Firebird Knight! Protector of the Broken Crown! She couldn't snivel like a little girl because she missed her shieldmates. She put the book aside. She didn't want to look at illustrations that weren't quite her world and think about things she couldn't control. She should be practicing for battle, or planning defenses.

Sorry, she signed again, more firmly. Then, *Thank you.*

"I thought we might go to the mall today," Ansel said kindly, taking his hand back and standing.

Mall. Tadra wracked her brain. Had he mentioned a mall before? She stood with him.

"It's a place with many stores," Ansel explained, before

she had to ask. "I still need to get everyone presents for Christmas. I was waiting until they left, I figured I'd have plenty of time, but...well, you showed up rather unexpectedly."

Tadra cocked her head at him. There was a whiteboard beside the couch where she'd been sitting. Ansel had talked a little about Christmas before, but... *presents?* she wrote.

"Gifts. It's a Christmas tradition to buy your friends and family small and thoughtful tokens." Ansel's whole face softened; the idea clearly brought him great pleasure. "You can help me pick a few things out."

What if? Tadra signed. She pressed the back of her hand to her head and feigned weakness. She hadn't had a spell since her second wave two days before, but she didn't want to be caught somewhere unsafe if it happened again.

"If you get dizzy, I can carry you back to the car and take you home at any moment," Ansel promised.

Tadra shook her head to think of someone carrying *her.* She didn't think she could get used to the idea of being helpless; it was completely counter to her nature.

"I'm hoping that it was just because you were in glass for so long," Ansel continued. "Maybe it was just a passing thing."

Maybe, Tadra signed. Maybe it was because Ansel wasn't her key, she thought, but she didn't try to sign that. Even if she'd had the words for it, it felt wrong to say.

"You'll want a jacket," Ansel said, and he opened the closet in the entryway to show a collection of outer garments in many sizes and colors.

Tadra would have made a noise of appreciation if she had been able, reaching at once to a collection of thick, black leather coats that hung together to one side. She pulled the stiff arm of one of them out. There was a bril-

liant red bird embroidered at the shoulder. A golden grif-
fin, a blue unicorn, and a green dragon adorned pairs of
matching garments.

"Heather made these for you guys," Ansel said, grinning at her. "It's the closest thing we have to decent armor
that you can walk around town in. We don't want to actually hurt any of the humans before we can get the dours or
whatever out of them, but they're going to be doing their
best to hurt us. Them, I mean. Padded leather seemed
sensible."

Tadra trailed her fingers over her shieldmates' coats,
grinning in pleasure, then gave hers a tug to pull it off the
hanger and pull it on. It was big across the shoulders, but
there was a belt to snug it close at the waist. It fell to the
tops of her thighs, and had big pockets, both inside and
out. The belt was sturdy enough to hang a weapon on.

She twirled to show it off and Ansel wholeheartedly
approved. "Heather said she could bring it in if you
needed, but she didn't want to before she could fit it to you
exactly."

That made sense; armor should be fitted to a fighter.
The arms were a little loose, but the length was good, and
there was a collar that could be stood up. Tadra flashed
Ansel a delighted double thumbs up and to her surprise, he
laughed uproariously.

"Ehhhh!" he said, returning the gesture. "I'll have to
show you episodes of *Happy Days*. I'm sorry so many of our
jokes are so obscure!"

It was strange, Tadra thought, exactly how much
humor they shared, considering that they were still finding
the common ground to build it on. They laughed over the
same kinds of bawdy jokes, enjoyed clever wordplay, and
took the same sort of joy in the antics of the pets and each
other. Part of it, she thought, was that he was never unkind

with his amusement. He didn't ever mock or tease, and he never took pleasure in her discomfort, even when she knew she must be ridiculous.

Ansel put on a very plain jacket by comparison, a puffy-looking orange and blue quilted thing with no particular styling.

Hat? Tadra signed at him. She had her own already on, a knitted cone with a puffy tassel at the top. She had learned her lesson from her first uncomfortably cold trip outside, and several since then, walking the dogs with Ansel.

"I've got this awesome fro to keep my ears warm," he scoffed, patting his hair.

Tadra eyed him curiously. His hair was so different than her own, in a thick, curly mane all around his head. *Sun,* she signed. *Your head, your heart. Keeps you warm.*

Ansel looked like he decided not to say something and took keys to the conveyance down from beside the door.

May I? Tadra wanted to know.

"Drive?" Ansel asked in horror.

He had shown her a video game of driving, and it didn't seem all that difficult. Tadra nodded eagerly. She wanted to try absolutely everything that this world had to offer.

"Let's work up to that," Ansel said. "It's a lot harder than it looks."

Tadra sighed and pulled her hat down over her ears. So much about this world was!

CHAPTER 12

*A*nsel wasn't glad that Tadra couldn't speak, but he did like that it gave him a perfectly reasonable and utterly platonic reason to watch her all the time.

It made driving a challenge, however, because he wanted to gaze at every fascinated expression she made with her face and her hands instead of paying attention to the traffic. He nearly ran two red lights on the way to the mall. It didn't help that the streets were slushy with new snow.

Ansel went over the things that he thought were important to warn her about as he parked. "Try not to touch things, or wander off. It might be crowded, so stay close to me. There will be a lot of noise and bright lights and interesting things. If we get separated, find a Santa Claus and stay with him, I will come and find you there." Ansel had shown her pictures of Santa Claus and attempted—poorly, he feared—to explain the mythology. "And above all, do not shift. People here do not change into tiny sizzling swans and it would draw a lot of unwanted attention."

Tadra nodded impatiently, and he locked the car and turned to take her into the mall.

She at least looked like everyone else, wearing jeans and light winter boots. Her leather jacket was open, and she had a knit hat over her loose hair. She looped her hand into his elbow and stayed rather closer to Ansel than he'd meant to imply she should.

He didn't mind it in the slightest, though he thought he ought to, and he smiled when one of the barkers just inside the door offered them a jewelry store coupon, "to get a gift for your girlfriend!"

Tadra exchanged an amused and rather wry look with him at that, and he politely turned the coupon down.

The mall, which was frenetic at the best of times, was in the throes of those madcap weeks between Thanksgiving and Christmas. There was a giant, tinsel-covered tree in the middle of the rotunda, and a Santa Claus was posing for pictures with a lengthy line of ill-behaved children and tired-looking parents. There was loud Christmas music from every store, overlapping in a din of sound like an ocean undertow to the chatter of all the shoppers and sellers.

"I have a list," Ansel said sympathetically. Tadra looked like she was shell-shocked, gazing around in wonder, her reservations clear on her face. "We shouldn't have to stay long."

But his plan to leave quickly was thwarted by Tadra's interest in absolutely *everything.* She dragged him into the gourmet chocolate store and when they walked out with a five-pound sampler bag, Ansel counted himself lucky that it wasn't worse.

They stopped in a bath boutique next.

Tadra smelled every sample that was out and tested the hand lotion.

"Pick one out if you like," Ansel offered, when she was drawn to a wall full of bath bombs.

She smelled several and selected one that was cinnamon and clove, half-closing her eyes in pleasure. He went to pay for it, passing cash over the counter to the clerk.

"You want a bag for tha—" the clerk trailed off and Ansel turned to find Tadra starting to put it into her mouth.

"It's not food!" he warned her.

Tadra froze with it nearly at her lips. She smelled it again, her eyebrows skeptical, then licked it defiantly.

The clerk choked with laughter at Tadra's expression of disgust and quickly coughed to cover her outburst. "Your change is sixty-seven cents," she said in a strangled voice as she passed the coins across the counter.

Tadra, looking as if she'd just been betrayed, dropped the bath bomb into the offered bag, then pointed the coins as Ansel was about to drop them into the charity box on the counter, signing a question.

"I'm donating the change to—" Ansel peered at the sign. He was still trying to banish the memory of Tadra's tongue. "Dogs for blind children, I think?"

Tadra shook her head, then pointed at the coins inside the clear plastic box.

"Oh, *money?*"

The clerk was staring across the counter at them with real confusion now.

"Let's talk as we walk," Ansel suggested. He gave the clerk a broad smile that hopefully said *We're just eccentric* and not *You should probably call mall security now* and hustled Tadra out with him before she could try to eat anything else.

He gave her the broad strokes of what money was and

what units it came in, showing her some bills and his credit cards.

She refused everything else that he offered to buy, looking thoughtfully at price tags.

Ansel pointed out the sign for the restrooms as they passed it and showed Tadra the map of the mall with its sprawling wings and food court and department store bookends.

Tadra carried a notebook to write on, but in most cases, she could point to items or signs, and they communicated with their improvised language. Ansel only realized how unique it was to them when a deaf woman caught their conversation and tried to sign something to them.

Sorry, he signed and shrugged, when she repeated a few phrases he didn't know and looked at him expectantly. She gave up quickly; they shrugged at each other and moved on.

Ansel explained his purchases to Tadra as he made them. "This is for Gwen. She really loves to play video games, but her current controller is starting to wear out. The engraved whetstone is for Henrik, who complains that his axe is never sharp enough." Tadra smirked knowingly and nodded.

There was a mini-karaoke machine for Daniella and Trey, and a loom for Heather. For Rez, a disco ball, and for Robin...

"They change size, depending on how much energy they've had to use and if...when...we win the day, I expect it will cost them a great deal," Ansel explained in the toy store. "They'll probably outgrow it over the next year, but I thought it would be nice for a while."

Tadra flashed him two thumbs up and craned to look inside the little house. There were half a dozen rooms in it, all of them furnished with perfect scale Victorian-style items with moving drawers and opening doors. The bed had a springy mattress and miniature bedspread, with tiny pillows and even tinier fringe. The kitchen didn't have plumbing, but it did have cabinets with minuscule dishes and silverware. Lights in every room turned on and off with wee switches.

Tadra clapped her hands with joy and moved to pick it up and carry it to the checkout.

Ansel stopped her. "We'll get one in a box, this is their display. They have some packed up that will be easier to take and this can stay out for other people to see."

Laden with bags and gifts, they left the toy store and moved into a stream of loud people. "Stay close," Ansel warned, then turned to find that Tadra was gone.

He scanned the crowd for her bright hair, but there were dozens of red-heads, and even more people with knit hats. Leather coats were common. "Tadra? Tadra!"

His call was lost in the Christmas music and hawker's cries. "Scarf for your girlfriend?" one of the sellers at a stand offered. "Real silk! For your boyfriend?"

Ansel brushed her aside.

"You had one job, idiot," Ansel told himself in disgust, juggling the multitude of bags and the giant dollhouse box. "Don't lose the firebird knight. Don't let the mute fae shifter from another world wander loose in a crowded mall. Great work, Ansel. Brilliant. It's no wonder they left you home with the dogs."

He wandered around the area for a while before he gave her up as truly lost and struck out for the rotunda where the line for Santa Claus was longer than ever.

Tadra wasn't there and Ansel caught the attention of one of the elf helpers. "Is there another Santa here?"

She popped her gum and looked bored. "Yeah, there's

one at the other end by B-Mart, but don't expect the line to be any less long."

"Thanks," Ansel said sincerely.

He walked as quickly as he could, burdened by bags and all of the gifts and hampered by the careless crowds of people, who seemed to be an even mix of shoppers who wanted to get in and out as quickly as they could and shoppers in no hurry who stopped in the middle of traffic to greet people and strike up conversations where they were most inconvenient.

He was just untangling himself from one of the latter, after nearly running over what appeared to be an impromptu family reunion, when he passed the hallway down to the restrooms and he happened to look up and see the castle-themed sign for the restrooms. There was a cluster of teenaged boys anxiously hovering outside the restroom.

Where would Tadra have gone? He paused there long enough to hear a male voice holler, "This is the men's room!"

CHAPTER 13

*T*adra found the format of the restroom rather strange and wasn't sure what the sink-like things mounted flat against the walls were for.

There was a picture explaining the curious flushing mechanism in a tiny cabinet with the toilet, though it was much different from the ones in Ansel's house, so that wasn't difficult to puzzle out. The toilet paper was considerably coarser than what Ansel stocked.

The sink was obviously a sink, but there was no apparent way to turn on the water to wash her hands when Tadra had finished. As she looked for a hidden handle underneath the spout, it rather suddenly came on, and just as suddenly turned off when she flinched back.

A group of laughing boys entered as she was trying to repeat her initial motion, hoping to coax the water into flowing again.

"Girl!" one of them exclaimed in a strangled voice, and they turned into a tangle of confusion and retreated immediately out of the door they'd come in, laughing loudly and tripping over one another as they pushed their way out.

Had they never seen a woman before? There certainly *seemed* to be plenty of others wandering the mall. Tadra returned to her task and was able to wash her hands in the intermittent and frustrating flow with some effort. She was turning and wiping her hands on her pants when the door opened again.

The man who barged in didn't notice her at first and went straight to one of the flat sinks hung vertically on the wall. Tadra watched him curiously, hoping for a clue to the thing's function, and he reached down and started to unzip his pants.

He glanced her way then and his gaze went from lazy to actively alarmed as he flinched and yelped and covered himself with both hands, nearly jerking himself into the wall. Was he having a seizure? Should she try to get him help?

"This is the men's room!" he hollered in clear outrage.

Tadra looked around and spread her hands in a signal of peace. She hadn't seen any signs restricting gender, but she had clearly betrayed some kind of social norm. She backed towards the door while the man fumbled to return his pants to closure, cursing loudly.

"Tadra?"

The door directly behind her opened and Ansel barreled into her. "Are you okay?" he asked. His arms were laden with the gifts they had bought and he barely fit through the door with them. Tadra caught one of the bags that started to slip from his grasp.

"Get your girlfriend out of here, man!" the stranger yelped.

"Sorry!" Ansel cried, herding Tadra back out into the hallway. "The bathrooms in Norway are all unisex!"

The giggling boys from earlier had clustered outside, and they fled as Ansel and Tadra exited the restroom.

"That was the men's room, couldn't you tell?" Ansel paused, and they looked back at the offered doors together.

One of them had a silhouette of a knight, the other of a figure in a dress with wings and a strange pointed hat. Tadra had chosen the most obvious of them; she was a knight, not a fable. She pointed at the door and then to herself and shrugged. It seemed obvious.

Ansel made a wheezing noise that turned into a whooping laugh and he leaned into the wall facing the doors, his gifts shaking in his arms. Tadra had to giggle, because his laugh was so infectious. The man that she had surprised stalked out and glared at both as he strode past.

"I didn't even think to warn you about that," Ansel said, when his chuckles finally subsided.

Still bemused by his reaction, Tadra shook her head. The people in this world were very strangely prudish about some things. Apparently, the division of gender spaces was one of those things.

"Let's get out of here before you pick a fight with security or something," Ansel said. "I think we've had enough of the outside world for now and the dogs probably need to go out."

Tadra took her share of the bags and together they wove their way through the crowd towards the exit.

"Here," Ansel said, glancing at the map as they passed it. "Let's go out through the department store. It's closer to where we parked."

The department store was quiet after the noise of the mall, its music subdued and its space less crowded. It was shiny and spare in a way that the rest of the sprawling building was not, and Tadra stared around in wonder. It was very...white. Everything was white, or shining metal, or glass. It even *smelled* white.

"Sample?" There was a woman dressed in as much

white as the store, and she was holding something in her hands.

The sample in the chocolate store had been Tadra's favorite part of the entire trip, so she nodded eagerly, extending her free hand just as Ansel started to say, "I don't think—"

The woman deployed some kind of tiny, poisonous spray weapon at her and Tadra instantly shrugged out of the bags she was carrying, throwing them aside and dropping into a fighting stance as Ansel squawked, "Wait a second!"

The white-clad woman gave a shriek of alarm as Tadra advanced and threw her tiny weapon uselessly. Tadra flung up an arm to deflect it, but realized that Ansel was trying desperately to diffuse the situation before she pressed a counterattack.

Enemy? she signed carefully to Ansel, not taking her eyes off of the woman.

"It's a perfume sample," Ansel explained. "She's trying to convince you to buy the scent." To the cowering woman, he said, "I'm sorry, ma'am, she's from...uh...Norway."

People paid money to smell this way? Tadra relaxed, but signed, *Are you sure?*

"I didn't know she was deaf!" the woman protested. "Or Norwegian!" She gathered up her spray device and backed away. It had spilled on Tadra's feet and she was now thoroughly soaked in the odor.

Ansel was gathering up the bags that Tadra had thrown off and Tadra sheepishly helped him. *Sorry,* she signed.

Don't be, Ansel returned. He looked like he was trying hard not to smile. When they had picked up all the bags, they hastened for the exit and finally escaped back out to the car. They unloaded the gifts into a deep, covered compartment in the back of the car and Tadra was successful in reattaching her safety harness.

The car starting was less alarming this time, and she could settle into watching the flow of traffic as Ansel made it go out into the stream of other cars and big trucks.

A driver in another car sped past them at one point and motioned at them with his middle finger up. Tadra started to return the greeting and Ansel quickly explained that it was a rude and derogatory gesture with its roots in self-pleasure. He looked flustered. "It's called flipping the bird," he said. "Or flipping someone off. You do it when you're angry. Robin does it a lot."

Tadra watched in interest as Ansel did the things with the wheels and knobs and pedals that made the conveyance leap forward and turn and brake to navigate the maze of roads and other traffic. It was a dizzying dance, the way they moved together, and Ansel seemed to be following some kind of insanely complicated choreography.

Even the straps that held her in like a saddlebag were confusing, sometimes holding her firmly back and other times letting her sit forward to crane her head around and look at things.

It was snowing heavily by the time they arrived at Ansel's house. It was so alien and perfect, with almost painful symmetry and all its straight, modern lines. She struggled with her harness until Ansel released it for her.

She helped him carry in all of his purchases and he let the dogs out into the snow. Vesta sniveled about it until Ansel went out with a shovel and cleared her a path out onto the lawn, muttering about spoiled pets and princess paws.

Fabio, on the other hand, bounced merrily through the

deepest drifts of snow and came in with clumps of ice collected in the furry feathers of his feet and tail. Tadra sat with him in the middle of the living room and pulled them gently out as he whined in joy at the attention and writhed with his feet in the air.

Ansel sorted the food and goods from their flimsy bags. "I'll let you help me wrap these," he said. "And hey, maybe we can go pick out a Christmas tree. It would be a nice treat for everyone to come home to one." He had shown her a calendar, explaining where the holidays fell in the boxes that represented days, and they frowned together over the New Year, when the veil between their worlds would be weakest and this world would be vulnerable.

"Do you want a snack?" he offered, wadding some of the bags into the recycling box that he had shown her.

Tadra could still smell the thick scent of the perfume she had been sprayed with and she shook her head, holding her nose and miming being sick.

"You want to take a shower?" Ansel suggested.

Tadra shrugged, not sure what he meant.

Ansel made a show of smacking himself in the forehead. "I never showed you how to work the shower! I have failed as a host. Come, let me teach you how to work the controls. You may agree that this world is actually worth saving once you've experienced the luxury that is a shower."

Tadra had to laugh at his earnestness, and she followed him lightly up the stairs to the bathroom. At the far end of the room, past the sink where Tadra bathed herself and the loud flushing toilet, there was a clear-walled chamber with a metal snake and handles on one wall. She had not been sure of its purpose.

Ansel pulled the round knob forward and showed her the markings that indicated temperature as water began to stream alarmingly from above the chamber. "Gwen's got some shampoo here. I'm sure she won't mind if you use it. Ah, just squeeze a little in your hand, only a little, and then massage it into your scalp and rinse clear. There's some kind of conditioner, but we're way out of my wheelhouse. I think it's got instructions on it. There's soap, that bar there. Your towel is here, hang it up when you're done with it or Vesta will chew it up or Socks will sleep on it."

The water was steaming now, and Ansel backed out like he was afraid of seeing more than he wanted to and shut the door before Tadra could sign her thanks. By the sound of it, he tripped over Fabio on his way down the hall.

Tadra stripped efficiently, stepped into the chamber cautiously, then slowly relaxed into the stream of heated water.

Ansel hadn't exaggerated the delight of the contraption. It was better than a bath, like a hug over her entire body, the pressure from the flow not enough to hurt but hard enough to stimulate every inch of her skin as she rotated beneath it in wonder. She could feel the heat of it soak into her bones, melting away the tension in her muscles. She turned in the stream and tipped her head up into it. It flowed down over her face and washed off the terrible smell of the perfume.

For a long while, Tadra simply stood in the shower, enjoying its decadence. Then she sighed and used the indicated soap and shampoo to complete her cleanliness. It was certainly more thorough than the cloth baths she had been taking in the sink, and the conditioner she applied according to the directions left her hair feeling deliciously sleek and silky. The smell was a great improvement over the perfume.

It took her a moment to figure out how to turn off the

curious faucet and she managed to get a bracing shock of cold water as she did so. Then she dried off, dressed again in her clothing, and hung the towel on the rack, mindful of Ansel's warning.

Fabio was lying outside the bathroom door and he bounced to his feet just as she would have stepped over him. She dodged him easily, skipping down the stairs. Ansel was standing near the window by the front door, his phone pressed against the side of his face.

Tadra wondered how he was able to see anything on the screen, then realized he was listening to it. He held a finger up at her and turned away, saying, "Daniella, hey, it's Ansel. I know I've left a few messages now, but it's been a couple of days and I haven't heard anything and I'm starting to wonder if I should, I don't know, alert the Ecuadorian police or something. Of course, that's going to be kind of hard to explain when they ask about your itinerary and such because you didn't arrive by plane and half of you don't have passports, never mind the fable. Anyway, call back when you can. Tadra's here and Christmas is next week. We're going to have to get a tree without you guys. So, yeah. Talk to you later. Soon, I hope."

He pulled the phone away from his ear and poked a button on the screen, then exchanged a long, thoughtful look with Tadra. "They're going to be crazy happy to see you."

Tadra made a sign that was a muddle of things ending in pulling her hands to her heart.

Ansel nodded in understanding. "You'll be happy to see them, too."

Tadra walked to the whiteboard. *Knight,* she wrote in the box where they listed words they wanted to learn to sign.

Ansel looked it up, and frowned. "It's not something

that comes up in modern speech a lot, apparently, people have a couple of different ideas of what it should be. We've had knights, historically, but it's not one of those words that has an official sign."

Tadra erased it and wrote *shield* instead.

Ansel found two signs for it. The first was a gesture as if she was holding and defining a shield on her arm, which pleased Tadra. The second was the verb for defend, with two fists raised protectively. After studying the tiny portal-images, Tadra raised her arms in the defense pattern, swiping to show the shield front, then finished with her arms crossed across herself.

"Shieldmate," Ansel said out loud.

Fraud, Tadra wrote, thinking of the woman at the store. This was another word with several options and they settled on one. Tadra touched her head with both hands and brought them out, spreading her fingers.

"Yeah, my head feels full, too," Ansel said. "I don't think I've strained my brain so hard since I was trying to take calculus three by correspondence because the class conflicted with my business theory schedule." He signed as he spoke, any of the words that he knew signs for.

Tadra hopped from her spinning chair and beckoned Ansel to follow her, leading him to the door out to the large conveyance room that had been clearly set up for fighting. It always helped her remember things if she followed studies with physical activity.

"You want to spar?" Ansel guessed.

Tadra nodded, mimed putting all her thoughts back into her head, then signed *question* and pointed at him.

Ansel looked conflicted. "Do I fight?"

Tadra had meant to ask what weapon he used. He certainly looked warrior fit, and he moved gracefully on his feet. She had simply *assumed* he was a fighter of some skill.

"I probably won't be much of a challenge to you," he said with humility. "Your shieldmates and Gwen have done their best to pound me into some kind of useful shape, but I am not their calibre." He moved to take a wooden practice sword down off the wall and tossed her a second one.

Tadra saluted him with the toy and dropped into a ready stance. Despite his dismissal, he took a practiced attitude and when she pressed a test attack at him, he was able to parry her away with ease and drop back with swift reflexes.

She was less easy on her next advance and they exchanged a flurry of blows on the silly wooden blades. Ansel was just enough slower than she was that she could penetrate his guard and lay a tap on his hip.

"Ah," he said, good natured as always when they backed away from each other. "I warned you. I've been training for just a year, not an entire lifetime like you lot."

You're good, Tadra signed honestly, and he used the distraction to attack while her hand was busy, coming forward under her guard to tap her knee.

You're smart, she added, from a safer distance this time. *Fraud.*

"That was the first thing they taught me," Ansel said with a laugh. "To use your enemy's weakness for your own advantage. Oh, what's that?"

He was convincing enough that Tadra's attention was momentarily drawn away, and he attacked with a curious combination of strikes that was distinctly different from the fighting style Tadra had been taught.

She laughed without sound and deflected his blows without effort; he was fast, but she was faster. He had the advantage of reach, but not by much, and his method was more cautious than hers.

They danced back and forth, testing each other and

scoring sound hits, until they had both worked up a fine sweat and earned a few minor bruises. It felt good to burn her muscles, and there was a comforting routine to sparring. Tadra was relieved to find that she had no dizzy spells or weird weakness as they did drills and sparred. She stopped him several times to demand that he teach her an unexpected form.

It was gladdeningly familiar to sparring with her shieldmates...and unexpectedly nothing like it.

Ansel was pleasant to watch and more than a little distracting. He was frank about his skill compared to hers, but Tadra thought he underestimated his own abilities; she was not inclined to take it easy on him. Theirs was a match of near equals, his strength and reach balanced to her skill and her handicap of having to taunt him with her hands instead of her voice.

When they came close in battle, or they had to touch each other to correct a handhold or stance, she found her heart quickening. The first time she feared one of her spells of weakness, but the second, she realized that she was reacting to his closeness. She had never found her shieldmates the slightest bit diverting, but she caught herself watching the play of muscles in Ansel's arms, and the movement of his legs, to her own detriment at times.

It wasn't only effort that flushed her cheeks when the dogs on the far side of the door howled for attention.

"That was a good workout," Ansel said approvingly.

He tossed her a towel that tangled her hands too much to speak with them, so Tadra only nodded, mopping off her sweaty face as she handed back the practice sword. Her time in glass had not softened her calluses, but the grip was a little different from the sword she usually used, and there were a few places that her fingers and palm stung.

Thanks, she signed, when her hands were free again.

Feels good. Better. She mimed putting things back in her head.

Ansel was always watching her, alert to her soundless speech, and he smiled now and nodded agreement. "You probably want another shower," he laughed. "I know I do."

Tadra made a gesture meant to indicate a shower and clownishly cleaning herself, nodding emphatically. Did she imagine the swallow he made, or the pursing of his lips? Was he as bothered by her proximity as she was by his? Did his light-hearted laughter mask the same kind of yearning?

It was hard to imagine feeling more than this for her key, Tadra thought longingly, as they greeted the dogs and Ansel scolded them for howling and reassured them that they hadn't been abandoned or neglected. "It's just a door, you guys."

Tadra ran the water in the shower rather colder the second time and thought fixedly of fighting technique and battle strategy so that she didn't wonder about Ansel's shower while she soaped the sweat from herself.

CHAPTER 14

*A*nsel left another message the following morning, this time on Heather's phone.

"I hope you guys are okay," he said briefly. "Call when you can."

He stumbled over Fabio as he went back into the dining room, where Tadra was eating scrambled eggs with her fingers as she diagrammed things on the whiteboard propped up in the chair next to her. "Can you lie anywhere else?" Ansel rebuked Fabio, then patted his head and scratched his ears in remorse when Fabio looked like he'd just been hurt and betrayed.

Tadra had drilled Ansel quite thoroughly on every detail of their previous encounters with dark forces in this world, and she had mapped each of them, with obscure shorthand and color coordination that represented blocks of time.

Timing important. Strength of bleak varies, she had written in explanation. *Anticipate. Be where they will be when they are in weak part of cycle.*

Although Ansel had not been directly involved in any

of the former conflicts—and Tadra didn't seem to think worse of him for that—the knights enjoyed retelling their adventures frequently and in great detail, and Ansel was able to recall pretty exactly how the battles had happened.

There were two numerical notes in the upper right-hand corner of the whiteboard. "What's that?" Ansel asked.

Tadra looked where he was pointing and did a comic impression of fainting and tapped her wrist. Those were the dates and times of her weak spells.

"Do you think those are related?"

She shrugged.

Talking with her would have been much more challenging with someone less expressive. Their vocabulary continued to expand with formal sign, but they made up as many words as they learned, and Tadra was unabashed about acting out her thoughts.

"I thought you might like to get a Christmas tree with me today," he suggested.

Tadra raised her eyebrows in interest and did a shrug-nod thing that suggested she was not sure what it was, but was intrigued.

"I was hoping that we could all go together when everyone got back," Ansel continued. "It's a tradition that you usually pick a tree with your family, but we're running out of time before Christmas, and they might not have good trees left at the lot if we wait too long. And it doesn't really feel like the holidays yet without one." He was struck by how much he wanted to share all the warm winter traditions he remembered from his childhood with her. Was it inappropriate to take a Knight of the Fallen Crown out sledding?

Tadra was looking at him in curious befuddlement.

"Wear something warm," he cautioned. "Just in case we do have to go tromping through the snow."

Tadra finished her eggs and wiped her fingers on her napkin, nodding agreeable. *Where?* she signed, then finger-spelled m-a-l-l?

"No. They have fake trees at the mall, but we're getting a real one. There's a tree farm about 45 minutes northeast of here. They've got a lot of pre-cut trees to choose from."

Tadra dressed in her coat and wrapped a scarf loosely around her neck, pulling her hat down over her ears.

Ansel had to stop himself from buttoning her coat and tucking the end of her scarf into it. He had hoped that the longer they were together, the less he would want her, that practice and pretend would eventually make himself believe he was only as fond of her as a friend. Instead, he wanted more than ever to turn her casual touches into something more, to linger when she touched him, to keep her close when she impulsively hugged him.

Her true key was coming, Ansel reminded himself.

And it couldn't be soon enough.

~

*T*he tree lot was crowded with last-minute tree shoppers. Apparently, the week before Christmas was prime tree shopping time. Parents chased hyper children through the prickly aisles, pausing to compare fragrance and branch thickness, standing them up from where they leaned on the dividers to eyeball their height.

Tadra made an expression of ecstasy, closing her eyes and waving the scent into her face with appreciation. She rubbed her stomach and grinned. *Which?* she asked.

They were sorted by type, and they quickly gravitated towards a balsam fir, Tadra following her nose. They examined and rejected a dozen, finding bare spots in the branches, or discolored needles.

It started to snow, as they picked out trees and held them upright for each other, carefully inspecting every one. Tadra found one she liked and hugged it, to her regret, laughing her silent, happy laugh as its needles poked her ungratefully. Ansel would have bought any one that she wanted. He would have bought her five of them, if he thought they'd fit in the living room.

He carried the tree, cursing as it scratched him, to the checkout, where they put it in a net, cinched it down, and wrapped it in paper. Tadra watched with huge eyes as it went from a broad tree to a narrow package.

"Make sure you water it frequently," the gray-haired tree-seller said by rote, watching children streak past with a gimlet eye. "Don't leave it outside overnight. You want me to clean up the end?"

Strapping it to the top of the car was a snowy, laughing endeavor that devolved into a short, brutal snowball fight. Tadra was utterly unstoppable, even after Ansel got a well-aimed snowball down the gap at her neck into her coat. She tripped him into a snowbank and showered him in armloads of snow as he pretended to object and managed to get as much snow back at her as she dealt him.

The other tree shoppers laughed at them as the fight turned into a grapple and skirted wide around their antics.

There was snow in Tadra's eyelashes and it frosted her fiery hair. Her whole face was alight with merriment, cheeks red, and Ansel didn't realize that he had stopped struggling until she signed a question at him. "Sorry," he said, realizing that he had taken a hold of her wrist at some point. They rolled away from each other and got to their feet. "Good fight," he said, trying to wrestle back his wholly inappropriate desire to pull her close and kiss her.

Friends, he reminded himself. They were only friends. He wasn't her key. He didn't get to kiss her.

Tadra made a sign he didn't catch enough of to remember and Ansel didn't want to ask her to repeat it so he could figure it out. He checked the tie-downs on the tree and they both got into the car again. Tadra had mastered her seatbelt and clicked it into place and put her hands primly in her lap. Ansel turned the heater on high. Then, as he was about to back out of his parking space, she tapped his knee and signed *I won!* when he looked at her.

"You certainly did not," he protested. "I was the clear victor here."

Tadra's expression was sly disbelief and a dancing grin, to Ansel's relief. *You were down,* she insisted.

"You're the one with half a dozen snowballs inside your coat," Ansel scoffed in return. "We judge the victor in this game by how soaked you are, and you are clearly wet clear through to your skin. I, on the other hand, am barely damp. See?" He unbuttoned his coat to show her that his shirt was still dry. "Some of us were sensible enough to close up our coats."

That was when Tadra revealed that she had smuggled in one last snowball. Ansel yelped as she dumped it directly down the front of his jacket.

"Vixen!" he exclaimed. *Fraud!* he signed at her frantically. "So cold!"

I won, Tadra signed again in satisfaction.

Laughing, Ansel put the car in gear. "You won," he conceded.

But watching her delight and joy as they forgot, at least for a little while, the grim fight that was pending, Ansel thought that he was the one who had won.

CHAPTER 15

The tree that Tadra had picked was set upright in a curious little bucket with spread legs and screws that anchored the trunk into place. It took a great deal of work to get it appropriately straight, especially with the dogs underfoot, wanting to smell everything. Vesta growled at it, and when Ansel cut off the netting that kept it cinched up, yelped in fear and ran to hide in the dining room.

It seemed much larger in the living room than it had at the place of trees where they had bought it, its branches stretching in all directions. They had to rearrange the furniture to give it more space.

Tadra still wasn't sure why they had it inside, as opposed to outside, where plenty of trees already grew, but it certainly made the house smell marvelous, and she could tell that it made Ansel very happy. His serious face softened when it was finally upright, and his shoulders relaxed.

"We'll decorate it once it's had a chance to relax a little," he said. "But it definitely needs presents underneath it."

The way he said presents was delicious, like he was thinking of something joyful.

Ansel fetched armfuls of the things they had brought from the mall, spreading them out over the dining room table in several trips. Vesta jumped up onto the table and tried to burrow into the crinkly bags. "Don't eat the presents, Vesta," Ansel scolded her, picking her up and returning her to the floor. They repeated this several times until Ansel gave in and let her lay on a bag that was full of scarves and mittens.

Fabio followed Ansel in and out of the dining room, right at his heels, in case he suddenly decided to leave and forgot to invite Fabio with him.

Then Ansel came in a final time with a half dozen brightly colored staffs that proved to be rolls of flimsy paper in bold patterns, plus a pair of scissors, a small device that Tadra didn't recognize, and a bag full of silvery ribbons and bows.

He cleared a space and unrolled the paper.

What are you doing? Tadra wanted to know.

"We want the presents to be a surprise," Ansel explained. "That's part of the fun of them, seeing your presents lying around but not knowing what they are."

He laid the box that held Gwen's gaming console into the center of the unrolled paper and made skillful cuts, like a tailor making a perfect square of cloth. He folded up the edges of paper, creasing the corners until the box was completely covered. The design on the paper was a bright red and white stripe, interspersed with clusters of spiky green leaves.

"Can you tear me off a piece of tape?" Ansel asked.

Tadra eliminated everything else on the table as *tape* and picked up the curious little thing she hadn't been able to identify.

"Yup," Ansel confirmed, holding the paper neatly in place. "That's tape. You see the roll in the middle? It's sticky on one side. You pull it past that cutting edge—careful, it's sharp!"

Tadra tested the serrated blade with her thumb. She could see that it might cut, with effort, but it felt too flimsy to be a proper tool. The tiny roll in the middle had some kind of flexible, clear material, and indeed, it was sticky on the bottom, but when she took her finger off of it, there was no residue on her skin.

"Just pull a little off the roll and then bring it down over the blade to cut it," Ansel explained.

It took Tadra a few tries, and one tangled sticky mess, to figure out the process of tearing off strips of tape to secure his packaging. A few applications, and the paper was neatly wrapped around the box, crisp and uniform. Ansel took a glittering bow from the bag, peeled a slip of paper from it, and stuck it firmly onto the box, completing the presentation. "We'd better get gift tags on these," he cautioned. "Otherwise, we'll forget who gets what."

Gift tags turned out to be tiny cards with a place to name the recipient and gifter, and these, too, were applied by tape.

Good, Tadra said. It was so quaint and lovely, a warm, generous custom that spoke highly of this world.

Partway through the next box, Ansel got up and turned on a music machine that didn't require winding, complete with singing voices. "You can't wrap presents without Christmas music," he said. The music seemed to vary greatly, from cheerful and nonsensical, to grim and full of grief. Ansel explained the lyrics, where he could. Tadra was particularly interested in the ones about Santa Claus, a generous, jolly man with the ability to stretch time and do impossible things.

He sounded like a useful ally.

They worked through the bags of gifts together. The easiest ones to wrap were in boxes, the hardest were the irregular and soft shapes. Robin's dollhouse required nearly a roll of the paper, and a seam in the middle that they covered with shining ribbon.

Ansel made a show out of making Tadra hide her eyes while he wrapped something for her. She wasn't sure when or how he'd managed to get her a gift, but the idea of it delighted her.

"No squeezing the presents," Ansel warned. "That's cheating."

It taunted her, a small, squishy-looking package at the top of the stack.

What about you? Tadra asked when all the gifts were wrapped. She tapped one of the boxes covered in candy canes.

Ansel shrugged. "Honestly, I get more happiness out of giving the gifts than getting them."

Tadra frowned. It didn't seem fair. But she had nothing in this world to offer him, so she let it slide. *Now what?*

"Now we decorate the tree!"

Ansel rummaged in the conveyance room where they sparred, Tadra and the dogs helpfully following him every-where, and came back into the house with a large clear box full of wonders. There were strands with tiny shapes of colored glass, glittery ropes of minuscule ribbons, and carefully wrapped pieces of awe-inspiring art that ranged from silly depictions of Santa to beautifully crafted giant snowflakes.

The strings of glass were put on first, secured end-to-end as they spiraled up the tree. Ansel fastened the last to a wire of power and the entire tree lit up brilliantly. Tadra clapped her hands in joy.

They hung the ornaments all around the huge tree, and Ansel told her the story behind each one of them as they went up. There were ornaments from when he was a child with stories about his foster parents, and an ornament he'd bought his first year in college (a training school, Tadra gleaned). There was a set of thin, colorful metal fish that he'd found in a place called Mexico one year that he was traveling over Christmas, and a clear globe with a building painted inside.

There were a few that he shook his head over. "I have no idea where this one came from," he confessed, holding up a fragile tear-drop in red and green with gold markings all over it. "I think an after-Christmas clearance sale? It's also possible that it just came with the house. It came with rooms and rooms full of miscellaneous junk. That's basically why I kept running the second hand store."

He looked sideways at her as if he'd just realized how much he was saying. "I'm probably telling you more than you want to know," he said sheepishly. "You don't need all the details from my life."

Tadra shook her head and gestured for more.

Ansel chuckled. "You already know more about me than the people who've been living here for a year," he said with a soft, crooked smile.

The very last thing to go up on the tree, high up out of the reach of anxious dogs, were the glass ornaments of Tadra and her shieldmates. She cradled hers in her hand while Ansel tied the golden string securely and tested the knots. They had to stand very close to do the work, and Tadra watched his clever fingers and reminded herself that he wasn't her key, no matter how good he smelled and how tenderly she felt for him.

Her real key would be a hundred times this, somehow, and Tadra's imagination failed at the idea of it. It seemed impossible that there would be someone she liked and trusted more.

But it hadn't been an instantaneous bond. He had *earned* her trust and affection and Tadra was conflicted by the idea that someone else might simply *have* that from her without merit. She comforted herself to think that of course her key would be worthy, she would just know it at once and not have to *learn* it.

"Where do you want to hang it?" Ansel asked quietly, and Tadra realized that they were still side-by-side, though he had long since finished the knot. "You don't have to, if it's too painful to see."

Tadra's fingers curled around it. The glass firebird had been her prison for an indefinable time. It had broken, and left her frustratingly unable to speak. The seams where it had been repaired were obvious in the fractured light from the Christmas strings.

But Ansel had put her back together. He'd taught her to speak without sound when her voice was lost.

She smiled at him and shook her head, then stood on tiptoe to put it in the last clear space on the side of the tree facing the room. *I want to see it,* she signed, pointing.

Ansel smiled slowly at her, perhaps guessing some of what she'd been thinking. Then he stepped back and looked critically at the tree. "There's supposed to be a star at the top of it," he explained. "Or an angel. I had a star last year, it ought to be in this box somewhere." He turned away, a trifle fast, and riffled through the bubble wrapping that had protected all the mundane ornaments.

Tadra laughed, and when he looked back up at her, shifted and flew to the top of the tree.

The dogs went wild and Ansel grabbed Fabio by his collar when his tail threatened the decorations dangling at his level. "You can't have the firebird, goon."

Tadra preened at the crest of the tree, trailing harmless sparks, then flew to land and shift back to her human form.

Ansel let Fabio go to greet her and Vesta pranced forward for her equal attention.

"You could be the star *or* an angel," Ansel said, shaking his head and chuckling. "Maybe both at once."

What is? Tadra signed.

"An angel?" Ansel's voice softened. "It depends on what you read. It's been a creature of both vengeance and mercy, a guiding hand, a guardian. Usually they are depicted in white, with feathered wings."

Wings like Robin's? Certainly Robin had been her guard and guide.

She didn't have a word for fable, but Ansel must have followed her thought. "A little less bad-tempered than Robin, usually," he said wryly.

Names, she wrote on the whiteboard. She should have signs to talk about her shieldmates. They had been making do with spelling, but that was awkward.

They picked easy to remember signs that started with the letters of their name. Robin was given the sign R touched respectfully to the forehead. Rez was an R that turned into a pointing finger, for his unicorn horn. Trey was a T that morphed into the wiggling-fingered sign for flame. Henrik's gryphon proved difficult to come up with a sign for, so they decided he should be an H with fingers turning to be a snapping beak. Daniella was a D that became the second half of the sign for sing, because that was how she reached the magic in this world. Gwen was a G that went to two thumbs playing a console. Heather was an H that became two knitting fingers.

That left the two of them.

Ansel signed toilet, because it started with T, and she

laughed and punched him in the arm. He proposed a T and turned his hand into a fist.

Tadra shook her head, dissatisfied with a name rooted in violence. She couldn't use the sign for fire, since that was already Trey's name.

Ansel made a T and made wings of his fingers to fly away. Her firebird. Tadra smiled and nodded.

That was when she realized that Ansel hadn't spoken aloud the entire time they spent deciding on names; they were speaking entirely in their silent language.

He gestured at himself and shrugged. *What name should he have?*

Without hesitating, Tadra made the sign for privacy at him. It already started with an A, and she had come to realize that he was a private person. Every story that she coaxed from him felt like a little victory.

Not her key, she reminded herself; what she felt for her key would be different, would be more. He was just a friend, and she only yearned for him from loneliness. She tapped his name against her mouth again with regret and she couldn't help remembering the feeling of his lips against hers when she'd tried to kiss him.

CHAPTER 16

I like it, Ansel signed, imitating her gesture. He held two fingers together from opposite hands. *Double meaning.*

But he didn't feel like he was private with Tadra; it was too easy to talk to her, to fill all the silent spaces with his own words. He had already told her more about himself than he'd ever shared with the knights and their keys, for all that they had lived there an entire year contrasted against most of a week.

He realized that he was gazing at her more tenderly than he ought to and schooled his expression. It was too early for dinner and normally he might watch television, but he'd seen what happened with the knights when they absorbed their knowledge of the world that way. Trey had entreated him to eat his shorts many times.

"Do you want to play a game?" he offered. "I think that Life or Monopoly would be a good way to talk about money and I'm pretty sure I've got Sorry and a chess board."

Play, Tadra signed agreeably. They had learned that word talking about the dogs.

Ansel found the games on a shelf in the garage and brought them into the living room with a triumphant honor guard of dogs. "Here we go," he said, blowing the dust off of them. "All we need to teach you about capitalism and economics."

The Game of Life fascinated Tadra and as he had suspected, it opened a can of worms involving ownership and careers.

Who owns, Tadra asked, waving her hand around and showing him a starter house card.

Ansel frowned self-consciously. "The house? I do. It's mine. It was...kind of out of the blue, honestly. I was looking into my parents—my birth parents, I mean. It wasn't really that I missed them, you know, but I got curious. I wanted to know where I'd come from. Roots, you know?"

Tadra nodded knowingly.

"My parents were dead, but I found an obscure great-uncle in Michigan. We met for lunch, he told me stories about grandparents I'd never known, and I figured that would be the end of it. But about a month later, he died and left me everything he owned, including this giant house and a second hand store and a warehouse that happens to be a weak place in the veil between worlds, though I wouldn't know that for a while. It's still all...pretty unreal. I was just lucky. Like rolling a dozen double sixes in a row."

He stopped. This wasn't something he *ever* talked about.

Did you mourn? Tadra asked, tracing an imaginary tear down her cheek.

"I didn't know him well enough to feel true grief,"

Ansel said. "But I mourned the chance to know him, to ever repay him for what he did for me. I wondered about it a lot, the timing of everything, I mean. Was it just luck?"

She squeezed his arm across the table, a kind, genuine gesture, and he missed her hand when it was gone.

Tadra signed more that Ansel didn't understand, then reached for the nearest whiteboard. They had to do that less and less every day, as their language expanded. *Magic?* she wrote.

"You think magic let us meet at just the right time?" Ansel wasn't as skeptical of the idea as he would have been a year before. Not looking across the table at a half-magic knight from another world. She was wearing normal clothing, and her hair was back in a modern-looking ponytail, but there was something about her eyes and her face that said fae. Something that said she was used to six impossible things before breakfast.

Magic can behave in unexpected ways if it's not well-directed, Tadra wrote. *You ask it to do what you need, but sometimes you aren't entirely clear what that is. That is why a knight's heart must be pure, so that our intentions are never clouded.*

"Robin once said that they thought it wasn't entirely chance, either," Ansel said quietly. "That it was part of something they'd cast years ago. They thought that each of the keys was in the right place at the right time to find their knights by a whole cascade of events that was set in motion long ago." But he wasn't a key, he reminded himself. He was just...the hound-keeper. The land-owner. The guy who'd divided the ornaments and sold them like they were just ordinary pieces of glass.

Tadra licked her lips thoughtfully and Ansel tried not to think about her tongue.

If Robin had some larger plan in mind, the magic might have known that even if they didn't, she wrote. *And big changes can be made with little nudges.*

Her last words were very small and running up the side of the board. She capped the marker and signed, *Play!* as she put her car on the board.

Tadra picked up the rules of the game swiftly and looked through the career cards in interest. *What?* she asked, pointing at Ansel. *What Ansel?* she signed.

It could have meant a few different things. "What's my career?"

She nodded encouragingly.

He told her about his job working as a freelance business consultant, analyzing data.

"It was something I turned out to be good at," he said modestly. "After college, I worked at a startup in Detroit and I ended up helping to turn the business around. It became a multimillion dollar overnight success and everyone wanted to hire me. That was when I inherited the house and...everything was sort of coming up roses. I kept raising my prices, because I didn't need the work, and now I charge an absolutely criminal amount to important people who don't really need my help to point out the obvious things."

Tadra looked skeptical and Ansel laughed. "Well, they're obvious to me," he said. "I never accept that there's only one answer to any question. I'm willing to search for unorthodox solutions and I'm good at looking at data and systems and figuring out where they're broken, and at thinking outside the box. It's just a knack."

She moved her car a few spaces and drew a card. Twins! she showed him, laughing. Ansel paid her, comically grudging, and signed *twice the farts,* because they apparently both had the sense of humor of eleven-year-old boys. They laughed until the dogs got wound up and Fabio thought it was an invitation to try to climb into Tadra's lap and lick her face.

When they finished Life, Ansel made pasta and garlic toast. Tadra helped in the kitchen, keeping the dogs back and handing him hotpads and colanders as he needed them.

It was a little frightening how much Ansel enjoyed this casual domesticity, he thought, straining the noodles into the sink. It felt so right to have Tadra dancing soundlessly around the kitchen island, teasing the dogs and tasting the sauce. He almost didn't want the others to return, because that would mean that he'd have to share Tadra with someone...with her key, he remembered with a jolt.

He'd have to watch her fall in love with someone else, and worst of all, he'd have to be happy for her, because he *wanted* her to have that connection. He wanted to see her with the unabashed joy that all the knights had with their keys. She deserved that fortune, to find that one other person who completed her.

And as badly as he wanted to be that person, he wasn't.

Ansel stuffed his despair down and loaded up their plates.

Meals tended to be quiet, Tadra's hands occupied by eating, and their conversations were largely by expression and pointing at items they wanted passed. They mimed an entire exchange about parmesan cheese, with Tadra pointing to the word on the container and waving a hand in front of her face in concern after Ansel had sprinkled it on his spaghetti.

Small milk, Ansel signed back at her. *Small*—he waved his hand in front of his own face.

She giggled soundlessly and enjoyed her meal with relish.

Ansel watched her from across the table, telling himself

that he was clinically monitoring her for communication reasons, not to watch her comically wrestle noodles and hope for a glimpse of her tongue. He wasn't really gazing besottedly at her.

Was he?

He schooled his expression with effort.

She wandered away while he was cleaning the pots that didn't fit in the dishwasher and when he was finished in the kitchen, he found her in the living room, gazing at the tree.

At the ornaments on the tree, specifically.

Uncharacteristically, her shoulders were slumped. Ansel felt terrible for focusing so hard on his own stupid longing that he hadn't thought about how hard all of this must be for her.

She was in a strange world full of strangers, and she missed her shieldmates. The other knights had at least had their keys to guide them and unlock their power, but she'd gotten stuck with the hound-keeper, everyone she knew mysteriously missing, with a deadline to save the world galloping down on them. It was too much to ask of anyone, even a Firebird Knight of the Fallen Kingdom, Protector of the Broken Crown, Bravest and Most Foolish of the Shieldmates.

"We'll find them," Ansel promised, coming to her side. "I promise, we'll find them."

He tried to gauge the distance between them just right, leaving enough space that they wouldn't accidentally touch, but close enough to provide her some comfort.

He forgot, though, that the knights valued touch, and he opened his arms without thinking when she stepped closer.

Embracing Tadra was like holding onto the sun.

She fit against him so perfectly, her cheek against his, her arms up around his shoulders. She was strong and gentle and warm. Ansel willed himself not to betray how much the feeling of her against him disturbed his self-control. He wanted her so badly, was desperate to turn and kiss the velvety skin that was pressed against the short stubble that he'd allowed to grow in.

This was for her comfort, he reminded himself, and he felt a desperate mix of joy and grief to have her so close, to offer her some solace...and to know that she wasn't his.

She gradually relaxed in his arms, and when she stepped away at last, she smiled sheepishly at him. *Thanks,* she signed. *Sorry.*

No, Ansel signed back. He could have spoken, but he didn't entirely trust his voice. *Don't. You are alone here. Sad is okay.*

Not alone, she signed back gratefully. *Ansel.* Her eyes were soft and bright.

Or maybe it was privacy that she was signing. Ansel only knew that he was going to need some privacy of his own soon, because his body was still reacting inappropriately to her intoxicating proximity.

His ardor was suddenly dampened when Tadra screwed her eyes shut and swayed in place.

He caught her as she staggered a step forward and nearly fell. This embrace was different than the last; she was limp and powerless in his arms, a shadow of the woman she'd been just moments before.

He helped her to the couch and pushed Fabio away when the dog came to lick at the face in his range. Vesta jumped to the back of the couch, but since she was out of the way, Ansel left her there.

"It's okay," he told Tadra, over and over as he covered her with the afghan from the back of the couch, displacing the nervous Italian Greyhound. "We'll figure this out."

Sorry, she signed, her face frustrated.

Ansel covered her hand on her heart with his own to still it and shook his head. Vesta found a suitable place on the back of the couch to curl up.

Tadra sighed and closed her eyes wearily.

Ansel laid a kiss on her forehead without meaning to, and his lips burned when he stood up to turn off the lights.

He left the Christmas tree lights on, softly illuminating the room, and made Fabio follow him out to the media room so he wouldn't climb up and crush Tadra while she recovered.

Fabio accepted a spot on the couch next to Ansel as a poor substitute for drowsing with Tadra. Ansel took up his keyboard with determination. He wasn't going to sit around feeling helpless. He had some use beyond feeding dogs and filling dishwashers, and he was going to use his skills to find Tadra's shieldmates...and her key.

He was sure that her key would be the answer to her debilitating spells, and he was big enough to put her happiness before his own loneliness.

Somehow.

CHAPTER 17

*O*ver the next several days, Tadra found herself being careful without meaning to, always pausing to check herself for weakness before starting a task. It was infuriating, frustrating, and...so random. She frowned at her notes on the whiteboard in the living room. There were neat records of times and any events they could think that might have triggered the attacks. They'd even tracked meals, working from Ansel's suggestion that it could be an allergic reaction to something.

She could not find a pattern in the frequency of them; there was no rhyme or reason to it.

Not being able to understand it was as irksome as the actual weak spells, which left her dizzy, drained, and unable to shift. She usually recovered quickly, but they left her feeling uncertain and helpless. She hated everything about them.

Ansel looked over her records of the dates and times thoughtfully with her. He had suggested seeing a medical doctor, but Tadra was certain that the experience was magic in nature. "There's not enough data," he said, looking over her notes. "It's not a regular, predictable pattern, or at least not one you can see at this scale. Maybe we have to back up from it a little."

He bumped her hip with his in a comforting, familiar manner. "And hey, every time it happens, we'll know a little more. That's something."

He was always so positive and optimistic, always ready with comfort and distracting laughter whenever she felt low or out of sorts or impatient.

And if anyone could figure out what ailed her, Ansel could. He was frankly brilliant, though he didn't seem to think that he was. He could outsmart her at many games, though he graciously suggested that it was only a matter of experience, and he had no trouble memorizing the hundreds of hand signals that comprised their communication. At this point, they could carry on complex conversations without a single spoken word, and he never let her feel any less for her continued inability to speak. They competed in their studies, on the sparring mat, and over games on the dining room table, the loser never complaining, only laughing in defeat.

Ansel taught her that opponents in this world often shook hands at the end of a match, as they did in greeting, and Tadra sometimes thought that was the best part, having her hand in his for a moment.

She glanced sideways at him. He was always watching her carefully, respectful but alert to her every gesture. She used his concentration on the whiteboard to study him for a moment, standing close at his shoulder.

He was like a shieldmate to her. And yet not, because she had never yearned after a shieldmate, or felt their skin set hers on fire when they touched.

He was such an appealing combination of things. Gentle, but strong. Kind, but certainly ruthless in their games. Humble, but confident. He had a knight's true heart and a poet's clear sight. She would go to battle with this man at her side given the chance, trusting that he was capable and unselfish.

He glanced at her and caught her watching him before she could look away. "We'll figure it out," he said reassuringly. "Maybe when Robin gets back with your key, that will fix everything, your weak spells and your voice…" he trailed off.

They shared a worry for the return of Robin and Tadra's shieldmates. He had made many phone calls, trying to track them, inventing a story about a lost sister using Heather's identity, checking missing persons and speaking with people at something called a consulate.

Tadra's concern must have shown on her face, because Ansel was swift to assure her, "I'm sure it will be soon! I've hired a private investigator and if anyone can find them, it will be this guy."

Tadra tried to smile.

"Mind you, he probably thinks I'm some kind of nut," Ansel told her with a coaxing smile in return. "'Sure, mister, I'm looking for my…uh…sister. No, I don't have her itinerary or know her passport number, but she might be traveling with three big dudes and a faery!' Anyway, he's a professional, I'm sure he'll get the job done. He'd better, for what I'm paying!"

Tadra tried to smile more successfully that time, then remembered that Robin would be returning with her *key*, because Ansel wasn't her key, and that made her feelings a hundred times more complicated.

Ansel was still watching her. "Would it make you feel any better to kick my ass a little with a wooden sword?"

Even the suggestion made Tadra feel better; Ansel knew her so *well*. She often worked out tangles of logic best when her feet were moving, when she was going through fast physical motion that didn't leave time for her brain to get wrapped up around itself. She nodded.

They changed into what Ansel called workout clothes, stretchy and loose-fitting and met again in the garage, leaving the protesting hounds in the house.

Tadra forgot to think about her lost shieldmates and mentor, let go of all the complex emotions that Ansel sparked in her chest, allowing her attention to focus on the fight at hand. Ansel was generally self-deprecating about his skill, but he was a strong and serious opponent, and Tadra knew that if she let her guard down, he wouldn't hesitate to take the advantage.

"I'm feeling lucky tonight," Ansel teased as they took the practice swords down. "And you look slow. You shouldn't have eaten all those sandwiches for lunch."

She flipped him "the bird" and curled her fingers in invitation and they stepped through a few familiar forms, step by step at first, expected thrust and counterpoint, dodge away, turn back. She had learned her lesson about trying to talk too much with her hands as they sparred and she ignored Ansel's attempt to goad her to carelessly responding so he could earn a hit.

They did several rounds of the dance and Tadra grinned in joy, completely immersed in the ritual and familiar flow. The practice sword was lighter than a battle weapon, but not so light that the exercise was without effort, and Ansel was a swift adversary. He wore an answering grin.

Her frustration eased away, and she forgot to fight like she might collapse at any moment, swinging her sword in broad arcs that Ansel blocked.

When he lowered his sword in sudden surprise, she remained on guard, thinking that he was trying to deceive her. Then she heard the telltale crackle of a portal and dropped her sword to turn and see a split open in the air near the center of the garage.

As it opened, there was a breath of warm, tropical air and an intense smell of green. There was a glimpse of jungle through the spreading doorway, and then figures so familiar and dear that tension Tadra hadn't even realized she'd been feeling melted away from her heart. Her shield-mates! They were as whole and hale and happy as they'd been in their photographs and they were back together with her!

She ran to throw herself into their arms as they forged through, pressing her forehead to each of them in turn as they embraced her in joyful hugs and lifted her with laughter and greeting.

"Tadra!" Trey cried, folding her into his arms.

"Shieldmate! Sister!" Henrik added, stealing her away to swing her up into the air with no thought for her dignity.

Then Rez had his arms around all of them with a roar of rapture and Tadra's feet didn't reach the ground and she didn't even care.

They were so busy talking over each other that it was a long while before they realized that Tadra wasn't speaking.

"Is your tongue broken?" Trey joked as he drew away, but he didn't seem concerned as Tadra shrugged and spread her hands without replying.

There were new figures coming through the portal with more warm, moist air. Their keys, Tadra knew. Heather, with sepia skin like Ansel's though they otherwise looked nothing alike. Daniella, with cream-colored skin and long dark hair pulled back in a braid. Gwen, with her sensible shorter hair and oval face. They were all quite dirty and tired-looking.

"This is my key," Trey said, drawing Daniella forward. "Daniella."

Tadra shook her hand in the polite Earth fashion and nodded, then did the same for the others.

Heather introduced herself. "We're *delighted* to see you in one piece!" She did not have to add that she was as surprised as she was delighted; they could not have expected her to be free of her glass prison.

"I'm Gwen," the last woman greeted her.

Then the final figures were coming through the battered portal and Robin—dear, familiar Robin, even if they were as distressingly small as Ansel had warned!—was stitching the fabric of the world together...behind her own key.

This was the moment that Tadra had been waiting for.

This was the moment that fire would return to her soul.

She should be filled with anticipation and relief. Here was her destiny, her weapon, forged to help her save this curious world that she was already half in love with. She would feel for this man emotions that she had never felt before and she should be giddy with happiness.

Hope and readiness ought to fill her.

But all that she felt was guilt and regret, because she'd already given her heart without meaning to, and she only wanted Ansel.

CHAPTER 18

*A*nsel wrestled back his prickly jealousy as Tadra greeted her shieldmates with unabashed enthusiasm and glee, embracing them without hesitation and letting them lift her into their arms for giant hugs and forehead presses. He was keenly aware of his sweaty condition and his unflattering workout wear.

The knights always looked like they were stepping out of a Conan movie or off the cover of a romance novel, no matter what they were wearing.

Then Robin was flying out through the portal with a stranger and Ansel knew beyond a shadow of a doubt that this must be Tadra's key. She spotted him as Robin sealed the portal and went stiff, backing away from Gwen, who had just introduced herself.

This was it.

This was Tadra's moment of connection with her key.

She would see him and love him and need him. Ansel would be forgotten in that instance, whatever fondness they had foolishly allowed to grow between them overshadowed by the greater bond of destiny. What Ansel had with her would be relegated to a perfectly platonic friendship, just as it was always meant to be. Just as it should have remained.

He could not make himself watch her, could not bear to witness the transformation that she must go through at the sight of the stranger. So he stared at her key, instead, and hated himself for hating the man who was going to make Tadra so happy.

The key was a tall, fit man with a grin splitting his tanned face. A mop of golden hair flowed back from a broad forehead. He had movie-star good looks and brilliant blue eyes and he moved like an athlete, effortlessly graceful. He didn't look once at Ansel, who was stepping back from the chaos of greetings, wishing he was anywhere else.

"This is Kevin," Henrik introduced. "A noble warrior of the land of California who was instrumental in our release from captivity."

Kevin. Ansel even hated his name.

Then he spoke, only to Tadra, "Hello at last," and Ansel despised his smooth voice even more than his name.

Ansel couldn't look at him any longer, and he gazed around at the rest of the room. Each of the knights gave him a swift embrace and a glad greeting.

No one asked why Tadra didn't speak, or how she had been released from her broken ornament and no one offered to explain their long absence or express any concern over the deadline they were facing.

"You guys cut things kind of close," he observed.

No one paid him any mind.

"Oh my god, I need a shower." This was from Gwen, who appeared to be covered in a fine, brown slime.

"Where are the dogs?" Daniella wanted to know.

That was his cue, Ansel reminded himself. He was the hound-keeper. "They're in the house," he said faintly.

Daniella opened the door to the house, and the dogs realized what was happening and poured in, howling and barking and wagging their tails as they greeted everyone eagerly. Heather scooped Vesta up into her arms and snuggled her close as she wiggled and whined. There was no sign of Socks, of course, and Ansel wished that he could slink off like her and hide until everyone went away.

"There was much heroism," Trey declared.

"And long captivity," Rez added, but he said it with a careless shrug.

"You had it easy," Robin needled him. "Talk to me when you do that again for more than a month." Of all of them, they looked the most battered...and the most unconcerned. They had been gone the longest, and clearly had been drained of their power; they were barely able to stay aloft after sealing the portal and had diminished to a size that would already almost fit in the dollhouse that Ansel had bought for them. This seemed like a terrible portent for the coming battle...which no one had mentioned at all.

Ansel felt guilty for his selfishness, and genuinely concerned. If Robin was this weak now, would the knights be successful in fighting back a full force of invaders in just a week? But Robin looked at him then and smirked. "Still better than living in your second-hand store was."

Something felt off, and Ansel looked back at Tadra reluctantly, wanting to see if she felt it too.

Kevin was shaking her hand in greeting, so she couldn't sign, and he was gazing at her with a look on his face that Ansel couldn't quite identify. Ansel could only see the lines of Tadra's shoulders—tense with emotion—not the expression on her face as she looked back at her soulmate.

"It's been quiet here," Ansel said, plowing forward. "Haven't seen any dours or read about any psychotic breaks in the paper that might be dark magic from your world. But tell me more about what happened. I must have left you about a hundred messages."

"It was a trap," Robin said without interest. "A bleak captured Kevin and used him as bait to capture the rest of us."

"It was noble Kevin's courage that freed us," Henrik said, clapping him on the shoulder.

Kevin staggered a little at the friendly blow and Tadra glanced back over her shoulder in Ansel's direction. Ansel looked fixedly at Robin so he wouldn't see the joy in her face. He wasn't strong enough to be happy for her yet. Robin looked distant.

"The same bleak that we've faced before?"

Robin shrugged again. "Only Kevin ever saw it directly. The rest of us were handled by humans. Did someone mention food?"

Still no one had commented on the fact that Tadra didn't speak, or even wonder how it was that she was standing among them.

Could she speak now? They had theorized that she might get her voice back when she met her key.

Ansel dragged his gaze to her again. He should cheer her on and be joyful for her. That's what a friend would do.

But Tadra's face was full of reservation, and her hands were making an urgent repeated motion. *No, key. No, key. No, key.*

Kevin wasn't her key? Irrational hope flooded back to Ansel's heart. "He's not her key," he blurted.

Everyone looked between them, bewildered, and even the dogs paused in their happy writhing.

"What do you mean?" Robin asked lazily.

"He's not her key," Ansel repeated. "That's what she's saying."

Tadra nodded crisply, looking relieved. *I'm sure.*

"She's sure."

Puzzled, Henrik asked, "She said that with her hands?"

"She doesn't speak?" Trey said in slow confusion, as if he was only now noticing.

"It's sign language!" Daniella realized. "I didn't know that you knew sign language!"

"I didn't," Ansel said, watching only Tadra, who was gesturing more firmly now, and stepping away from Kevin. "She says there's no connection, that there's been a mistake, that he's not her key." He tried hard not to sound too glad about it. The relief was like being snapped with the rebound of a rubber band.

Kevin, to Ansel's surprise, didn't look the slightest bit concerned by this news. He only looked...smug.

"Maybe the reason that she feels that there is no connection is related to the reason she can't speak," Robin said dismissively. "Perhaps the key bond itself was damaged when her glass prison was broken. I'm sure it will work out. We're all ravenous, what about an early dinner?"

Ansel stopped looking at Tadra long enough to look at Robin, confused. The fable looked like this was all of no particular concern. No one else looked the slightest bit bothered, either.

"I am starving," Daniella said merrily. "I have been dreaming of a hamburger with a side of fries for two weeks."

"Don't you guys want to talk about this? Or our game plan for the end of the year?" Ansel suggested leerily. "We've been discussing strategy while you were gone…"

"We should do takeout from Brewer's!" Gwen said, as if he hadn't spoken.

"They have the baskets of fowl in the shape of fingers," Henrik said, nodding.

"Do you want to catch me up on this trap you walked

into? Should we be concerned?" Ansel asked desperately. He glanced at Tadra's hands. "Tadra wants to know if you encountered superdours there. We wondered how wide-spread they'd gotten."

"It is of no moment," Rez shrugged.

"An order of the spicy peppers, breaded and stuffed with fine white cheese!" Trey added, as if nothing in the conversation was more important.

Something wrong, Tadra signed firmly. *Is not...* she made the sign they had invented for shieldmate. ***Wrong.***

Ansel had already come to the same conclusion. None of the knights seemed the slightest bit concerned about the fact that Tadra did not recognize Kevin, or even that she couldn't speak. They didn't seem to care about the coming battle or their captivity. All of these things were dismissed as unimportant as they shed their weapons and tromped out of the garage into the house. They acted nearly drunk, skipping away from any topics of significance, fakely jovial like a troupe of mall Santa Clauses.

"I'll call in an order!" Heather called.

"First dibs on the shower!" Gwen countered.

Then they were all out of the garage, the door swinging slowly shut behind their happy chatter, and Kevin, Tadra, and Ansel were alone.

"I wondered if you'd be trouble," Kevin said thought-fully to Ansel, moving between him and Tadra.

"I wouldn't be if you were her true key," Ansel answered. He'd been completely prepared to let Tadra find her happiness with her key, but if Tadra said this wasn't him, Ansel was just as ready to fight him as he'd been to welcome him.

Maybe more ready, to be honest.

Tadra stepped forward and Ansel had to divide his attention between them. *Who?* she signed.

"Who are you, really?" Ansel asked for her.

Kevin didn't answer, but he turned his gaze to Tadra and grinned. "I'm your key, of course."

Fraud, Tadra signed angrily.

Ansel balled his hands into fists.

Kevin's gaze swiveled back to him. "Don't get any fancy ideas about hurting me. I may not be her soulmate, but her key bond is mine and I have her reins tightly in hand. Anything you do to me will only harm her."

Ansel could not doubt his sincerity, and it filled him with white-hot rage.

"The key bond is their weakness, you know, not just their strength. Robin was a little trickier, but I know every crack in *their* armor and *pride* was always their greatest flaw." He glanced scornfully at Ansel's clenched fists.

He faced Tadra. "It's a shame that your firebird is tangled so deep with your human self. I have no need for this shell you inhabit, but I need your firebird."

Then he was making a sweeping motion with one hand and Ansel watched in horror as Tadra sucked her breath in and collapsed in place, like a puppet with all her strings cut. Before he could take a step, not sure if he was going to try to help her or attack Kevin despite the man's warning, Kevin turned his blue eyes—unnaturally blue, they seemed now—to stop him in his tracks.

Ansel had read descriptions, in horror books mostly, of blood running cold. None of the fanciful literary turns of phrase really did the feeling justice. It was like he had spikes of ice stabbing him from the inside of every vein. And then, just as swiftly as it started, it was gone. Ansel stood still for a moment, trying to make sense of what had just happened to him, and Kevin turned back to Tadra as if dismissing him as a threat.

"My little firebird," he said, kneeling to pat Tadra's

head as if she was an obedient dog, then tipping her chin up. "You don't have much power here, do you? More than my bleaks now, though. They have been away from our world too long, and they can't use power like you can, they can only use it *up.*" He clucked in disappointment. "It's been much easier to get things done since you woke up, but I'll have to be careful about how much I take at once. I only need enough for the portal home, at the end of it, where my full army waits."

Ansel turned to get one of the knights' discarded weapons, then caught Tadra's tiny, urgent sign out of the corner of his eye. *Stop. Stop. Cold.* She was making the hand motion discreetly, looking up at Kevin with a slack expression of wonder and fear.

No, it wasn't *cold.* It was *freeze.*

"Poor little mute bird," Kevin said. "I wasn't sure how my spell was going to work. I didn't have much time to figure out the enchantment, or how Robin had altered it as it was cast. Henrik's counterspell only confused things, of course, but in the end, I got what I needed. Not all of your shieldmates, unfortunately, but you alone ought to be enough for my endgame, and they have been neutralized."

Tadra's hands were still fluttering. To an observer, it might have just been nervous motion, but Ansel watched her fingers avidly, trying to figure out what she was saying. *Game? Play a game? Play along? Pretend?*

He itched to do something, to attack Kevin while he was turned away, to get between him and Tadra. But it terrified him how much control the man had over Tadra; he'd been able to drop her with a mere motion, and it sounded as if he *did* have the key bond, whether it had been meant for him or not. Ansel balled his hands into fists. Was *Kevin* the reason behind Tadra's weak spells all this time?

Play along, Tadra repeated.

Kevin glanced back to Ansel, who forced his hands to relax and tried to make his face look vague and confused. If Kevin was controlling the others, it was an easy assumption that he was trying to do the same to Ansel.

"Were we going to order food?" he asked blandly. "I think I have a coupon for one of the delivery services."

CHAPTER 19

*A*nsel's indifference was so convincing that for a terrible moment, Tadra was sure that he'd been caught in Kevin's spell and she despaired of ever getting him back. She was alone in this world in truth now, adrift and truly powerless against an enemy she knew nothing about, facing a man who claimed to be her *key*.

Then she saw Ansel's hands lift to reply with the sign she'd given him, just as subtle as hers had been. *Play along.*

Relief flooded her.

"Tadra appears to have fallen," Kevin said, and Tadra made herself look even weaker than she was actually feeling.

"She probably just needs some sleep," Ansel said off-handedly, and Tadra was looking at Kevin's face at the right moment to see his mouth curve into a satisfied smirk.

Ansel continued. "This happened a few times while you were gone, I think." He even scrunched his brow, as if he were struggling to remember.

"It's no big deal," Kevin said smugly. "Let's get her to bed."

Tadra saw the flash of fury in Ansel's face and she made a show of struggling to her feet with his help to help distract Kevin from seeing it.

"Sure," Ansel said, and if his voice sounded somewhat strangled, he had made his face look serene and careless by the time Kevin looked at him. "I wonder what the others have decided to order. I should make sure there's something I can eat."

Tadra made herself allow Kevin to pull her back up to her feet, not feigning all of her weakness. She gave him a slow, sleepy blink, like she couldn't focus her thoughts, and that seemed to be what he expected.

"Oh, here, I'll help," Ansel offered casually when she could not quite keep herself from flinching away from Kevin. She tried to make it look like a wave of weakness, rather than an act of disgust and was grateful for Ansel's steadying arm. "She's got a room upstairs. I've got you set up in the last guest room downstairs by Daniella and Trey. Just a futon, but I'm sure it's a step up from whatever bleak prison you guys were in." He chuckled and shrugged.

Kevin didn't protest. They had come out into the living room, and Tadra's state did not go unnoticed.

"Tadra, are you unwell?" Trey asked.

"Is something wrong?" Henrik wanted to know.

Rez furrowed his brow, like he was confused about something.

Their keys didn't even seem to notice.

Ansel, copying their careless lack of concern, shrugged off the questions. "She just gets these dizzy spells. It's probably nothing to worry about, she'll be fine in an hour or two."

If Tadra had held doubts before that something was wrong with her shieldmates, those doubts were cemented into certainty now by their casual acceptance of Ansel's brush-off. At any other point in their long history, the other knights would have taken action, suggesting solutions, offering comfort, insisting on solving what was wrong with her. Now, although they looked sympathetic to her discomfort, they were painfully suggestible to the idea that it was of no great concern. Rez didn't even offer his healing power, as if he'd forgotten he *had* it.

"Feel better soon!" Heather called cheerfully. She was sitting in Rez's lap, looking over one of the menus from Ansel's fridge.

"Rest works many wonders," Henrik said with a knowing nod.

"I can take her upstairs," Ansel offered, sounding almost *too* casual.

Kevin shot him a suspicious look. "I'll get this arm," he insisted.

Tadra wished she had the energy to pull away, but didn't want to betray her cognizance, so she laughed and let the two of them support her up the stairs as if she had merely indulged in strong drink.

The door to her bedroom was not wide enough to walk three abreast, and Ansel reluctantly let go of her there. She felt his hand squeeze hers, briefly, and then Kevin was walking her into the room and lowering her onto the bed.

Ansel breezed in behind them and shut the curtains. "There we go," he said cheerfully. "You'll be right as rain in no time, Tadra. Kevin, why don't I show you where you'll be staying and you can put your order in for food. What would you like? Michigan cuisine isn't all that much to brag about, but there's a great pizza place downtown. Daniella works at a cafe with good all-American food, we'll have to take you there some time."

He sounded just like the others had, bubbly and

unbothered by anything. It was incredibly un-Ansel of him and Tadra wanted to warn him away from overacting.

But Kevin didn't know Ansel at all, so Tadra feigned sleep and tried not to shiver when Kevin pulled the comforter up over her. Between the two of them, Kevin seemed to be satisfied that his mischief was working. Tadra lay with her eyes closed for a long moment after they left together, then crawled from the bed to open the door and cling to the doorframe, wishing that her weakness had been entirely an act, too.

Robin. If any of them could shake off an enchantment, it would be Robin, the wisest and strongest of them. She had to get them aside from the others, try to pry up underneath the veneer of the spell. With Robin on their side again, she and Ansel would be able to free the others.

Except that she couldn't speak to Robin, unless she risked writing. No one but Ansel understood her.

She tried to stand at the doorframe and failed; all the strength was gone from her legs so she slid down and sat in the open doorway. She could hear merriment from downstairs, and she listened to the distant sound of it with her heart in her throat. They all sounded so joyous and familiar...and so fake. They looked like her shieldmates, but they'd been tampered with, damaged, and she was angry and dismayed.

And worst of all, she was helpless.

She set her jaw. Kevin, or whoever he was, had taken her vigor, but he had not taken her will.

There was a shout from downstairs, and loud laughter.

"Be right back," Ansel called from the bottom of the stairs, and Tadra felt her spirit lighten. Ansel was still on her side, was still the warrior of light that he'd always been.

She swung her door open a little wider as he came up the stairs and down the long hallway, but he put his finger to his lips as he passed by. He was soaked; clearly he had spilled something on himself to give him an excuse to change. Clever Ansel. Clever, and brave, to try to fool someone like Kevin, clearly a dark magician of some skill.

Ansel ducked into his own room and grabbed a dry shirt, then stood in the doorway and signed from there as he continued to make obvious noises in his bedroom. Anyone listening carefully from below would know that he was there, far away from Tadra's door. Too far for normal conversation, but not too far for *them.*

Tadra was apparently not entirely out of energy, because watching Ansel take off a soaking wet shirt and getting a good look at his finely sculpted chest before it was covered with a dry garment was enough to make fire rise in her blood despite the lethargy in her limbs.

She let herself enjoy it; it wasn't like she could look away and risk missing some of the signs he was making, and Kevin *wasn't* her key, so she now owed him no loyalty.

Break...magic...shieldmates. Ansel was asking how to break the spell over her shieldmates.

Tadra had to shrug, and lick her lips a little. She made the sign for Robin, an R to her forehead.

Ansel nodded and Tadra signed, *apart, alone.* They had to get Robin alone.

Ansel nodded again. *Smart. How?*

Tadra gestured to her eyes, covered her wrist and shrugged. *Watch and wait.* She pointed at him, then her mouth with a frustrated frown. Only Ansel would be able to talk to Robin.

We'll fix this, Ansel signed. He made the sign for protection and pointed at her.

Ansel would protect her.

Tadra was surprised to find tears welling in her eyes. She had never guessed that she would want someone to protect her. She was the firebird guardian, a champion of the powerless. But it didn't feel like weakness to accept Ansel's shelter and support. It felt like home.

In a world that had taken a terrible unsteady turn under her feet, he was still solid and trustworthy, a partner she could depend on.

He had already taken longer changing his shirt than the act really warranted so he reluctantly shut his door, loudly, and whistled as he walked past her room down the hallway again without slowing. She couldn't decide what to sign him as he went by and it ended up a muddy mixture of *thanks* and *sorry* and *good*.

She curled the sign for *I love you* into her lap when he had already passed.

CHAPTER 20

*K*evin was looking at him suspiciously when Ansel came down the stairs in his new shirt.

Ansel kept his face as neutral as possible, trying to funnel his memories of stoners in his college classes. He was suggestible, he had no suspicions, he was completely normal and not-at-all paranoid. As far as he knew, everything was going exactly as it should, he had no doubts or reservations or independent thoughts.

The others made it easy, talking about a whole lot of nothing that he could join in on easily. He caught them up on the dogs, who were blissfully absorbing all the attention. He detailed the many things that Vesta had destroyed and everyone laughed at his comic descriptions of Fabio's heartbreak.

"I'll pay for the damages," Heather assured him, cuddling Vesta in her arms like a baby. "She was just missing her mama, weren't you! I was gone for so long!"

"She does that when you're in the bathroom," Rez pointed out wryly.

"Socks is...somewhere," Ansel told Gwen when she came down, freshly-showered.

"She'll come out in her own good time," Gwen said without worry. Socks was pretty independent, but Gwen's nonchalance still seemed a little over the top.

They all admired the trimmed Christmas tree and exclaimed with guilt over the presents that he and Tadra had wrapped and placed under it.

"You should go shopping tomorrow!" Ansel suggested as casually as he could manage. "Take Tadra to the mall and show her Santa Claus." Robin wouldn't be able to go somewhere as public as the mall, which would leave them home, alone, with Ansel.

"We can get photos in Santa's lap!" Daniella joked.

"I am not sure if I like the idea of you in this Santa's lap," Trey protested with mock jealousy.

Then the delivery driver arrived, and the dogs exploded into a frenzy of greeting and guarding.

Once the driver had been tipped and sent on his way, Ansel went to the kitchen while the others unpacked it in the dining room. "Who wants drinks? Kevin, what'll it be? We've got sodas, some beer, water…?"

"Don't drink Ansel's almond milk!" Heather and Daniella chorused.

Kevin chuckled and Ansel had to grit his teeth and hope that it looked like he was smiling.

Kevin had been at the last battle for the faery world, he said, which meant that he, too, was from that place. He didn't appear to be a bleak and he didn't have the same awkward puppet-blankness that a human who was ridden seemed to have. He clearly didn't think he was being controlled. So what was he? A human? A human witch who had fought at the side of Cerad? Ansel had been under the impression that Cerad's army had been one of darkness and dours, and Kevin seemed too big and blond and *tanned* to be a faery.

Gwen came into the kitchen to help him bring out drinks, and Ansel tested her cautiously. "So, you guys had a bit of an adventure, I guess. How did you get hurt?"

There was a purplish bruise at her temple, and Gwen's face crumpled in concentration as she touched it. Then her face seemed to clear. "It was no big deal," she said, with a shrug and a smile. "We're back in plenty of time."

"Time for what?" Ansel asked pointedly, glancing at the open kitchen door.

"Time for Christmas," she said carelessly. "What else?"

The end of the world as we know it, Ansel thought, thoroughly unsettled. "What about the...end of the *year?*" he asked. He didn't want to accidentally trigger some kind of protection that Kevin had laid on her, and he didn't know how this magic of control really worked. Were they all brainwashed? Would Gwen tattle to Kevin if Ansel was too obvious with his questions?

"We should get fireworks," Gwen said breezily. "Oh, we're almost out of cola. Put it on the shopping list? We'll need to go out tomorrow and battle the Christmas Eve crowds."

That wasn't at all the battle that Ansel had been thinking of. "Good idea," he said faintly as she bustled out with an armful of bottles and glasses.

It reminded him of something, and after a moment, he finally realized that Gwen's behavior matched the aftermath of a dour. The host never really acknowledged that they'd lost control of themselves, or that anything was ever wrong. They came up with an explanation for what had happened, no matter how incomplete the story seemed, and everyone around them accepted it without question.

Except Tadra...and Ansel.

It made some sense if Tadra was immune to Kevin's magic if he was using her own power. But Ansel was only human. Only human...and not Tadra's key.

Ansel closed his eyes, listening to the din of the merry chatter coming from the living room.

He'd gotten used to the quiet: just himself, and the dogs, and silent Tadra, and he ached to have that back. He'd missed his friends, and Robin, but that wasn't who had come through the portal. These were strangers. Worse, they were strangers wearing the faces of his friends. *Frauds.*

"Anything wrong?"

Kevin.

Ansel opened his eyes. "I was just thinking how weird it was to have all you guys home again. It was really quiet without everyone here, and there was some reason I was really anxious to have you back, but I don't really remember why now." He shrugged like it was no big deal and forced a big dumb smile onto his face. "Guess I just missed you all."

Kevin's satisfied look made Ansel want to slug him. He wrapped his fingers around the handles of the serving tray instead. "I have to put cola on the shopping list," he said, trying to sound the right amount of dreamy and distracted.

Robin's chair and table had remained set up on the dining room table, but the scale was large for them in their much-diminished form. That didn't seem to be a bother to them—nothing seemed to be a bother to any of them.

Ansel ate with the others, forcing tasteless food into his mouth as he pretended as hard as he could that he was just like them, under some kind of careless enchantment where nothing mattered at all.

CHAPTER 21

*T*he mall, which had been a scene of noise and chaos the first time Tadra went, was much, much worse without Ansel.

Tadra thought at first that it was just that she felt completely on edge around Kevin, knowing the lie behind his too-nice grins and light-hearted humor, hating how she had to smile and act like everything was normal.

But it was also the way that none of them could understand anything she signed at them. Writing on the notepad she'd brought was awkward and time consuming, and they didn't remember any of the signs that they'd practiced together just that morning. She had learned many new things with her shieldmates and she knew that they ought to remember at least the basics of what she and Ansel had taught them, but the thoughts seemed to run through their minds like water through a sieve.

Tadra felt like she was out of step with all of their conversations. She had nothing to add, and they seemed confused about how to include her.

And most of all, it was the way they all acted like *nothing at all was wrong.*

There was no hurry in any of them, no anxious awareness that they needed to be worried about the pending thinning of the boundary between their worlds. They acted like there was no danger, no pressing need to do anything but select gifts for other people and eat messy food in a loft filled with tables and chairs.

They sat crowded close together at the noisy meal and Tadra could barely make it through her own dish, a greasy pile of fries and a round meat sandwich with a sugary drink of bubbles. None of it was to her taste, least of all the company. Kevin was wretched, but her shieldmates were worse, because none of them were *real.*

She might have asked to return to Ansel's house, perhaps even feigned weakness. She was fully recovered from what she now knew was Kevin's use of what little magic she had. But she had to keep them all occupied long enough for Ansel to break Robin from his enchantment...if he even could.

Everything was awful and loud and a stark contrast to Ansel's quiet safe house, and his agreeable, genuine company.

"Let's go shopping!" Daniella said eagerly as they threw their copious trash into a bin. "Christmas is the day after tomorrow and I haven't found anything for Trey or Kevin yet."

She led the way down the moving stairs towards a shop full of incomprehensible electronic things and Tadra trailed along, trying to look dazed and not just dismal.

How long would it take for Ansel to talk with Robin and break the spell on the fable? Tadra couldn't let herself wonder if he would be able to at all. Ansel was wise and smart, but he didn't know faery magic, and Kevin was clearly a witch of great skill.

And he was using *her* power.

She had to turn away to look fixedly at a rotating Christmas display, her hands in fists at her side, because she desperately wanted to attack the charlatan. She knew that if she did, he could merely drain her strength, and worse, that her shieldmates would take his side, which was a chilling and depressing realization.

"Don't worry," Gwen said warmly at her elbow. "I know that money is a little strange at first, but we can cover a few small gifts for you and steer you right."

Tadra looked at her pleasant oval face, at her soft brown eyes. There was a real person in there, she reminded herself. These keys were cut from the same cloth as knights, true-hearted and good. It was her duty to release that person, to free *all* of them, from Kevin's evil influence.

Tadra lifted her chin. This was all no more than a slight setback; she had a mission to focus on and there was no room for self-pity or doubt. She would figure out how to sever Kevin's control and bring them all back.

"Have you thought about anything you might like to get for Ansel?" Daniella asked Gwen. "He's so impossible to shop for." They were standing in front of the colorful map of the great mall.

"What do you get the guy who has everything?" Gwen agreed.

Ansel. A *present* for Ansel. The idea of choosing a gift for him was a ray of light in the gloom of her heart.

Tadra found her pencil, which had dropped to the bottom of her pocket and pulled her notebook out. *I know!* she wrote.

CHAPTER 22

The house was weirdly quiet with all the knights and their keys gone again, but Ansel found himself missing silent Tadra most of all. It was unsettling not to have her in the house with him, and he was surprised by how much he'd gotten used to having her nearby in their few weeks of companionship.

He kept looking around to make sure he wasn't missing her hand signs, to let himself drink in her beauty under the pretense of maintaining communication. He found himself wanting to make observations to her, to explain something about his world's technology, or just to see how she was reacting to some new wonder. She was so interested in everything, so alive and full of life.

Even if everyone else had been home, the house would be empty without *her*.

But it wasn't. Robin was still here, and Ansel had work to do.

"Robin? Hey, Tinker Bell?"

Robin wasn't watching television, or lounging in the

living room. The dogs, feeling very miffed that their people had finally returned and then abandoned them again, clearly forever, followed at his heels through every open room and up the stairs and back down.

Ansel finally found Robin in the dining room, sitting at their little table-on-a-table, on a chair close to their scale as they browsed the Internet on a phone propped up beside them. They shut off the screen when Ansel and the dogs came in.

"Looking up faery porn?" Ansel ribbed him as Fabio flopped down in the doorway so he couldn't escape.

Robin flipped him off. It was uncanny how true to their character they seemed, and how quickly that illusion was broken when Ansel asked pointedly, "I want to know what we're going to do when the dark forces from your fallen world break through the weakened veil in about a week."

Robin had been looking at him, and their gaze simply slid from Ansel's like he'd been oiled, just as all the knights' did whenever any serious topic was brought up.

"I was just thinking how much nicer this place was than that hole of a warehouse I stayed in for a whole year," they said casually. "I should have squatted at the Marriott or something. Better room service, too." Robin acted like the pending battle hadn't even been brought up, just as Ansel had expected.

"I don't remember you paying any rent," Ansel pointed out as he sat in one of the chairs facing Robin. "You know, you're pretty ungrateful for a freeloader. We're here because we're prepping for the invasion from your dark-sparkle faeryland, remember? We should plan our defense."

"I was in the middle of a game of Candy Crush," Robin protested.

"End of the world, *faery*," Ansel pressed. "I think this is a *little* more important."

"I'm not a faery," Robin said, as if that was the sticking point of Ansel's statement.

Ansel suspected by now that a direct discussion would go nowhere. His previous attempts to crack into whatever compulsion had been cast on the knights and their keys had ended the same way; they simply could not absorb the conversation, it ran off of them like water off a duck.

But he was hopeful that a sideways attack might work. "Robin, if there was some magic at work that kept someone, say me, from talking or thinking about certain topics, how would I go about getting free of that constraint? Theoretically, I mean. You're a fable who would know how to do that, right?"

Robin looked suspicious, but slightly flattered, and just as Ansel wondered if this was going to be a dead end, too, they shrugged. "I'm a creature of magic. I don't need trappings and ritual. I would simply burn the foreign magic from my system."

"How do you do that if you don't know that you need to?" Ansel persisted. "Is there...an...I don't know, like a cleaning cycle you could run to just sort of scrub out any spells that you wouldn't know about?"

"I would know if I were enspelled," Robin scoffed. "I am—"

"A fabulous magical fable," Ansel finished for them. "But if you *didn't* know?"

Robin's familiar scowl hesitated just a fraction and Ansel pressed at the possible weakness. "You've been mistaken about things before. What if you were wrong about this, too?"

"I'm not wrong," Robin said, but they said it thoughtfully. "If I was..."

"Theoretically," Ansel added.

"If I theoretically was under a spell…" Robin closed their dark eyes and Ansel, watching them carefully, didn't see anything change until their eyes opened again, blazing in anger. "This is a violation!"

Then, to Ansel's surprise, their face changed to an expression of grief and guilt. "What have I done?"

"Can you talk about it now?" Ansel said cautiously. "Will you remember this? Can you remember the coming battle and how Kevin…"

"Cerad," Robin snarled.

"Cerad is controlling Kevin?" Alarmed, Ansel started to rise to his feet. "Is Tadra in danger? The others?"

"Cerad *is* Kevin," Robin said flatly. "It's just a name that he assumed here. We have all been his puppets."

"Why didn't the knights recognize him?" Ansel remained on his feet, hands flat on the table.

"Only I ever knew him. And I was already compromised when they got to Ecuador." It was hard to look at Robin now, they were so angry. Ansel felt like they were glowing without light; there was an energy coming off of them that wasn't light or heat, but some other under-the-skin kind of power. Even their voice was different, deeper and vaster and more musical.

"He doesn't know," Robin growled. "He doesn't know that I have slipped his leash." As quickly as they had angered, the energy seemed to drain away from them. Ansel wondered if he imagined the fact that they were a little smaller than before, and he frowned to think what breaking even just that much of the spell had cost the fable.

Ansel was the focus of a sudden sharp look. "You and Tadra have eluded his enchantment?"

"Not for lack of trying," Ansel told him, settling back

into his chair. "Her dizzy spells. He said he took the key connection, and he's able to drain her power. He tried to use it to enspell me."

Robin's eyes narrowed. "And you shook it off. How?"

Ansel shrugged. "I don't know. We've just been playing along as best we can, pretending that we can't hold a thought in our heads, like all the rest of you."

"He sometimes only saw what he was looking for," Robin said. "He must have stolen the bond that would have made her your key during the battle when we first came to this world."

Ansel felt like he'd just been stabbed with hope. "I'm Tadra's key?"

But Robin shook their head. "No. I think you would have been; that is why the magic took us to your warehouse. But there is no way to reset that kind of connection. It is Cerad's now as surely as if it had been made for him." They chuckled dryly.

"And he can just keep using it to drain her?" All the hope turned into fury inside Ansel's chest. If he had hated Kevin, he didn't even have a definition for the depth of emotion that he had for Cerad, for the man that had *stolen* the connection he might have had with Tadra and was using it for his own evil purpose. "Can we…can I...kill him?"

Ansel had never thought of himself as a violent person; he felt that there was always an alternative to hurting someone. And although he had grudgingly become skilled at sparring with the knights and their keys, he could not imagine using that hard-won expertise to harm another person. Until Kevin. *Cerad.* "Is he human? Mortal?"

Robin's face was a mixture of anger and sorrow. "He was. He is...with one major difference."

After a long silence, Ansel asked, "Are you going to tell

me what that difference is or just lean into that whole mysterious asshole persona that you have spent your years on Earth cultivating?"

Robin chuckled without humor. "Cerad is my fault. It was my error that made him what he is, and my guilt that kept me from correcting it with his death before it was too late." They stood on the edge of the table and should have looked ridiculous, like a doll propped up for a children's game, but they never did.

"I am not merely a fable. I am *the* fable. I have been the crown of faery for as long as faery has existed. Time and memory there does not flow as it does here, so I cannot say if I am centuries or millennia old, but after a time alone in the world of my own wonder, I desired more complex companionship. I had the ability to create anything I needed but not the imagination to conceive of it. Which was when I discovered a world just next to mine, separated by only a thin veil."

Ansel absorbed this revelation. "You're the crown. The broken crown they talk about."

"All this time, you didn't know you had a celebrity living in your warehouse."

"I might have left out milk and cookies if I'd known."

"That's Santa Claus, asshole."

Ansel had to laugh dryly, then ask, "And the stories of the faery queen stealing human children…?"

Robin's smile was wry. "Most stories have seeds of truth, however far they may be from their roots. Suffice to say that the time I came here two years ago was not the first time I have crossed this boundary. Your world has changed in ways I never thought possible."

"And Cerad?" Ansel wasn't ready to let go of the topic of stopping him.

"I raised him beside me as an equal, whatever he

thinks now about how I wronged him. He had every power at his disposal, every luxury and advantage. I even gave him the tools to tap magic without being magical himself. I *trusted* him."

"And it wasn't enough, because humans are shallow and petty?" Ansel guessed.

"You've read the wrong books," Robin said reproachfully. "He fell in love. He fell in love with a mortal woman. She...died and left him hurting so badly that he begged me to free him from the torment of it. I didn't wish to lose him as my brother, so I took his pain away from him, and created a monster instead of a man."

"You took his pain?"

"I took his grief away and left a hole for chaos and darkness to grow. His sorrow was tangled irrevocably with his love and with neither of them, there was no heart left in him. I created a pocket for evil to live. I didn't realize at first what I had done, and the taint spread before I knew how to stop it. It poisoned the deepest cores of our magic, causing chaos and destruction in the form of the bleaks and dours, even before Cerad realized that he could control and direct it with the anger and malice that remained inside of him unchecked by compassion. I was almost too late to save any of the magic at all. I only had enough untouched for four vessels."

"The knights," Ansel realized. Trey. Rez. Henrik. *Tadra.*

"I took my truest human warriors and gave them the last of the pure magic from my world, to protect it. They were at first my final hope to save my kingdom, and now, the only hope to save yours. I broke my crown to make them."

Ansel let his breath out in a hiss of understanding. "Do they know?"

Robin's wilting posture told Ansel as clearly as words

that the knights did not know. "I could not put that weight on their shoulders, too. I thought...I honestly thought that it was a kindness. They know me only as a mentor and friend, and they thought that the crown fell long before they came to duty, not that I broke it to *make* them."

"Tell her," Ansel said fiercely. "Tell them all. They deserve the truth."

"I was trying to protect them from the truth!"

"What truth?" Ansel demanded. "The truth of who you are? The truth of what they are? Or the truth of how you failed Cerad? You can't pick and choose what to tell them and expect them to fight on your side just because you *say* it's the right one. We all have to be able to make our own destinies, with all the hard choices that come with it."

Robin drew themself up in bristling fury and Ansel had a moment of wondering if he'd badly overstepped at last— he was, after all, scolding the crown of faery, however diminished, like they were an errant dog. The air seemed to crackle.

Robin's anger faded into sorrow and they shook their head in chagrin. "Being immortal and all-powerful didn't always mean I was particularly smart."

They gave Ansel a long, appraising look. "You asked if you were supposed to be Tadra's key. Do you..." they paused.

"I love her," Ansel said, and the words were so raw that they seemed to burn his mouth. "I love her. I tried not to, believe me, but it was like trying to stop the tide or turn back time."

Robin gave a great sigh and turned their face away. Were they disappointed? Did they—rightly—think that Ansel wasn't worthy of a woman like Tadra? A woman who held a quarter of the remaining magic of faery, one of the truest of the crown's knights.

Then they looked back. "Does she feel the same?"

Did she? Did Ansel imagine the warmth in her eyes or overestimate what was only friendship and affection? "It doesn't matter," he said mournfully. He wasn't her key, even if he might have been. He couldn't anchor her to this world and allow her to access her power. He couldn't keep Kevin from draining her to her bones whenever he wanted.

"It matters," Robin countered softly. "That could be why Cerad can't enchant you. It could be why Cerad can't enchant *her*. Love is its own kind of magic, and it can be stronger and wilder than even the deep magic of faery. It can undo whole worlds. The key spell wasn't just meant to connect two people magically, it was meant to find people who could love each once they were connected."

"I don't want to undo worlds," Ansel said. "I just want to undo what Kev—Cerad has done. You never said whether I could kill him or not."

Robin frowned. "I don't know what harming him would do to Tadra. They are bound together, whether they should have been or not."

It wasn't a risk that Ansel could take, and his helplessness made him ache. "Then we find another way to stop him. How do we break the spell he has over everyone?"

"The enchantment he's using is very simple and requires almost no power; it merely builds on one of the most basic magics of faery. The human brain already tries to fill in gaps—I'm sure you've seen those visual tricks where colors don't actually exist, or read the articles about how witnesses can be influenced."

"People are sheep?" Ansel supposed sourly.

"Not sheep," Robin said. "They are complicated

vessels of emotion and imagination. Their minds *want* to protect them from confusion and pain, and it can be easy to lead them to comfort with gentle falsehood. This magic simply makes an easy path for that. You merely blank out the parts you don't want them to feel or think about and let their own imaginations do the rest. It isn't the same as controlling them, as manipulating them like puppets, and it isn't the same as removing their memory. It simply cuts off their will in very particular ways. It is, in some ways, the light side of what dours do, the way that they enhance all the greed and anger without specifically directing it. I suspect that Cerad does not have the power here to do any more than this, or he would be more flagrantly using the knights' unlocked magic. He, like all of us, is limited in your world."

That made sense with what Ansel had witnessed. The enchanted knights and their keys slid off any topics that might cause distress, to the absence of caring about anything but each other. They laughed and seemed merry, but it was all dulled by a lack of depth.

"How do we break it?" he asked again.

Robin paced the table, their wings gleaming behind them. "If I had more power, I could do it directly. There was a time I would have been able to do it with a thought." They looked down at themself with frustrated resignation. "It will have to be subtle, but the spell must have weaknesses. There are topics that won't allow any purchase—the coming battle, I would guess, and doubts about Kevin himself, possibly even knowledge of their own power. But perhaps we can go in sideways, find a place that is still tender, that will allow us to infiltrate the indifference and get through to the real person behind."

"While not letting onto Kevin—Cerad—that we know

who he is and what he's doing," Ansel said wryly. "That's all. Can he re-enchant you?"

Robin's dark eyes went flinty. "I know what he's doing now," the fable said firmly. "He won't have luck with that again."

CHAPTER 23

*T*he first few times Tadra had come back to Ansel's strange house from being out in the even stranger world, it felt nothing like a home. Now, with her shieldmates and their keys...and Kevin...Tadra was filled with relief and comfort at the sight of it. This was where she belonged. Not the noisy mall, or the cold streets, but here in the house that was so filled with her memories of Ansel.

Even the sight of the excited dogs gave Tadra gladness and relief.

She couldn't help but wonder anxiously, had Ansel been able to get through to Robin? Was there any hope that he had been able to crack through Kevin's enchantment?

Ansel greeted them all with his fake-jovial act and Tadra watched him for any clues that he had genuine good news, hopeful for a sign of optimism or victory.

But they were both hyper-aware of Kevin's scrutiny and Ansel gave no hint of any thought beyond greeting them and getting the dogs back out of the way as everyone

flowed in. He was friendly, offering up the table in the
dining room for wrapping gifts and coming to direct the
unpacking of the groceries. He was so convincingly light-
hearted that Tadra was actually worried he'd fallen under
the spell until he signed a quick *Play along* at her.

"Tomorrow, we feast!" he joked. "You must have
bought half the store. Where are we going to put the
turkey? I hope you got one that was thawed! Here, let's put
the potatoes in the pantry, they'll be fine there until we
have more room in the fridge."

He flashed Tadra a thumbs up, but Tadra was not
certain if it was meant to be a casual greeting for the
benefit of the others or a message that he'd talked to
Robin.

Real Robin, not the dazed, distracted version of Robin
that was a farce of their real self. She caught Kevin's suspicious glance and smiled in what she hoped was a
compellingly cheerful way. She had the bag with her gifts
in her arms, and she clutched it close, like she was trying to
hide it.

"Let's wrap presents," Daniella invited. "Girls first!
Guys out!"

Tadra was herded into the dining room with the keys,
and she was keenly aware of how different it had been to
wrap gifts with Ansel. They chattered merrily, gossiping
about what they'd gotten their knights, what they were
making for dinner, what they hoped to get.

They did their best to include Tadra, but she could
barely converse with them, as much because she didn't
understand their slang and obscure references as because
she couldn't speak. They were all from this world and lived
in it effortlessly.

Once she'd wrapped her gifts—they were unimpressed
by her hardwon skills with the tape—she slipped back out

to the living room with the bright-covered packages in her arms.

Robin was standing on a footstool in the empty room, gazing at the lit tree. All the overhead lights were off, making it glow in the dark space, and Robin was edged in silver and flickering with green and red.

But was it Robin? Had Ansel been able to crack Kevin's enchantment, or was this only the hollow shell of Robin, moving through the motions of life without their full will?

She must have made some small noise, or perhaps Robin merely sensed her, because they swiveled to see her, and gestured her closer. They glanced behind her, and pressed a finger to their lips—a useless reminder, since she could not speak. Tadra went to the tree and put her gifts with Ansel's beneath it.

From the dining room, there was more laughter and someone turned on Christmas music. They chattered and scolded each other for peeking.

Tadra turned back from the tree, searching Robin's face for clues.

"I am myself," they said quietly, to her crashing relief. "I remember our purpose and know about Kevin's falsehood."

Tadra sank down to her knees before them. *So worried,* she signed, even though Robin wouldn't know the words. She wasn't even sure if they were official sign language or words that she and Ansel had made up as they struggled together learning to communicate.

They sighed. "I owe you many things," they said, in a voice uncharacteristically filled with regret. "Most of all, the truth."

Tadra looked up at them, confused.

"I always told you that the crown you were meant to

protect was broken, but I never told you how, or why...or that I was the vessel of the crown."

She pointed at them hesitantly and mimed a crown upon her head.

"I was the crown of the kingdom," Robin said.

Tadra felt that she ought to be surprised. She wasn't sure if so much had happened that she was merely numb to shock...or if some part of her had always known. There was something about Robin that hinted at greater power, a deeper well of wisdom, and they had always discouraged talking about themself. The crown...had felt like a distant abstract, and Tadra saw with unexpected clarity that the crown that Robin had taught them about was the ideal of themself.

A dozen of their disparaging remarks came into ironic focus.

If she had not already been kneeling, she would have then, so she merely bowed her head. She did not have a sword to raise, so she made the sign for shieldmate and kept her fists crossed across her chest.

"Tadra," they said warmly. "Tadra, the bravest and most foolish of my knights. In some ways you are the wisest."

She looked up and caught a smile across their face, a smile that didn't quite reach their eyes.

"There is more…"

Tadra could not speak and keep her arms crossed, so she released them and shrugged. *What else?*

Noise from the doorway behind her made them both freeze, but whoever it was moved on to the kitchen without pausing.

Robin sat on the footstool, and speaking quietly, told her a story that was familiar, with new details that changed the truth she'd known completely. Kevin was Cerad. Cerad had been Robin's companion, and Robin had tried to help him heal from grief and made a terrible mis-step.

"I didn't understand the power of the heart, or the complexity of human emotion," Robin admitted with humility. "I had boundless magic energy, but I could not spare him his suffering without changing the basic blocks of who he was...*what* he was. I told you that Cerad betrayed me, that he wanted power, and that was true, but it wasn't the truth. I betrayed him, by doing as he asked me to, and he is only trying to fill the void that I left in him."

Then Robin gave her a sharp look and stopped speaking.

Tadra did not lower her gaze, suspecting a test. How could she express that she did not blame Robin? She could not repeat the vows that she'd made as a knight out loud, but she was not going to cast them aside because she learned new details that didn't change her loyalty.

Robin went on. "When I realized what I'd done, when I saw how the magic of our world was being tainted by the darkness I'd crafted, I was desperate to save it. I took what was left and divided it into four vessels." They stopped, glancing again at the doorway behind Tadra but there was no need for them to say more.

Four vessels.

Four knights.

Her magic half was not merely a gift of intangible power to aid in her mission, it was a pillar of their world. When Robin told them that they were the protectors of their kingdom, of the broken crown, they had not meant it metaphorically. Her firebird was a *part* of the deep magic, one of the last unsullied pieces of her world.

Tadra mimed pulling from her chest, offering her hands back to Robin. Could she give it back? Would she lose her firebird altogether? It was hard to remember a time before the two of them had been one.

Robin's face softened, and they shook their head. "I do not believe that it would be possible. The power has bled into every pore of your being, like a dye staining wool. If it was taken from you, it would not leave enough to live as merely a human."

Like when Kevin—Cerad!—drained her of what little magic she had and her human form could barely stand.

Tadra let her breath hiss in her mouth.

Cerad had control of her. And all the knights, if not to the same degree. Which meant that he had access to all of that power that he needed. And his purpose was not different now; he wanted the riches and wealth of *this* world for his own.

Tadra made the sign of a key into her hand and it was universal enough that Robin knew it at once. "Cerad has the connection of your key, the magic that would have anchored you to this world. But he is not from this world, any more than you are, and magic has a different flavor here. I believe that his access to your magic is limited just as the other knights were limited before they bonded with their keys."

What now? Tadra asked. *Stop him.*

Robin drew their chin up with determination. "I don't know how to make everything right again, but I will not let this world fall because of my mistakes with my own. I will find a way to break his power over all of you."

Tadra felt greatly comforted. Robin was the fable she knew again, her teacher and friend. She trusted that they could do as they vowed.

Then they looked searchingly at Tadra. "Ansel. You have feelings for him."

Ansel. Even the sound of his name made her feel weak.

A knight should not have distractions from their goals, Tadra realized with shame. She gestured to her heart and covered her ears, shaking her head. She couldn't listen to her foolish heart.

Robin took to the air and touched their forehead against Tadra's where she still knelt.

"Your heart is the greatest part of you," they said firmly, taking her face in both tiny hands. "Always listen to it and never underestimate it the way that I did."

It was hard to focus her gaze on them so close, so Tadra closed her eyes and soaked in the comfort of her mentor...her crown. Her breast burned with mixed feelings.

Robin retreated back to their footstool. Tadra shrugged her helplessness. What should she do next? Cerad had all the power of her firebird at his command.

"Keep on as you have," they advised, either guessing her question or simply moving to the next logical step. "I do not understand Cerad's plan yet, to know how best to thwart it. I suspect he is waiting for the time that the veil is weakest, to call over his bleaks for a swift victory."

Tadra scowled and gave the sign for her firebird, then shook her fists in frustration.

"There is one—" Robin cut themself off as Daniella came sailing into the room with Gwen, both of them laden with gifts.

"Yes, yes," Robin joked. "I see how it is. All the gifts for the knights, none of them for the fable. Never mind, I'm fine, I know my lot in life. A whole year in Ansel's odiferous warehouse, I suppose this will still be an improvement over that."

The keys teased the fable back, saying Robin clearly didn't need the presents that had been picked out for them if they weren't going to appreciate the gesture.

Trey and Rez swept in after them, making a show of squeezing and shaking their presents over the protests of their keys.

Tadra pretended to laugh along, but she watched them cover her presents with their own and wistfully wished them back, whole and real again, or not here at all so that she could enjoy this time alone with Ansel again.

CHAPTER 24

"*Y*ou aren't calling your mother?" Ansel asked Gwen, when he caught her alone in the media room. "Daniella and Heather are both off doing their daughterly duty."

Gwen was playing some kind of zombie shooter game and she looked back over her shoulder at him. "I'll call tomorrow, when everyone's in a food coma. Mom is less likely to give me a hard time about wasting my life if it's Christmas proper, but Christmas Eve would totally be free game."

Ansel glanced out down the hallway behind him and decided that shutting the door would be too suspicious. He came to sit beside her on the couch, using the excuse of sharing from the open bag of popcorn that she had on the coffee table her feet were propped up on.

"I won't get butter on the couch," she promised.

"Clean it up if you do," Ansel said casually. "Hey, Gwen, do you think there's something a little weird going on?"

"Weird how?" Gwen asked, grimacing and pounding

on one of the buttons with her thumbs. "Weird like flying fables and tiny dogs and what Henrik did to the microwave? Dammit, that's not what I was trying to do. This controller is on its last legs; I'm hoping they have a sale on them after Christmas."

"Weirder than that," Ansel said more directly. "Like there's something—*someone*—messing with our minds."

Gwen looked at him a moment, confusion crinkling her brow as she seemed to think about it. "Like who?"

"Like Kevin," Ansel suggested. "Don't you think he's a little...off?"

He was watching her carefully and saw the exact moment that he said Kevin's name and her brain seemed to switch off. "It's nothing," she said, shrugging as she gave Ansel a giant, false smile. "It took all of us keys a little while to connect with our knights, you know. It's no big deal. Don't push them, it'll work out." She turned back to her game in time to make a spectacular save. "Aw, yeah. Eat it, Gamer69."

Ansel felt like he was witnessing a telemarketer reading from a script.

"Think about it, Gwen," he pressed. "The veil to the other world is going to be thin at the end of the year. A week away. Shouldn't we be a little concerned about that?"

Gwen gave no indication that she'd even heard him, concentrating on her game as if she'd forgotten about Ansel altogether. He reached forward and snatched the controller out of her hands. "Listen to me," he insisted. "I want you to think about you and Henrik, facing off against the superdours just a couple of weeks ago. Remember that? Remember how seriously we were taking everything then?"

She gaped at him, looking shocked by his action, but still not as alarmed as she ought to, just confused. She tried to take the gamepad back, but not with the kind of effort Ansel would expect from her, like all of her reactions were muted and slow. Gwen had always had fighter-honed reflexes, so it was particularly obvious in her motions. He racked his memory for some way to get through to her.

Robin had said that love was a special kind of magic. "Henrik," Ansel said desperately. "Aren't you worried about Henrik? What if someone is messing with *his* brain, trying to control *him?*"

"Control?" Gwen stopped trying to get the controller back and her brow furrowed at Ansel, like she was trying very hard to figure something out. "Henrik…"

"Henrik's wrapping your gift right now," a silky voice said from the doorway.

Ansel turned to find Kevin standing behind them with his fingers spread, but not before he saw all the tension fall away from Gwen's face, to be replaced by a silly smile.

"Oh," she said, snatching the controller back from Ansel. "I wonder what he got me! It's probably socks, oh my gosh, you should have seen him when I took him to Big Mart, waxing eloquent over the *vast* selection of knitted footwear."

"Oh, no!" Ansel said, forcing himself to laugh and lounge back on the couch, letting his face go slack. "That's awful, because I got you socks, too. Dammit, now I'm going to have to go buy you something else!"

Gwen punched him in the shoulder. "You don't have to buy us gifts," she reminded him.

"We could make it a theme," Ansel said, looking over his shoulder again at Kevin, who had his arms folded. How much had he heard? Robin said he was suspicious, but that meant he couldn't tell for sure. "Kevin, you should get her socks, too."

"Oh my god you guys," Gwen said, giggling. "Don't do

it. Don't! I'll end up being like my Aunt Mina who gets everything flamingo even though she can't stand them because someone told someone else that she liked them, and after that it was this giant joke. I want more than socks for gifts the rest of my life, have pity!"

Ansel took another handful of popcorn.

Trey appeared in the door. "Tadra has fallen," he said casually, and it was everything that Ansel could do to swallow the tasteless, dry popcorn in his mouth and not react, because Kevin was watching him so closely.

"Do you need to translate for her, Ansel?" Kevin asked pointedly. It was like he wasn't even trying to be subtle with his test.

"That's what the whiteboards are for," Ansel said lazily. "I mean, if you need me, sure, but Gwen's got the dungeon level coming up…"

"Her shieldmates can assist her to bed," Trey said nobly.

"She'll be fine," Ansel insisted, taking another handful of the popcorn so he had something to do but ball his hands into fists. He wished he could turn to watch Kevin's face, to try to decide if he'd been satisfied with Ansel's answers, but he feared that he would betray his anger if he looked at him too long.

Kevin followed Trey out, and Ansel breathed a silent sigh of relief. Gwen went back to playing her game as if nothing at all had happened.

"About Henrik…" Ansel said quietly.

"Mm-hmm," Gwen said, her hands fast on the controller as her avatar navigated a minefield.

Ansel knew that his opportunity had ended, at least for the moment. He had a stab of concern, wondering if Robin had been swept under again when Kevin reset the spell. Had he and Tadra lost their only ally against Cerad?

CHAPTER 25

*T*adra woke to the sound of Vesta running up and down the hallway outside her room in unbridled glee, followed by the tromping of Rez and Henrik down the stairs, whooping in celebration.

"Sorry!" Heather said, when Tadra came to the door to investigate. "Merry Christmas!"

"It is six in the morning," Gwen complained as she emerged from the room she shared with Henrik, rubbing her eyes.

"Rez has been awake and begging to go down since five," Heather said without pity. "He's more wound up than Vesta. C'mon, let's go and open our presents."

"As long as there is coffee." Despite her grousing, Gwen seemed just as excited as the knights.

No one asked if Tadra was feeling better, or seemed to remember her collapse the night before. She glanced cautiously back at Ansel's door, but it was open and his room appeared to be empty. She followed Gwen and Heather down the stairs into the living room. The lights on the tree were all on, flickering in green and red and white.

The rich smell of coffee was coming from the kitchen and Tadra followed her nose to find Ansel pouring cups for everyone.

Excited? Ansel signed, making it a question with his face.

Presents! Tadra signed back eagerly.

Almost normal, he signed back. *I remember Christmas. Real Christmas.*

Tadra knew what he meant. On the surface, it felt like his descriptions of the holiday, light-hearted and happy, everyone full of anticipation. But they both knew that the merriment was only a facade.

Play along, she signed wryly.

But not everything about this was pretend. She was honestly dying to give Ansel his gift. She had a gift for Kevin from their shopping trip—a clever watch of some kind that wasn't really from Tadra in any way, as she had no funds and played no role in actually picking it out, just nodding and agreeing when the keys made suggestions. She'd found small things she knew her shieldmates would love. But for Ansel…

I'm excited for your present, she signed at him, only wondering as she said it if he'd think she was only excited to get a gift from him, which wasn't what she meant.

Tadra had never given a gift before, and she was surprised by how nervous it made her. Would Ansel like it? Did he already have one? People of this world had so much stuff already, perhaps it would be basically meaningless to him. She fretted over the idea that he might not appreciate it, that it would fall short of his expectations.

"What did she say?" Trey asked, puzzled, as if Tadra was not standing right beside him.

"She's excited to give presents," Ansel said, grinning, and Tadra's heart was warmed to know that he'd understood her exactly. How much more terrible would this whole farce be without Ansel in her corner?

"It is a wonder, how much you can speak without words," Trey said approvingly. He gave the sign for *shield-mate;* it was one of the few signs that he'd memorized.

Tadra said it back to him, and Trey folded her into his arms affectionately. Tadra hugged him back, wishing there was some way to free him from Kevin's influence so that she could have her brother-at-arms back in truth, not just *most* of him, like this.

There was hot coffee cake being pulled from the oven by Daniella, who insisted that everyone eat a piece before they tackled presents.

"Truly, the wait is grueling," Trey complained. "Can we be done with the food and go right to the presents?"

"You have at least had the luxury of enjoying this day once previously," Henrik pointed out. "Consider how it is for your shieldmates, our very first Christmas! Do not deny us the pleasures of this ritual!"

"It is true that I am superior in many of the ways of this world," Trey teased.

"Not by so much as that, shieldmate," Rez scoffed.

Tadra made a rude gesture with her hands that required no interpretation.

"Is it time for presents?" Heather asked plaintively.

By unspoken consensus, Ansel was put in charge of sitting by the tree to distribute gifts and Tadra had to remind herself several times that she shouldn't look at him with too much fondness as he took the task with the same stoic air that he used for his more unpleasant hound-keeper duties.

"For Henrik!" Ansel announced, handing him a sloppy, sagging present. "Tadra wrapped this one."

He did a good job of making sure every person had a

present at hand for most of the lengthy event, spacing them out with efficiency, and if it had not been for Kevin watching over them all with his knowing smirk, it would have been an utterly lovely morning.

The paper that had been so wondrous to her only a short few days before was ripped from the gifts without care, and it gathered in drifts all around them as they each amassed a little pile of new goods and heartfelt trinkets. She exchanged an amused look with Henrik, who was as boggled by the waste as she was. Their other shieldmates had already become accustomed to this aspect of the world.

The package from Ansel that Tadra had wondered over for so long proved to have fingerless gloves in a glittery red yarn, perfect for keeping her hands warm but leaving her fingers free to sign clearly. *Thank you,* she signed sincerely.

She got other gifts, from her shieldmates and their keys. They were thoughtful and kind, and gave Tadra great hope that they were, beneath Kevin's meddling, still the kin that she remembered. Trey gave her a volume of faery tales from this world, Rez gave her a pretty string of bright beads and red feathers made of metal, and Henrik gave her a warm bathrobe.

Heather had knitted her a long, soft scarf, Daniella gave her something called a bluetooth speaker that would make music from her phone, and Gwen gave her a small, useful-looking knife with a blade that folded invisibly into the handle. Kevin got her a fluffy white hat with matching mittens that was as impersonal as her gift for him. She refrained from pointing out that they weren't as useful as the fingerless gloves but was shallowly glad.

I will be warm and well-defended, she signed, and Ansel translated to peals of laughter. She signed a heart-felt *thank you* with each gift and received one in return for each of hers.

Tadra watched her present for Ansel slowly appear behind the other packages as more and more of them were handed around. Then he was lifting it, and giving it a theatrical shake and Tadra felt like she must be feeling the Christmas spirit he had talked about, because her insides were fluttering with excitement and anticipation.

It was a small art kit with a pocket sketchpad, a selection of pencils in various hardnesses, a tiny metal sharpener, a soft eraser, a short paintbrush, and a miniature pan of watercolors, all wrapped in a leather case emblazoned in gold with a bird in flight. It did not look exactly like her own firebird, with a shorter neck and a less graceful silhouette, but Tadra thought it was close enough to meet the purpose of something personal.

Ansel met her eyes and signed a sincere thank you. *I like this. A lot.*

No one else knew that you were an artist, Tadra replied, shaking her head. *Privacy,* she signed. Or possibly *Ansel.*

Ansel shrugged as he repeated the sign to her, then added. *But I like that you know.*

"What are you saying?" Kevin asked, entirely too casually. He was wearing the smart watch that Tadra had technically given him, and the scarf that Heather had made him.

"I was saying thank you," Ansel said, his face a careful mask of nonchalance. "Although it doesn't look a lot like her," he pointed out with a chuckle and he put it in the pile with his other gifts like it was no big deal, even as he signed *favorite* to Tadra and *it fills my heart.*

Robin's dollhouse was the big finale and they looked rather dazed by the gift. Tadra wondered how much of their reaction was an act for Kevin, and how much of it was that they were genuinely overcome by Ansel's generosity. The price tag had been rather alarming once she had a scale for their money to measure it with.

The keys and Trey went to the kitchen to prepare a more substantial breakfast, while the knights and Ansel began the complex task of assembling the house from the many parts. Tadra wandered between the two groups, helping where she was able and trying to keep her casual avoidance of Kevin unremarkable.

She itched to strike him, to fight him outright, but she knew that Kevin—Cerad—had too much power over her. He would only drain her if she tried something, and it was more useful to maintain their charade.

So she stewed inside and kept her expression faintly bored, and wished that she could hug Ansel and draw comfort from his closeness. They passed each other unremarkably, only a subtle flicker of their hand language between them when they could. *Sorry. Hang on. Play along.*

CHAPTER 26

reakfast was a magnificent affair and Ansel sat across from Tadra so that he could easily translate for her. They spoke a great deal as they plowed through the pancakes and sausage and biscuits with gravy. Out loud, the conversation they had was only for the food, jovial and shallow.

But privately, in their secret language, much more was said.

I love gift, Ansel told her.

You have art inside, she replied. *Your heart. Your eye. Beautiful.*

You're beautiful, he replied, somehow braver for knowing that they were talking right across the others and no one knew. Even Kevin seemed thoroughly engrossed in his meal and his conversation with Henrik. Ansel had to take a plate of bacon that Heather was handing down the table and caught only the last part of Tadra's reaction.

She was flushed, even the tips of her ears going pink, and had a mixture of delight and chagrin on her face. Daniella, next to her, asked if she was okay and Tadra quickly mimed taking too hot a bite of food.

"It's not proper breakfast gravy if it's not served at one degree less than the temperature at the surface of the sun," Heather sang.

That led to a serious discussion out loud about the temperature of the sun, while Tadra silently said, *You are my sun.*

Her *sun*, but not her *key*, Ansel thought achingly. If he were, he could break Kevin's control over her. If he were, Kevin wouldn't *have* any control over her.

He cracked a joke with Rez and made himself pry his fingers off the fork he was starting to mangle in his hands.

After breakfast, everyone helped clean up, holding their sides and complaining that they'd eaten too much. Heather took over in the kitchen to start preparing for dinner and Gwen vanished with Henrik into the media room to test her new controller.

Tadra and Rez politely offered to assist Heather with the food, and Kevin quickly added, "I'd love to help, too."

Ansel concentrated on not grinding his teeth and knew it would be too obvious to throw himself into the task as well. Once the table was cleared and the dishwasher was running, he returned with everyone else to the living room, to laze on the couches complaining goodnaturedly about how full he was and to enjoy his newest gifts.

"Are you going to draw us something, Ansel?" Daniella asked.

Ansel resisted his urge to clutch the sketchbook that Tadra had given him to his chest. He almost put his hand in an A to his lips: the sign for privacy, and the name that they had picked for him. He forced himself to smile and laugh instead. "Oh, it's nothing to see," he said deprecatingly. "Not much more than stick figures, really."

They might have politely insisted, Ansel thought, if

they'd really been themselves. But like everything else, it was shrugged away, bent into a weird illusion of normalcy.

He turned a few blank pages and listened to the voices from the kitchen. It was strange to have voices in the house other than his.

The day dragged on like a bizarre kind of torture. Ansel and Tadra were vaguely friendly to all appearances and reassured each other in sign whenever they could.

"What is that sign?" Kevin asked with suspicious languidness when he caught them communicating in the kitchen. "You've made it a lot."

Play along.

"It's just an expression," Ansel improvised. "'So it goes,' kind of?"

Tadra smiled and nodded vacuously.

Kevin seemed convinced, and shortly after wandered out of the kitchen.

They skipped lunch, browsing from the leftover coffee cake and platters of cheese and crackers if they were hungry. Christmas movies were interspersed with football in the media room, but Ansel couldn't get excited about eating or entertainment. He laughed with the others, and ate dry crackers and wandered through the house flitting from task to task, feeling like the whole thing was hollow.

He was emptying the dishwasher during a lull in the kitchen when Robin found him.

"Merry Christmas, Meatbag," Robin said, alighting on the windowsill above the sink.

"Merry Christmas, Tinker Bell," Ansel returned.

"Any...progress?" Robin asked, glancing behind Ansel carefully.

"It's hard to catch anyone alone long enough," Ansel said quietly. "And when there's two of them, it's like being boxed into a corner. A big, bland, everything's-fine corner." Like a chess game, with Kevin moving the pieces at every turn.

Robin frowned. "I hesitate to blow our cover by attacking directly," they said thoughtfully. "But I have been unsuccessful in more oblique methods of removing what he has done with them."

"Why doesn't Cerad use the knights directly?" Ansel asked. "They have their own unlocked magic, can't he just tell them to do stuff for him?"

"The glamor he has on them is a sideways thing," Robin said. "It's subtle. If he ordered them to do something truly against their nature, he might lose his control altogether. It's better for him to simply sideline them, and use Tadra's power as he can."

Only days of practice kept Ansel from clenching a fist or punching the counter. It was infuriating that Cerad had power, but it was worse that it was Tadra's power. There was nothing Ansel could do about it, and he wasn't sure that anything had ever made him so angry.

Robin hissed in warning and when Ansel turned, he had managed to scrub his emotions from his face. "Kevin," he greeted. "Heather. Cute Santa apron."

"That bird isn't going to cook itself," Heather said merrily. "Want to give me a hand stuffing a turkey?"

Ansel thought grimly that he'd love to, but that Kevin would probably put up a fight. Beside him, Robin snorted with laughter, as if they had followed Ansel's thought.

"I'd love to," Ansel said brightly. "Have baster, will broil!"

He didn't have another chance to talk with Robin alone that day.

Dinner ran late and was as false as breakfast had been, as false as everything since the knights had returned with Robin and the keys. Ansel excused himself afterwards and went to his room shortly after dessert, citing the early morning and the pending tryptophan coma.

He sank down at the edge of his bed, but didn't lie down. He missed the dogs.

They had crowded him and stolen the comforters, Vesta had chewed a hole in one of his pillows, and Fabio could fart to make his eyes water, but there was something comforting about their aliveness and their dumb interest in everything.

Maybe he could get a pet of his own, something well-behaved and mellow. Maybe a big, gentle dog, like a Newfoundland, or a Saint Bernard. But was it cruel to adopt a pet when the end of the world was coming anyway?

He thought he imagined the tap on the door the first time. It was just the sound of the house settling, or a creak of the baseboard heat somewhere. Maybe Socks, prowling past.

Then it came again, a soft, swift tap-tap at his door.

Ansel rose to open it, hoping and knowing who he'd find.

"Tadra," he said, achingly. She was dressed in the fuzzy red bathrobe that Henrik had given her, one bare leg rubbing the other nervously beneath the hem. Her hair was dark in the shadow, with a halo of red-gold. "You probably shouldn't be here."

The hallway behind her was quiet—there were voices from downstairs, but Henrik and Gwen had gone to bed even before Ansel. Probably not to sleep; their door was shut.

Tadra made a gesture that wasn't a sign but was obviously a scoff, then put her hand in the letter X and tilted it down. *Need.*

"What do you need?" Ansel asked, equal parts reluctant and hopeful. He knew what *he* needed, and he was too used to not having it.

Ansel, she signed, moving closer. Or maybe *privacy.*

Someone was coming up the stairs. Ansel opened the door wider to let her in and shut it but didn't latch it, afraid that it might catch the attention of whoever was coming upstairs.

She stood very close when he turned around, close enough to make his breath catch.

She moved her hands like they were water, smooth and graceful and Ansel didn't think that any of the motions she made were words at all, but he knew exactly what she wanted before she put the letter A against her mouth.

Him.

Ansel made a sound with no translation. "I'm not your key," he reminded her quietly. It was hard to think straight and stay noble with her standing that close, looking at him so trustingly. He *might* have been, he reminded himself.

She pointed to him and scooped her hand back to her chest, flattening it there. *You are my heart.*

It was dark and the noises in the house were all distant, making everything seem out of step with time itself. Ansel seemed to feel his own heart seize and stop beating.

"Tadra," he said quietly. "Tadra, my love…"

She closed what space was left between them, slipping her arms up around his neck and kissing him passionately. Ansel didn't even try to maintain self-control this time, catching her up into his arms to open his mouth to her hungrily. He kissed her with all the regrets and desires he'd been battling back, all of his thirst for her there on his lips as he claimed her tongue and pulled her tight against him.

She was so long and lean and alive in his arms, at last. Her hair was silky and her skin as velvety as her plush robe. Ansel could not have her close enough, could not kiss her hard enough to make up for all the days he hadn't dared to touch her.

It was minutes later, panting for breath, that he remembered the door behind her, cracked open to the hallway, and the risk they were taking. Gwen and Henrik often slept with their door open so that Socks could come and go as she pleased, and their bathroom was on the opposite side of the hall. Heather and Rez, at the far end of the house, might need to let Vesta out unexpectedly. He wasn't sure what they might do, how deep Kevin/Cerad's grip on them went. Maybe they'd simply forget anything they saw, but maybe Kevin had them honed to act as his observers, as well.

He drew away from Tadra, just far enough to whisper near her ear, "Are you sure?"

She didn't let go of him, but Ansel could feel her hand at his back as she curled in her ring and middle finger and spread her thumb apart. *I love you.*

He latched the door as quietly as he could manage while he was still kissing her, then took her face in his hands, threading his fingers up into her hair the way he'd been longing to do for so long. They stood, kissing for an unmarked time, savoring every touch, every unspoken confession, until a sound in the hallway made them freeze together.

A door creaked and closed.

They were still for a moment longer until Ansel could wait no longer. He kissed her again, more fiercely yet, and she untied her bathrobe belt and let it slip off of her shoulders.

She was naked underneath, as gloriously nude as she been when he first freed her from her glass prison. Ansel thought that she was even more beautiful now than she'd been then, because he knew how amazing she was inside.

He didn't speak, and she couldn't, but words were unnecessary. Every fingertip was a tome, every kiss was a pact. He was unable to stop touching her to even attempt to undress himself, and they retreated to his bed and toppled onto it together, trying to keep it from creaking as their urgency for each other swelled.

Tadra straddled him, only his pajamas between them, and spread her hands over his chest and rubbed against him like a cat in heat. Ansel bit back his groan and reached to take her by the waist and roll over with her, kissing the place where her neck met her shoulder, down to her collar-bone, cupping her breast and making her writhe and silently beg, clawed fingers pulling him closer.

He kissed down to worship between her breasts, teasing her nipples with his thumbs. It felt so good to use his hands on her at last, to touch what he'd yearned for so long, to talk with her in signs on her flesh. He kissed everything he could reach, working his way slowly down her responsive body, stroking her sides and making her arch up at him in quiet, desperate need.

I love you, he signed, touching the core of her pleasure reverently as he kissed her belly.

I love you, she signed back, before his mouth closed on the folds of her vulva and her fingers dug into his back.

Ansel licked her gently, as patiently as he could manage, touching all the places that made her surge and clench, until she stiffened and released, her breath going quick and then slow.

Just as he'd gone down on her, he worked his way back up, kissing her belly to her breasts as she caressed his shoul-ders and buried her fingers in his hair. One of her hands made it down, inside his pajamas, and took a commanding hold of his hard cock.

Ansel almost choked at the touch, and it took every

ounce of his willpower not to make a noise, gritting his teeth and holding himself still so that he didn't accidentally cause too much exquisite sensation. He finally put a finger to Tadra's lips. *Wait.*

He rolled off of her and she sat up to watch him go in concern. But he didn't go far, only to the bedside table, silently cursing the noise of the opening drawer. It took more rummaging than he wished—his hopeful condom had sifted rather further down in the junk that had accumulated than he expected; it had been a very long time since his life had included a companion in his bed that wasn't one of the dogs.

Tadra furrowed her brow as she observed him, then she smiled as he ripped open the package with one hand and his teeth and slipped off the rest of his clothing with the other. He unrolled the condom down over his cock, and if she wondered what it was or why he wore it, she was much more interested in being laid back down on the bed as he covered her and claimed her mouth again.

She spread her legs eagerly and Ansel had to pause and gather all of his self control at the hot, wet feel of her, at the touch of her lips against his, the hiss of her breath. One of her hands was between them, her palm flat on her chest making tiny circles: *please, please.* Her other hand had the same message, pulling at his shoulders to draw him closer.

It was a moment from a movie when everything went to slow motion as he slid gently into her. She threw her head back and pressed up around him, tight and blazing hot around his cock. Every thrust was deeper and harder and hotter, until Ansel could not tell what was pleasure and what was delicious torture and they were moving together to a crest of release like nothing he had ever experienced before.

Not crying out, trying to stay silent, was one of the keenest challenges he had ever faced. He wanted to roar in triumph, to shout as she shivered and slackened in his embrace and he came at last.

They lay together a long while after, tracing patterns on one another's skin, making blurry signs that weren't quite conversing, kissing whatever was closest, tangling limbs and fingers in hair.

He didn't have to be her key to know that they were meant to be together. She was his, and he was nothing in this world without her.

adra tried to speak, because an act like that, a physical joining so acute and profound, might have healed even her voice as well as her heart, but she was not terribly surprised to find no sound in her throat. When she closed her eyes and reached inside for the magic of her firebird, it fluttered as muffled and distant as ever.

But that didn't diminish her joy at all.

Ansel loved her.

He loved her with his warrior's heart and his beautiful body and his clever fingers. He loved her the way that she loved him. Theirs was a true connection of two souls that saw each other and longed to be one. A bond of friendship, strengthened by attraction and sealed with pure, unselfish love.

Ansel left her with a last, reluctant kiss to stand and strip off the curious clear cover he'd put over his cock, twisting it and tying off the end of it. Tadra mimed a child and *stop*. She knew how babies were made, even if she'd never considered that she might have one of her own. She was a knight, not a mother, and the very idea of it filled her with a knot of complicated feelings.

Ansel nodded and signed, *Not now.*

Not now, she agreed. Not now, with a great battle looming and her shieldmates compromised and her own world lost. Not now, but maybe someday. Someday...with Ansel. He returned to the bed from throwing away the device and drew her into his arms once more. The room was chilly and there was sweat cooling on their skin. He was her warmth and safety and Tadra curled up with her arms around him and buried her face into his neck with a sigh. The creak of the bed was loud in the quiet room.

She wasn't sure how long they lay together like that before there was a scratching at the door that made them both freeze together.

"Probably Socks," Ansel whispered near her ear. He got up quietly and opened the door a crack before she could yowl.

Robin's whispered swearing dispelled this assumption, and the fable slipped in and then leaned against the door to close it behind them. Ansel snatched his robe from the hook and put it on, looking deeply chagrined; Tadra had wondered how much of his weird prudishness about nudity had been that he didn't want to admit his attraction to her.

Apparently not all of it.

He brought her the robe she'd dropped on the floor and she shrugged into without embarrassment.

Robin, she signed respectfully.

"Don't mind me," Robin said sarcastically. "I wouldn't want to interrupt anything fun when the end of this world is nigh."

"I'm not sorry," Ansel blurted.

"Good," Robin said with a chuckle. "As long as *she's* not sorry."

Not sorry, Tadra signed with a smile, even though she flushed. Everything about her felt better. If her shieldmates were still enspelled and there was a terrible darkness waiting to unleash over the world in a few short days, at least she would go to her battle with Ansel at her side and in her heart. If he wasn't her key, he was still hers in every other way. When he sat gingerly on the bed, she snuggled shamelessly up against him.

"If we could get to business?" Robin suggested.

Tadra mimed choking herself, signing her firebird and then smooshing her hands together.

Robin glanced at Ansel.

"She's asking if there's a way to keep her power from Cerad. Can she take it from herself somehow? Destroy it?"

"The deep magic is part of you," Robin said, speaking to her directly. "Destroying your firebird would kill you, just like your human body dying would take the magic with it. Because of the key connection, you would probably doom Cerad with you." They said it thoughtfully, as if they hadn't considered it before.

Tadra squared her shoulders. It was the ultimate sacrifice, and she thought she could make it, as terrifying as the idea was. This was the kind of choice she'd been trained to make, her greatest final duty.

"That's not an option," Ansel said fiercely, his hand finding hers.

"I agree that it is a very last choice," Robin said grimly, but they didn't bother to deny that it might be one she might have to make.

Why? Tadra mimed dropping something.

Ansel looked at Tadra's hands as she signed. "Why...drop? Why break...? Oh. Why didn't breaking her ornament destroy her magic half?" He looked at Robin. "How *was* I able to put her back together? What role does the ornament itself play in her...whole existence?" That was more than Tadra had asked, but she nodded in agreement. Sometimes, it felt like Ansel knew what she meant even when she didn't have the words to sign.

Robin frowned at Tadra. "Like most magic, it is...an interpretation of what is actually happening. The spell was to make them fragile, and the way that the magic and this world translated that was to make it seem as if they were literal glass. The truth is more complicated, and the ornament is really only an illusion."

"I put it back together," Ansel protested. "It was real glass, I felt it, I held it in my hands. I...kissed it. It was a real, glass ornament."

"It is *real*, but wasn't *all* of her," Robin tapped their chin. "The rest of her was suspended not-here, not-real. When you repaired her avatar, you had to draw her back as well. If the pieces had been separated, if they had been too small to put back together, you would not have successful in that endeavor."

Ansel rubbed the bridge of his nose and Tadra made a rude noise with her lips. "I feel like this is one of those fringe science quantum mechanics things that no one really gets, where the more you think you know, the less you actually do."

Robin smiled. "I'm trying to illustrate the complexity at work. Every assumption you make is an approximation of what is actually there. Your brain wants reasons and limits, and they don't always exist."

"Like the ways each of the keys has a different way of tying their knight to the magic forces here?" Ansel said, like he was trying desperately to wrap his mind around what Robin was trying to explain.

"Exactly. It is similar to the way that these glass vessels

are indeed tied to the physical being of their knights, and to the way that it is not at all what they are."

Robin looked piercingly at Ansel. "You did not merely put her glass vessel back together, or Tadra would not—could not—be here. You healed her beyond the physical, your will stitched her back from broken parts. You concentrated on it, didn't you? Focused entirely, thinking only of the cool glass, of mending every seam, of all the broken places in your own soul that longed for her. And that focus let you do what you didn't know you couldn't."

Tadra's hand squeezed Ansel's, and he looked at her with raw, dark eyes. "I wanted to be a part of this whole magical quest, to have a greater purpose," he said quietly. "And I wanted you. I wanted *this.*"

You found me, she signed at him with her free hand. *I love you,* she mouthed.

Ansel leaned in for a swift, hungry claim of her mouth that prompted Robin to make a noise of disgust so loud that they all looked in worry at the closed door.

"Let's keep that stuff to a minimum," they said much more quietly. "What we're trying to do here is not to make out like horny teenagers, but perhaps figure out a way to stop Cerad. We are running low on time and opportunity."

Tadra signed and had to repeat it as she mouthed the words for Ansel to understand. "Does that mean the ornament doesn't actually matter?" he asked for her.

"Did you listen at all?" Robin scoffed. "They are *entangled.* You would not have been able to bring her back without repairing the physical anchor. But glueing some pieces of glass together would not have worked without great magic." They turned to Tadra. "Your human form, your glass avatar, your firebird, and your key, they are all connected. Shattering the ornament would disrupt a part of the balance. If you broke it into enough pieces, the human body would break just as surely."

"She survived the first time because it wasn't badly broken?" Ansel asked. "The white glass ring wasn't damaged at all."

"I believe that it all would have turned out much differently if it had been," Robin said. "I do think the damage to your glass avatar is why you cannot speak."

Tadra found herself touching her throat, where one of the seams in the glass had been. So many tiny pieces of luck. That Ansel had the skill to repair her and the will to bring her back. That the injury of her avatar had not been worse. The loss of her voice seemed a very small price to pay for her resurrection.

Ansel was watching her, like he always did, and Tadra was happy to return his gaze without pretending that she wasn't.

They were interrupted by the sound of scratching at the door, this time very definitely Socks as she howled her affront at the closed door that was keeping her from claiming a spot on Ansel's bed.

Ansel swiftly opened the door for the cat, who immediately decided that she didn't want in after all.

Ansel returned to the bed after he'd shut the door carefully behind her again. "Destroying Tadra's firebird is no kind of option. We need another way to stop Cerad."

"We must free my knights," Robin said decisively. "With their power, we could keep Cerad from opening a portal and win against the bleaks he has already on this side."

"Would he hurt Tadra when you did that?"

Tadra decided again that she liked having Ansel feel protective of her. He was so adorable and ruffled and it was such an unexpected joy to be under someone else's wing. She made a dismissive gesture and he scowled at her. "I have a real problem with that possibility."

"He needs her power," Robin said. "I believe that the key connection works for him, but it also works against him. His bleaks were able to find a way to use human anchors, but his connection with Tadra prevented him from doing the same; he couldn't forge a new conduit. He has been powerless in this world without her and I do not believe he would lose that again unless he had a better option."

"He said it was easier since she woke," Ansel said, just as Tadra remembered it as well.

Ansel, Tadra signed suddenly. He might hurt Ansel if he thought that he wasn't safely enspelled.

Robin guessed her mind. "Cerad would have no reason to keep Ansel alive if he thought he was any danger to his plans."

Protect, Tadra signed. *Protect Ansel.* She liked the idea of protecting Ansel almost as much as she liked the idea of him protecting her. It was a complete alignment of both her values and her affections.

Robin looked at Ansel for translation, but Ansel was gazing at Tadra. "I don't want you to worry about me," he said tenderly.

I am shieldmate, Tadra signed proudly. She didn't have signs for her vows, but Ansel knew them by now. *I protect.*

"You are the Firebird Knight of the Fallen Kingdom," Ansel said, taking her hand and kissing it. "You are a Protector of the Broken Crown. You are Robin's bravest knight, and the most foolish."

"You are *disgusting,*" Robin said, rolling their eyes. But they were smiling, and Tadra knew that her mentor approved of the direction that her heart had taken her.

Someone out in the hallway stumbled to the bathroom

and they all hushed, listening, until the toilet flushed and a series of doors closed again.

"We should not be caught," Robin said. "If Cerad knows that we have escaped his influence and are working against him, we will not have the freedom we have now. Go on as you have before, and I will also attempt to break my knights free on my own."

They gave Tadra a quick touch of their forehead, pinched Ansel, and slipped out the door to return, no doubt, to their new dollhouse downstairs.

Tadra took her leave more slowly, kissing Ansel a reluctant goodbye. She wished she could linger, and lay in his arms much longer, perhaps even make love again. As thoroughly as he had satisfied her hunger, he had awakened new ones, and Tadra knew that no bed would be restful without him again. She twined her fingers into his thick hair and stroked the rough stubble on his jaw and wished she had her voice to tell him exactly how dear he'd become to her as she lay her forehead on his and breathed his breath.

She wasn't even sure what words she might use if she could speak, because what she felt for him transcended her ability to express it. Like Robin describing magic, the way she loved him wasn't a matter of logic or limitation.

He didn't offer any words of his own, and he didn't have to; Tadra knew his heart like her own, and his hands said plenty.

At last, reluctantly, she kissed him one last time and made her way back to her own bedroom.

Hours later, when Socks decided to claim a spot on her bed, she was still awake trying to puzzle a way out from underneath Cerad's control that didn't in any way risk Ansel's safety.

CHAPTER 28

For Ansel, the next few days were a blur of trying to bluff his way through every interaction with Cerad. He translated for Tadra as needed, careful to keep their real conversations subtle. They maintained a perfect cool facade, friendly, but not close. He caught Cerad watching them and he feared their secret language would be cracked, so he kept his interpretations near the truth and his physical reactions to her locked down as hard as he could whenever Cerad was around.

It was easiest to keep distance between them, because she made his skin tingle with proximity, and it was hard not to smile foolishly if she brushed up against him or let his hand linger if they both reached for something at the table. It would be even worse to flinch away at the electric touch of her, so Ansel practiced keeping every motion lazy, every expression distant, and they kept away from each other without looking like they were deliberately doing so.

It was hard not to watch Cerad, too, to try to figure out if there was suspicion behind his icy blue eyes. Ansel got good at letting his gaze slide sideways off of anything he was looking at.

It helped that Cerad didn't seem concerned...about anything. He wasn't bothered by the dogs, he didn't have strong opinions about meals or entertainment. He seemed mild and emotionless, and aside from the way he watched everything with smug, narrow-eyed interest, he could have been just a friend visiting from California.

It would have been impossible for Ansel to continue his charade if Cerad had staked any claim on Tadra herself, but to their relief, Cerad's interest in her seemed purely for her firebird's power. He drained her several times over the week, for purposes they could only guess, but not to collapse, only to slight faintness. Ansel pretended to shrug it off with the others and inwardly hated Cerad more than ever.

At night, they made up for their cool outer expressions with hot, desperate touches. Ansel had to smuggle new condoms in during grocery runs, feeling like an errant teenager with his first girlfriend, but it was worth every frustration to have Tadra in his arms, to kiss her and lay her back on his bed—or on the floor if the bed wanted to creak too loudly—and tell her without words all the ways that he loved her.

There was nothing in the world that was better than those stolen moments with her legs wrapped around him, speaking only in sign and skin, bringing her to gasping pleasure and falling with her into a sea of satisfaction.

The biggest risk to each tryst was unexpectedly Socks, who took a closed door as a reason to yowl for admittance, even when she didn't actually desire entrance.

Twice, the Siamese cat was an interruption at the worst of times, and finally, fearing that his closed door, or Tadra's empty bed, would draw unwanted questions when the cat woke one of the others, Ansel took to leaving his door propped open just enough for her to come and go as she pleased as he had before.

This necessitated making love to Tadra more quietly than ever, and Ansel thought that having to stay quiet and secret only heightened the sweet elation that they found together.

Each night, he found new discoveries in her kisses and on her gorgeous body. She had a scar that matched the one on her nose in the small of her back. She had to write the explanation for it, dragonvine, which didn't clarify much until she drew a rough botanical sketch of a thorny vine with grasping tendrils. Ansel traded her for the story of falling down a flight of outdoor stairs into a barrel full of recycling. "I was lucky it was mostly plastic," he said, showing her the scar on his leg. "But there was one glass bottle."

It wasn't all sex and comparing scars. They also plotted, filling whiteboards with lists of things they knew about Cerad's plans, weaknesses they observed through the day that they hadn't been able to share, anything at all they might use to stop him.

Robin joined them in these war sessions sometimes, though they always waited until very late at night, giving them evening privacy without comment or complaint.

During the days, the three of them each took acting cues from the enspelled knights and keys, floating around as if they were in an opium haze, happy to joke and go through all the motions of a normal life, shying away from any topic too serious or any reference to danger or future. They didn't spend any more time with each other than with any of the others.

The keys had all previously arranged to take time off from their workplaces, originally planning to spend this week preparing for the great battle, and it felt a little like they were all on a retreat together, determined not to think about the work waiting for them.

Ansel chipped away at the others as he could, when privacy was possible, usually coordinated between the three of them. His early experience with Gwen suggested that an approach dealing with their partners might be most successful; suggesting danger to their keys did seem to crack through the creepy veneer of carelessness.

Twice, Ansel thought he was going to get through, first with Trey and later with Heather, but each time there was some interruption—Cerad once and a choking dog emergency the second time—and when he tried to follow up, he found that he was starting again from scratch.

Tadra and Robin had no better luck.

"I might be able to break the spell working at it directly with magic," the fable said late on the second to the last night of the year. "But it would not go undetected and..." They looked down at their hands unhappily.

They didn't have to finish.

"We'll need every scrap of what's left of your power to close the portals back to your world when Cerad opens them," Ansel finished. They were all sitting on his bed, Tadra cuddled against his side, Robin cross-legged on a throw pillow.

As far as they could guess, Cerad was simply biding his time until the veil thinned, when he could most easily use Tadra's power to open a portal for his forces on the other side. His bleaks on this side—they still had no idea how many there were—had some power, but Robin guessed that it was not enough to hold portals to faery open for long.

With the knights' power unlocked by their keys, it should have been an easy task to subdue Cerad and any bleaks on this side, leaving Henrik and Robin to seal any portals. But the knights had been sidelined, even if Cerad couldn't use their power directly, and Robin was badly diminished.

"I don't like the risk, but we can't wait any longer," Robin said firmly. "If I can break the spell, we will have the knights' power and Henrik has enough skill to close a portal without me. Tomorrow is New Year's Eve. Cerad is going to make his move and if we have any chance of stopping him, it is now, tonight."

Tadra put her fist to her chest.

"All of us?" Ansel said. He squeezed Tadra closer to his side.

Robin shook their head. "Let me try alone. You two will be our fallback plan if I fail. That he doesn't know you are free is the ace up our sleeve."

Ansel looked down at his hands and thought wryly that it was kind of Robin to include him as any kind of asset. He didn't have any magic, he wasn't Tadra's key, and he was a mediocre fighter at best. He was the hound-keeper, the land-owner. What good was he going to be in any final battle? Was it possible that Robin thought he'd be a liability and that was why they didn't want him there? Tadra was a warrior, but Cerad would be able to neutralize her with a thought. There was nothing of Ansel to neutralize.

Tadra stirred against him and Ansel realized she'd been signing.

"We'll be…" Ansel frowned at her hands and guessed, "rearguard?"

She smiled at him in delight and nodded and Ansel's heart squeezed. She was so beautiful, so brave. She never complained about Cerad's theft of her magic, though Ansel knew that it filled her with frustration. She never stopped trying to find patterns in the information they had, filling whiteboards with notes and theories, all of them meticulously erased before she went back to her own room. Ansel had never even imagined a woman with a spirit so invincible.

Robin cleared their throat and Tadra sat up from Ansel and bowed her head, crossing her fists across her chest. Robin floated to touch their forehead to hers and they were still that way for a lengthy time. Robin said something low and private and Ansel looked away, trying not to overhear.

"Good luck," he said gruffly, when Robin left her to touch his own forehead. Their hands pressed briefly at his temples.

"Thank you," Robin said. "For your hospitality and your courage. You are a valuable ally and an admirable man. I watched you for a long time during my first year in your warehouse and took your measure well. You are a credit to your world and have a true heart. I am honored to have you at my side in any battle."

Ansel was sure that there was a formal response that Robin would expect from his knights. "Sure thing, Tinker Bell," he joked instead. "Break a wing."

Robin snorted with laughter and gave Ansel's forehead one final knock with their own. "I know why Tadra likes you."

Then they were gone, slipping out the door and disappearing downstairs.

Socks oozed in as the fable left, giving an offended little mrrt. Ansel latched the door behind her and returned to the bed to gather Tadra back into his arms.

Robin would take on Cerad directly, and they would

win. Ansel had to believe that, because the alternative was so awful. The fable *would* break the spell and free the knights. Tadra clung to him; her worry and uncertainty didn't need any hand signs to convey. There was no way to know how the battle would go, how or when Robin would initiate it.

When she lifted her mouth to his, Ansel kissed her desperately. Robin was their only chance, and Ansel knew that both of them were wondering if the fable would be forced to kill Cerad to save the world...

...and if Tadra would die with him.

It wasn't worth it, Ansel thought. Let the world burn, as long as he could keep Tadra safe.

But even as the idea occurred to him, he knew that he wouldn't do that even if he could. Tadra wouldn't want to live at anyone's expense. She was selfless and pure-hearted, and she would offer her life before she asked it of anyone else.

Ansel felt her thumbs on his face and realized that his cheeks were wet with tears. "I love you, Tadra," he said. "I love you more than I ever knew was possible."

Her cheeks were tear-streaked, too, and Ansel bent to kiss them away. This wasn't the end, he couldn't believe that it would be.

Robin would find a way to save them all, to stop Cerad and keep dark forces from toppling their world. Ansel had to trust that the fable would win the day, because he couldn't think of any other option.

He worked his way back to Tadra's mouth for a desperate salty kiss as she wrapped her arms around his neck and kissed him back.

Ansel felt the moment that Cerad tapped into their key connection, in the sudden stiffening of Tadra in his arms and the subsequent weakness that made her go boneless.

But it was much, much worse than usual. She jerked and struggled weakly, her head lolling away from their kiss, and then went terribly, deathly still.

"Tadra!" Ansel cried, not caring if anyone in the house heard him. "Tadra, no!"

CHAPTER 29

Tadra woke slowly in the dark, lying in an unfamiliar bed, feeling like she'd been rolled flat like a pizza and then baked. Her muscles felt like melted cheese.

She giggled a little to herself, because cheese was such a joke between her and Ansel. They had so many wonderful jokes together.

"Tadra?"

The bed wasn't unfamiliar, it was Ansel's, and he was curled up around her on one side. On her other side, a warm, heavy lump began to purr.

Tadra found Ansel's face and patted it. He sounded so worried, and when he exhaled, she felt his breath against her skin. Dear Ansel. Dear, kind, good Ansel, with his big heart and knight-like loyalty.

The memory of her collapse flooded back as Tadra banished the last of her weariness and sat up.

Socks stood up, stalked to the foot of the bed, and started grooming herself as if she'd been embarrassed to be caught purring.

Robin? Tadra signed.

"I don't know," Ansel said achingly. "I couldn't leave you. I don't know what happened. Robin never came back."

Cerad had reached for her power, taking more of her than he'd ever taken before, but what had the outcome been? Had Robin been able to break the spell? Or had Cerad triumphed over the fable when they battled?

The house was quiet and the light around the curtain suggested that it was morning...morning of the last day of the year, when the veil between worlds was the weakest.

"Are you okay?" Ansel wanted to know, tucking a stray lock of her hair behind her ear. "Is there anything I can do?"

Good, Tadra signed. She tilted her hand back and forth. *Sort of.*

Out in the hallway, the door at the far end of the hall opened and there was the sound of a small dog streaking out. Shortly after, there was the thumping of a larger dog coming up the stairs and the two of them did laps of the upstairs and downstairs, eager for outside and food.

It sounded heartbreakingly *normal.*

Rez, grumbling, went down the stairs to let the dogs out and Gwen came stumbling out of her room for the bathroom.

Tadra tested her limbs and found that her strength had largely returned. *Better,* she said, and Ansel caught her hand and kissed it. *Best,* she signed.

Socks, having finished her grooming, jumped off the bed and walked to the door to meow demandingly.

Ansel and Tadra exchanged a complicated look with no words. Were her shieldmates freed of the spell or did they still need to pretend? If they were to maintain their charade, Tadra would have to sneak her way back to her room. Was it worth even trying any longer? Whatever was going to happen today was going to happen. There was no stopping it now.

Socks yowled again and Tadra gave Ansel a quick kiss and rolled off the bed to her feet. Her legs were steady beneath her and she pulled her robe tight around her and padded to the door. She cracked it open and then walked boldly out, nearly tripping over Socks, who was second-guessing which side of the door she wanted to be on.

Tadra had only gone a few steps when Henrik emerged from the room he shared with Gwen.

"Shieldmate," he greeted casually, moving to let her pass to her room. He didn't seem curious that she was coming from Ansel's room in her robe, or pause to comment on her purpose. Tadra's heart sank and hope that she didn't realize that she was holding onto faded to ash. Henrik was still enspelled, more sunk in his careless stupor than ever. The real Henrik would have at least been curious.

Robin had clearly failed in their quest.

And that begged the question of what had happened to Robin themself.

Tadra dressed quickly and finger-combed her hair. By the time she had emerged from her room, Ansel was coming out of the bathroom, already dressed.

They descended the stairs together, but distant out of habit, carefully separate and not looking at each other long.

Daniella was standing in front of the Christmas tree. "No one watered it," she observed dreamily. If anything, she seemed more dazed than she had the day before. The needles were falling off of it in sheets and many of the branches were already bare. "We should take it down."

Robin? Tadra signed at her, full of dread.

Daniella only looked at her blankly. Did she not remember the sign, or had Robin become one of those topics that their minds slipped away from?

"I have the box for ornaments," Trey said from behind her.

Tadra woodenly helped pack away the decorations, listening as Ansel went into the kitchen to help with breakfast, both of them going along with the flow of things because they weren't sure what else to do.

The glass avatars were wrapped up last and placed at the top of the box, and no one seemed to give them any kind of significance. They were just ornaments, with no more meaning than the plastic Santa Claus or the hedgehog with a candy cane.

While Trey and Daniella wound up the strings of lights, Tadra went prowling for Robin, trying not to be obvious about her search as she poked around in corners. They weren't in the dollhouse, or in any of the places they liked to perch and watch things.

She was startled to run into Cerad as she walked the hallway to the media room where she could hear the television going, and wondered how successful her bland expression was; he looked at her a little longer than usual, furrowing his brow.

"Are you feeling okay?" he asked casually.

Tadra shrugged and nodded, keeping her eyes lazy and her motions slow as she passed him.

He didn't follow, and Tadra breathed a sigh of relief.

Robin was watching television with Heather, some kind of rowdy game with many pauses called football. The sight of the fable made Tadra halt in dismay.

If Robin had been diminished before, now they were moreso, barely the size of a fist. Where they hadn't been able to fit through the dollhouse doors without ducking the night before, now they were almost too small a scale for it.

They looked up at Tadra's entrance and grinned. "Can you believe this game?" they asked. "They call it a contact sport, but stop the play the moment there is a hit, even though they are wearing ample armor!"

Was it part of their ruse? Tadra wondered. Or was nothing left of Robin behind the joviality?

She signed their name, but they were already looking back at the screen, watching a noisy and bright commercial for a car.

Tadra took a seat on the couch nearby and waited until Heather left to refill her coffee to close the door behind her and face Robin. *Robin,* she signed. *Good?*

Their vacant expression remained, despite the fact that they were alone. *Robin,* she tried again. *Shieldmate. Magic.*

They glanced at her, then back to the screen.

There was a whiteboard in the room and Tadra took it up. *You are under a spell,* she wrote frantically. *But you can break it if you try. Purge yourself of influence.* Ansel had convinced them to do that once, would it work again? Robin was so much smaller now, so diminished. *Kevin is Cerad.*

Robin looked at her skeptically when she held it up for them to read. "I wonder if we've got some of those pizza rolls in the freezer."

Tadra gazed at them in dismay; they were engrossed again in the television. For a moment, she wanted to snatch them up and shake them in her hands, desperate to awaken them again.

Robin, her mentor and her crown, was lost. Only Ansel was on her side now.

She hastily rubbed the words from the whiteboard with the side of her hand and left it with the marker on the couch.

She paused in the doorway of the kitchen and met Ansel's glance. *Robin lost,* she signed.

He balled his hands in frustrated fists and then signed, *Sorry. Next?*

What did they do next? How could the two of them, powerless, hope to defeat Cerad?

Tadra had to drag her gaze away from Ansel, because she knew the answer to that question and she knew that he would try to stop her. *Wait,* she said, letting no hint of her intentions reach her face. Then she repeated herself firmly, tapping her wrist. *Wait here.* She walked into the living room where Trey and Daniella were closing up the box of decorations.

I'll take, she signed, smiling cheerfully at them, and although she didn't think they remembered the meaning of her gestures, they didn't protest when she took the box and went to the garage with it. Fabio trailed her curiously and she carefully nudged him back with a foot and shut the door behind her.

The garage was quiet, compared to the house, and starkly lit.

Tadra walked slowly towards the shelf that the Christmas box had come from and set it down on the concrete floor, lifting the lid with a heavy heart.

She unwrapped each of her shieldmate's avatars, and then her own, holding it aloft to gaze at the cool reflection of her firebird. Every seam and broken place caught the light.

It looked so fragile.

It *was* so fragile.

Tadra curled her fingers around it and yanked, breaking the string that held it to the white outer ring. All she had to do was shatter her firebird and she would drag Cerad into death with her, release her shieldmates, and fulfill her duty as a knight. That was the only possible ending to this story now, and she had to do it now, before Ansel realized what she was doing and tried to stop her.

Knowing how Ansel would hurt was the worst of it. She was not afraid to sacrifice her own life; she had always been prepared to fight to her own death in the name of light. But she had never loved the way she loved Ansel, and he loved her back with the same intensity. Losing her would break his gentle heart and Tadra flinched at the thought of it. He would know why she did it, but he might never truly forgive her and the pain that she would cause him made her hesitate, turning the red glass in her hand.

Tadra had read the stories of the phoenix in the faery tale books of his world, but she knew that there would be no rising from the ashes for her. This was a one way choice, her final charge of duty.

She set her jaw and lifted her arm, only to find that she could not complete the move—or make any motion at all —as the door behind her opened.

She didn't have to see him to know that it was Cerad, and she realized in despair that she had delayed her destiny a few moments too long.

CHAPTER 30

*A*nsel waited in the kitchen, pretending that he cared how the dishwasher was loaded, until he thought that he could follow Tadra out into the living room without looking too suspicious. He stopped in the doorway for a moment, trying to decide why things looked wrong.

"You guys took down the ornaments," he realized. The Christmas tree, which had been shedding needles at an alarming rate for days, was bare of decoration.

Most alarmingly… "Where are *your* ornaments?" They hadn't been moved back to the kitchen window, out of reach of the pets.

"They're in the Christmas box," Heather said, as if they were nothing more than Hallmark collectibles. She was knitting, and the clack-clack of her needles droned in Ansel's head like she was deliberately trying to hypnotize him.

"Where's the Christmas box?" Ansel pressed, as a terrible thought occurred to him. "Where's Tadra?"

"She took the box of Christmas to the garage," Rez said. He was lazily sweeping up the drifts of needles beneath the tree, knocking as many more off as he was picking up. "Perhaps the sucking machine that the dogs hate?" he suggested.

"We should take the tree out first," Daniella said, from her seat on the couch next to Trey. But no one actually stood up and offered to make it happen. If anything, they all looked more mechanical and out of it than ever. Gwen and Henrik were sitting on the loveseat opposite from them, and Gwen was looking at her hands with a frown, as if she was expecting them to do something, but she couldn't remember *what.*

Had Robin had some small success in chipping through Cerad's spell, even if they hadn't been ultimately successful? Were the others trying to break free, struggling beneath the increasingly glassy surface of their enchantment? If Ansel could shake them the rest of the way out of it, maybe there was still a chance.

But first he had to stop Tadra from doing something terrible. "Where is Kevin?" he asked in alarm.

Rez shrugged one shoulder at the garage door. The same door where Tadra was...with the Christmas box that held her own fragile ornament.

Ansel wasn't sure which part of this equation dismayed him the most. He abandoned his charade in full and bolted for the garage door, pushing a protesting Rez from his path. He had to vault Fabio, who was confused by having people on multiple sides of a door, and he crashed into the garage to witness a tableau of his worst fears.

Tadra was kneeling by the open Christmas box. Her firebird was clenched in one fist, held high above her head. She was stone still, baring her teeth at Cerad, who was standing above her with a smug, lazy smile that Ansel wanted to strike off his face. He was holding a bleak's black sword, turning it thoughtfully in his hands.

Cerad looked around at Ansel's noisy entrance, but didn't look alarmed. "Why Ansel, are you here to help pack up the Christmas decorations?"

Should he bother to try to continue to bluff? They were out of time, and whatever Cerad was planning to do, he was clearly planning to do it soon.

While Ansel was still deciding what to do, Fabio realized that Tadra was down at a height he could reach with his tongue. The dog barged past Ansel, straight for the kneeling knight.

Cerad made a little growl and twisted one hand. Fabio was suddenly tumbling back with a yelp of pain and protest. He shook his head as he regained his feet, tucked his tail between his legs, and fled the garage, confused and upset. The door slammed behind him with a flick of Cerad's fingers.

They were definitely past pretending.

"Let her go," Ansel said. He was good at odds and he could taste the futility of his statement.

Cerad only smiled. "You've been biding your time, hoping to find a weakness. I knew that Robin couldn't have broken free of my will without outside help."

"Robin told me what happened," Ansel said as evenly as he could manage. Could he circle around to the wall where the weapons hung? Did he have a chance against Cerad with a blade? And what would happen to Tadra? Ansel felt like his lungs had forgotten how to breathe. A real hero would be in motion, making something happen now.

"They told me what they did to you," he continued, trying to buy himself time to figure out what to do. "But it doesn't have to be like this. You were a decent person once. Maybe you could be, again. You could have that back."

For one brief moment, Cerad didn't answer and Ansel had a flash of hope. If Cerad wasn't irredeemable...

Then the wizard laughed and the sheer hollowness of the sound made Ansel feel like someone had doused him in cold water. There was no soul in Cerad, no warmth at all. It was like there was a well of invisible darkness there, oozing out of his glacier-blue eyes. The garage seemed to chill by several degrees.

"I wouldn't want it back, even if it were possible. I am a better person *now*," Cerad said easily. "Not so distracted by petty things like love and mercy."

"Love and mercy aren't petty," Ansel said with conviction.

"They are weaknesses," Cerad said dismissively. "You could have stopped me long ago, if you had not been so afraid of hurting her. She could have destroyed her firebird long ago, if she had not been afraid of hurting you."

Tadra was still, not even blinking. She still had her firebird aloft, as if she'd be caught right as she planned to dash it to the ground.

She probably had, Ansel thought, and his chest hurt so badly that he almost believed that Cerad was right: it really would be better not to feel so keenly in order not to suffer so badly.

Then he had to smile, because he wouldn't have given a moment of his pain in exchange for the joy of loving her.

Cerad looked puzzled at his smile, then frowned. "It doesn't matter, hound-keeper, you're too late now." He lifted one hand and made a grabbing motion.

Ansel, knowing what was going to happen before he even heard the sizzle of a portal, dived for the nearest thing that could possibly be a weapon, the lid from the Christmas box, and he swung it desperately, even as Cerad heaved Tadra, unprotesting, to her feet and dragged her through the brief portal.

Ansel got one chilling glimpse through to his warehouse, crowded with dark figures, as he flung himself after Cerad.

CHAPTER 31

*A*nsel staggered through the space the portal had been into the garage wall, holding a perfectly sliced half of the lid from the Christmas box. The rest of it had gone through, but he hadn't been quite fast enough, or started soon enough. He wasn't even sure if it was a mercy that he hadn't himself been caught halfway between places when it closed.

"No! No, goddamit, no!" He smashed a fist into the drywall. It cracked around his blow, leaving a crumbling crater.

Ansel flung what was left of the lid away, detoured far enough to pick the first ornament he could grab from the open Christmas box and skidded back to the house, letting the door slam against the wall behind him. The dogs exploded into barking panic, but Ansel had no time to soothe them.

"Robin! Robin, dammit, where are you!" But Robin was lost again and no use now.

The knights were all lounging in the living room and they looked up at Ansel's noisy entrance with lazy expressions of disinterest that were the last straw to Ansel's serenity.

"Damn you all," he snarled. "Kevin isn't Tadra's key, he never was. He was Cerad, and he's been playing all of you."

Just as it always did, the information merely slid off their placid faces.

"He's got your shieldmate!" Ansel shouted. "He's going to use the last of her magic to open a portal to your world for his dark forces so that he can take over this one, too."

Was there the barest flicker of interest in Henrik's eyes? Did Trey hesitate just a moment before taking another sip of his coffee?

Knowing Tadra was in danger wasn't quite enough to crack through their enchantment. Knowing the invasion of his world would start soon wasn't sufficient. But he knew who they cared for even more than that. Ansel held the ornament aloft and looked at Gwen. It was Henrik's glass prison. "If you don't snap out of it, I will break Henrik's gryphon."

Everyone else smiled at Ansel in amusement, as if they thought he was making a joke. Even Henrik was chuckling.

Gwen alone seemed vaguely alarmed and Ansel pried into that crack in her armor of indifference. "If I break this, he dies, and you know it. I'd do anything to save Tadra, even shatter your knight's avatar if that's what it takes. He'll die and it will be your fault!"

Ansel was not sure that he actually had the guts to dash Henrik's ornament to the ground. But Gwen didn't know that and Ansel had spent weeks in the most intensive acting crash course imaginable, first pretending that he wasn't falling desperately in love with Tadra, and then that he was under Cerad's enchantment. He made his words and face convincing and raised the ornament over his head as Gwen got to her feet.

When Gwen's fist connected with his eye, much faster than he expected, Ansel thought wryly that he probably should have picked a different key to try to enrage. Daniella and Heather were both mediocre fighters at best, but Gwen was a black belt in Tang Soo Do.

Ansel staggered back into the naked tree, knocking it completely off the base as he struggled to protect the ornament in his hands. Henrik rose to his feet, fire in his face for the first time since they'd come back from Ecuador.

"Yes," Ansel hissed as he struggled to stay upright, backpedaling over the fallen Christmas tree. "Fucking feel something at last!"

"I do!" Henrik roared. "I do feel! Gwen, my key!"

Gwen was staring at Ansel in horror and astonishment, the first genuine expression he'd seen on her in the whole long week that Kevin had been controlling them.

"You were going to hurt Henrik!" she exclaimed.

Ansel held up the undamaged golden gryphon in its glass ring. "I hoped you would believe that I was." He put his other hand over his throbbing eye. "Ow."

Henrik was looking at his shieldmates now, both of them watching, slack-jawed, from the couch as if they were merely viewing television, each of them with a casual arm around their keys. He shook his head like a dog with a bee in his ear.

"What has happened to them?" Henrik asked in horror. He and Gwen clung to each other, looking a little like they'd just both been drenched in cold water.

"The same thing that happened to you," Ansel said. He might have wept in relief, but all he could think of was Tadra. "Kevin is Cerad. He's using Tadra's magic, and he's going to open a portal to your world and let all the darkness over."

"How long? What day is it?" Gwen asked in alarm.

"New Year's Eve," Ansel said. "In the morning. We're cutting it a little close."

"Why did you not awaken us earlier?" Henrik wanted to know.

"You think we didn't try?" Ansel snarled. "You think we haven't been doing every goddamn thing we could imagine to get you to snap out of it?"

"What we?" Gwen said, still looking at the oblivious knights and their keys on the couch. "Were we all like that?"

"Tadra and I haven't been affected," Ansel said impatiently. "And Robin was free...for a while. But Cerad got his claws back into the fable, and he's got Tadra *now*. Those weak spells? Those were him."

Henrik furrowed his brow. "Weak spells?"

"You and Tadra?" Gwen said sharply. Of all of them, Gwen knew Ansel most of all.

It was too much to explain, too much to fill in. "We don't have time for this," Ansel said impatiently. "We've got to get these guys out of their trance and back on our side and go get *Tadra.*"

Would Cerad kill her once he'd opened the portals? He didn't care for any life, his purpose only for his own power. When he had no need of her...

Ansel turned on Henrik. "Break the spell on the others," he commanded.

Henrik snapped him a bow with his fist over his heart and then turned his attention to their rapt, enchanted audience. Gwen closed her eyes and held her hands just in front of her. They stood this way a moment then turned to each other with puzzled expressions.

"It's not working," Gwen said.

"If I were in my magic form…" Henrik suggested, and he seemed to flow into a huge golden gryphon, filling the living room and knocking the abused Christmas tree back even further when he shifted.

Nothing changed as far as Ansel could see; there were no fireballs or flashing shields. He had to trust that Henrik was doing *something*, but the slack expressions on the knights and their keys didn't waver.

After a few moments where the only sounds were the dogs whining and panting, he shifted back into a man. "It is a clever and persistent spell," Henrik said gravely. "It will take time and care to break it."

"We don't have time," Ansel said flatly.

"Their ornaments," Gwen said, setting her jaw.

Ansel handed her Henrik's glass gryphon and turned back to the garage, where he gathered up the last two ornaments. The white ring from Tadra's firebird lay at the top of the box and Ansel picked it up with the others, desperate for any part of her. *I'll fix this*, he thought forcefully. *I'll fix this and get her back.*

There was no other option.

Henrik had no luck threatening Daniella and Trey with breaking his ornament and Ansel watched his performance critically. Gwen did no better. Daniella looked worried, as if she was watching a tense moment in a movie, but didn't even get to her feet.

"Give me that," Ansel said finally. He took the green glass dragon and ripped the string holding it in the ring. "I'm not screwing around any more," he told Daniella, and he lifted it into the air. "Cerad has Tadra," he told her flatly. "And I don't have anything left to lose."

She believed *him*, rising with a cry that set the hair at the back of Ansel's neck up.

Heather and Rez were next; Heather had been knitting and she stabbed at Ansel with her needles before he could dodge away.

"Oh my gosh, I'm sorry," she said, when she'd shaken her head clear and he'd caught her up on what was happening.

"I remember most of it," Rez said, looking around in alarm. "But it is very distant."

"Robin explained it, but I don't have time," Ansel said. "Cerad is at the warehouse now, and if we don't go stop him, the same thing that happened to your world is going to happen here."

It might have been heartening, the way that they all sprang into action, gathering their weapons and donning the leather jackets that passed for armor, if Ansel wasn't remembering Tadra's last look of despair as Cerad dragged her through the portal. He pulled on Tadra's jacket himself; it wasn't a perfect fit, but he had no intention of sitting this battle out, and it was the closest thing he had to armor.

He impulsively picked up the ornaments that had been left on the table, including the ring from Tadra's firebird, and tucked them all into an inner pocket of his coat, in case he needed to break Cerad's control again.

He glanced up to see Henrik watching him do it and he glared at the knight in challenge. Henrik only nodded his approval.

"I know it's the end of the world," Daniella said grimly to Trey, "but *damn*. You look good in black leather!"

Trey smiled and smoothed the leather down across his chest. "There is nothing impractical about going to battle well-dressed."

Robin appeared from the media room, completely unconcerned by the fuss.

"Will one of you otherwise uselessly large people start some pizza rolls before you go out?" they asked, as if everyone was not dressed for a back alley rumble and Rez was not handing large, blunt weapons around. They would try not to harm ridden humans, and had been practicing knock-out and tackle techniques.

Ansel didn't have an ornament or a key to threaten Robin back to themself with, and didn't know otherwise how to snap them out of their enchantment. He did the next best thing he could think of, snatching the fable out of the air and stuffing them into one of his pockets.

The knights stared in horror as Ansel zipped up the pocket and Robin struggled and swore creatively.

"We might need them," Ansel said flatly to the knights, ignoring his squirming jacket.

"Fuck you!" his pocket said.

Hopefully Robin wouldn't chew their way out in the time it took to save the world.

Ansel gravely accepted a sword from Rez. He wasn't a warrior, and he didn't relish the idea of killing anyone, or even knocking them senseless, but he had seen at least one bleak and a host of ridden humans waiting at the warehouse for them, and he would do whatever he had to do to save Tadra.

"Ansel?"

Henrik was watching him expectantly, one hand in the air, poised to open a portal.

They were waiting for his direction, Ansel realized. He'd gone from hound-keeper to hero...and he wondered why he'd ever wanted this weight on his shoulders.

"Let's go save the world," he said, and Henrik ripped a portal to the warehouse where their destiny waited.

CHAPTER 32

*T*adra willed her limbs to move and couldn't.

It was worse than being unable to speak. It was even worse than her long imprisonment in glass.

It wasn't worse than the grief in Ansel's eyes, or knowing that she'd failed. If only she had hardened her resolve a little sooner. If only she had moved faster. If only…

Cerad yanked her through the portal and released his iron hold on her, catching the firebird when she might have dropped it from her nerveless fingers. He didn't bother to catch her, and Tadra fell to her knees. He paused to turn the glass in the flickering light of the warehouse and chuckle. "I cast a spell to make you fragile," he scoffed. "I did not realize how fragile you would actually be. It doesn't help that this world is dry of magic."

Tadra wasn't frozen any longer, but she was drained, and she feigned more weakness than she actually felt. *You are the fall of the kingdom, and you will pay for your crimes,* she signed, knowing that he could not understand her and that it was an empty threat.

Cerad laughed and tucked the firebird carelessly into his pocket. Tadra watched where he put it, wishing she'd had the courage to stop him sooner.

He left her in the charge of a pair of guards—one bleak, reeking of evil, and one human whose jerky motions reminded her of trying to walk with chilled joints.

There was an innocent under that veil of darkness, Tadra thought achingly. If she had her full power, she'd be able to release them and perhaps gain an ally. But she could only touch a tiny portion of her firebird magic and Cerad could steal anything that she accessed.

She let herself slump down to lie on the cool concrete floor, in every way a picture of collapse, as she watched and waited for her chance, hoping that her strength would renew quickly. Cerad had not taken that much to bring them here, and she wasn't sure how accurate his sense of how much power she had actually was, so she pretended she was much worse off than she felt.

Robin said that time passed differently for fae than for humans. Something about the way that memories were set down made time stretch and bend with magic. Tadra felt every cold moment as it trudged past, listening to the gathering of Cerad's army as portals opened and his forces swelled.

She braced herself for the portal to faery, but it was clear that Cerad was being careful with his power use; these portals were only from Earth, a gathering of his forces on this side before he opened the gates to her home world and let the darkness beyond through to complete his conquest.

The tactician in her thought that this made the warehouse a brilliant place for a glorious strike, to take out all the dark army at once, forever.

But there was no one to make that glorious strike. Her

shieldmates were compromised, Robin was lost, and Ansel…

Tadra felt a hot tear slip down one cheek. Ansel would take them all on if he had any way to get here, with no hope of winning, because he was as brave and foolish as she was. She was glad that he wasn't here, because Cerad would surely destroy him for fun, merely to make her suffer. She had only one way to stop things now, and she had to bide her time and wait for the right opportunity, hoping against hope that her chance didn't come too late.

When she heard the sizzle of a portal behind her, at the far side of the warehouse she assumed it was another of Cerad's allies, a belief that was quickly dispelled by the cries of alarm that were immediately raised. Tadra rolled and sat up, hoping she had enough strength to use whatever was happening as the distraction she'd been hoping for. She gained her knees, and had a chance to see down the warehouse behind her, where a shining portal was disgorging a welcome sight.

Her shieldmates, not in the sad, human lethargy that had muted their spirit, but in their full, glorious faery fighting form charged out, tails lashing and wings spread. Their keys ranged beside them, dressed in their black leather armor. Of them, only Gwen was armed, but Tadra could hear the ring of Daniella's strong voice, and Heather was already weaving her hands in the air as Rez charged to skewer a nearby bleak.

And at their head, dressed in her own armor, was Ansel.

Tadra felt her heart expand a hundred times. Brave, foolish, beautiful Ansel.

He was holding one of the heavier practice swords, and he ignored every one of the ridden humans who stepped forward to stop them, slapping away their attacks or letting the knights do their work at his flank. His gaze swept the warehouse in search of her.

He caught sight of Tadra just as Cerad arrived at her side, laughing his cold, humorless laugh. "They're too late," Cerad said, sending his bleaks to intercept the attack.

He took Tadra by the shoulder and hauled her to her feet. She let herself stagger against him, pretending to be limp and disoriented, and he grinned down into her face. "You have what I need left inside you," he said, and he wrenched her back to arm's length.

"Behold, little bird, the end of their world as they know it." Cerad raised one hand and traced not one but two portals in the air, spreading wider and wider out onto a chilling scene as Tadra glimpsed her world as she'd never seen it, an impossible dark force waiting on the other side to flow over and complete Cerad's claim on this world.

Tadra felt the power draw out from her bones and her heart to power the portals opening, and she flung her hand out in one last, desperate motion, releasing the glass firebird that she'd smuggled out of Cerad's coat to fly through the air.

It would strike the ground and shatter, but Tadra feared she was once again moments too late.

CHAPTER 33

*A*nsel felt his heart stop when he saw through a gap in the fighting as Cerad lifted Tadra to her feet, and he saw the flash of red in her hand as Cerad started tracing the great portals between worlds with her power.

Ansel knew what Tadra was going to try to do. They didn't need words, or even signs. She was going to break her firebird and hope it kept Cerad from accessing what was left of her power in time to keep him from opening the portals.

Ansel felt rage and fear and frustration burn through him. *Tadra, no!* he signed, but she wasn't looking at him, and even if he shouted, his voice was unlikely to carry that far over the sounds of battle raging between them.

If he'd been her key…

Ansel screwed his eyes shut. He *should* have been her key. They were meant to be together in ways that he'd never imagined were possible, even if there had been no magic to make it obvious to them. Every part of his heart was fitted to every part of hers, like the interlocking parts of a complicated system.

Cerad had stolen the magic connection, but he couldn't take their destiny...and love was stronger than magic.

His eyes still shut, Ansel cast his memory back to holding the pieces of Tadra's firebird back together. He shouldn't have been able to mend her the way that he did, it defied logic and sense. If he could lay aside the constraints of his mind, let go of his own human limitations...if he could believe that he could do anything...maybe he could.

Something clicked into place as Ansel remembered the drawing he'd made of the four white rings, overlapping in the middle. Tadra's ring had never broken.

His eyes flew open, just in time to witness Tadra use the last of her strength to raise her glass firebird and dash it towards the ground.

Her act was too late, because Cerad had already ripped a portal open, a shimmering slash through the warehouse, and then a second one, and the great dark host that waited in faery was already gathered—a dire wind preceding it through.

Stop, Ansel signed, and he set his teeth, dropped his sword, and caught Tadra's firebird just before it could shatter at her feet from all the way across the warehouse. His chest felt like it was on fire as he lowered it slowly to the concrete floor.

It was impossible.

And if he could do that impossible thing…

Ansel remembered the seams of broken glass that he'd glued together, the way they went invisible when the light was right, the satisfaction of fixing the un-fixable things that had always inspired him. He became aware that the heat at his chest wasn't metaphorical. The inner pocket that he'd tucked the ornaments into was glowing through his heavy jacket.

Robin was still swearing from Ansel's outside pocket and drumming at his side with tiny feet.

Ansel listened to the battle turn against them as the bleaks from the other side came through the open portals, wispy shadows brandishing black swords, dark hounds howling at their heels. It was an insurmountable host, an unstoppable force, crowding through the portal into the howling warehouse.

Even the three knights and their keys at full power could not hope to keep them back, and Ansel was dismayed to watch them regroup to try. Tadra was limply struggling in Cerad's grip, and he was grinning down at her, ready to take the last of her power to clinch the victory, holding the portal open against Henrik's best magical efforts.

Cerad wouldn't be able to do it if he didn't have the key connection.

Ansel clutched at his chest where the rings felt like they were starting to burn through to his skin and pulled the ornaments out. The mythical animals were all cool glass, but the rings...the rings were the real magic, Ansel realized. That was why Tadra hadn't been lost when her ornament first broke. She was entangled with the magic in the unbroken ring, anchored, and that was why Ansel had been able to find her again.

And maybe–just maybe—he'd been able to release her because he was *supposed* to be her key. Ansel yanked the ornaments off their strings, and returned them to his pocket carelessly as he stacked the rings in his other hand.

These were vessels of the magic of faery. *These* were the pieces of the broken crown.

It was everything he could do to hold on to the burning

rings and he thought he could smell his own singed flesh. They were shining so brightly now that his fingers glowed red around them. He could not tell where one ended and the next stacked on top of it; they were a single circlet of power.

A crown.

Ansel was holding a whole crown, and it was blinding him, but he didn't dare to close his eyes or look away from it. Tears rolled out of his eyes and he gritted his teeth against the pain and brilliance.

Ansel looked to find Cerad glowing with power as the portal to dark faery grew larger and wider, Tadra struggling like a wounded bird in his grasp. Was he drawing the magic from the crown through his key bond with her because Ansel had unlocked it? Was he only making things *worse?*

"Break the crown!"

Robin had squirmed free from Ansel's pocket and was hanging in the air before him.

"Break the crown and the power ends. All of it! It's the only way to save your world."

It was the only way to stop what was happening.

Ansel could destroy the crown and *all* the magic, leaving the dark forces no foothold in his world. The portals would close. It would protect Earth and seal the fate of the fae kingdom that had fallen. Tadra and the knights would probably be destroyed, their human selves dragged to destruction with their magical halves, and the only magic in the world left would be whatever was naturally here. Robin...Robin would diminish to nothing.

The only way to save billions of innocent people who had no idea that the fate of their world was hinged on a battle in a warehouse in Michigan that night was to sacrifice his friends and his love.

"You have to do it!" Robin cried, battering themself against the crown like a desperate moth; they were too small to wrest it from Ansel and throw it to the ground, but they were trying gamely. "It's the only way to stop him!"

"Your knights…" Ansel said achingly.

"You know they are prepared to make such a sacrifice!"

It was true, Ansel knew. They would not hesitate a moment to do whatever they considered right.

Ansel lifted the crown, prepared to dash it down, then paused.

This was the hero moment, he realized. The moment he made the hard choice and clinched the fate of the world. The moment he'd always wanted to be a part of. He had to do it, this terrible act with no happy ending.

His fingers tightened hard around the burning glass.

There was always another choice, some out-of-the-box solution. That was what he excelled at, finding the unexpected path. His inability to find another answer was only a failing of imagination, all he had to do was stop limiting his own inventiveness with boundaries of his own making.

Ansel shook Robin off the crown and clamped it down onto his own head, taking all of the power of faery for his own, instead.

He knew he'd made a terrible mistake as the magic seared down into him.

It was too much for a mortal to bear. He was a fool, he was too weak, too human for such power and it drove him nearly to his knees. He was unworthy, unfit. He'd let everyone down, lost his chance to save at least one world.

Then he seemed to feel Tadra's hands, cool, over the top of his. Her ring and middle fingers curled in. *I love you.*

Resolve hardened in him, like he was fighting against a strong wind and suddenly had a handhold. He was aware of everyone, everything. He could see the battlefield, spread out as if he was watching it from above. The battered warehouse. The arches of the broad portals and the scarred landscape beyond. The knights, fighting in their magic shapes at the sides of their human keys.

Most of all, he saw Tadra, kneeling with her unbroken firebird in her hands.

Ansel felt Kevin—Cerad—give a shudder of alarm and the attention of every bleak and dour and ridden human turned unerringly to where Ansel stood, the magic of the crown spilling down around him like a cloak of lightning and music.

The dours flung themselves at him and dissolved away at his touch, because he imagined that they *would.* The ridden humans raised weapons, then dropped them as they regained their own will, because he believed that they *could.* The bleaks howled into nothingness, because he knew that they *should.* The warehouse exploded outward in all directions, opening the roof to the dark sky above.

The power was dizzying. It yanked at his mind like a whole kennel of dogs on leashes trying to pull him in every direction. It was like trying to keep his attention on a single thought in the middle of a tornado of sparks, each one of them worlds. It was like scrolling through an infinite spreadsheet of data and trying to make sense of a completely unknown system. He felt everything at once, saw everything, smelled it and tasted it and was deafened by the sound of it.

Ansel had unspeakable power, all the deep magic that had been the pillars of an entire faery world were at his command, and he could feel it coursing through his veins. He could smite Cerad where he stood, take him apart to his very molecules, destroy what remained of the man that had been and stop the war in its tracks.

I created the evil, Robin had confessed. *I took his grief and left a hole for darkness.*

Ansel looked at the light that streamed from his palms and fingertips. What would burning Cerad away leave room to grow? Was there more to magic than destruction and pain?

Every key's interpretation of magic was different. Daniella heard music she could make harmonies with. Heather saw fibers she could weave. Gwen saw her power in controls and dialogue boxes like a video game. He saw it as fire, like snaking vines of raw energy, capable of burning away anything in its path.

It was just a way for his mind to make sense of a power so vast and complicated that human minds weren't meant to understand it.

But that didn't mean that it was limited to what he thought he could do with it. He didn't have to use fire to burn, he could do anything with magic that he could imagine...

He didn't have to destroy Cerad, but Cerad did not know that, and he raised his sword for a last defense as Ansel appeared before him, unconstrained by distance and physical reality.

"I give you imagination," Ansel said, laying a glowing hand on his forehead.

Imagination was lock-step with compassion; no one could understand someone else if they could not imagine themselves in other shoes. Where Robin had taken Cerad's grief and left emptiness, Ansel gave him *empathy*, pouring it down into Cerad as if he were an empty vessel.

Cerad staggered back in horror, dropping his black sword with a cry before he went limp and fell to his knees. Tadra toppled beside him. What remained of his army collapsed in confusion. All Ansel had to do now was close the portals, and the danger to earth would be done.

Ansel was still on unearthly fire, and he could feel himself losing his last sense of himself. His mind was not magic, and no mortal could control this power so long without letting it consume him completely. His only chance at surviving this was to cast the crown off now.

Beyond the portals, he could see the faery world, still blackened and broken, and he knew in a brilliant moment of clarity that the only thing stopping him from fixing it all was his own sense of limitation.

He also knew what it would cost him.

Could he sacrifice the last shreds of his humanity to save a world that was already given up for lost?

He closed blazing eyes and remembered how Tadra had been ready to smash her glass firebird. She'd been willing to give up her life and all of her magic to try to save his world. He could give his mortal mind for the world she loved.

Ansel—already feeling more crown now than man, like he was composed entirely of light—reached out with all of his strength and will and imagined the dark world unfurling new green, clear water washing out muddy streams, bright sky bursting through storm clouds. He touched every ridden human, burning back their dark riders, and purged the taint from the leylines beneath the surface of the land, chasing it back to every corner of the world: every deep place and every high breath of air.

He was everywhere at once, too much, spread too thin in an inferno of magic and when his final, gasping breath drove the last of the darkness away, he felt suspended in nothing for a moment, exhausted and undone.

There was nothing left of himself, only ashes.

CHAPTER 34

*T*adra felt the full power of her firebird when Ansel unleashed the crown, but she could do nothing but struggle uselessly while Cerad held the reins to it through their wretched, wrong key connection.

Cerad cackled, sure of his victory as his forces swelled and paraded in through the portals. The fight of her shieldmates took a turn for the defensive; she could barely see their desperate light through the swirling darkness.

Cerad threw her easily aside, and she landed by her miraculously unbroken glass firebird. The seams where Ansel had repaired her sparked in the angry light.

Did she have a third chance to make this right? If she broke the glass avatar now, was it too late anyway?

She didn't even have the opportunity to raise it above her head before everything suddenly hushed and the warehouse walls and roof blasted out. Cerad's army seemed to collapse in on itself, dours disappearing, bleaks shrieking to nothingness. Dazed humans stepped out of shadows, lowering weapons and shaking themselves.

Ansel himself was standing before them, but he wasn't

Ansel at all, he was the crown, all the power of faery shedding off from him like roaring wildfire as Cerad raised his
sword. He laid one hand on Cerad's head, fingers glowing,
and Cerad collapsed.

Beneath them, the earth heaved and groaned and if
Tadra had been standing, she may have fallen. The power
from Ansel was blinding, and it swept over her to the
portals of faery like a vast, inexorable wave. She didn't look
to see what he was doing with it, if he had any control of it
at all now; she knew that Ansel needed her, that he was
flying to pieces in the maelstrom he'd created, and that she
would lose him if she didn't act. She surged to her feet and
wrapped her arms around his flaming body.

She didn't have a hand free to sign to him, and her
voice was still silent when she tried to speak, to tell him
how much she loved and needed him. All she could do was
beg him, silently, to stay, to open her whole heart,
completely.

He shuddered in her embrace and tried to speak, and
when he couldn't, Tadra took his face in her hands and
pressed her forehead to his, feeling the crown burn into her
brow.

He still didn't answer, and Tadra felt as if he was
dissolving in her embrace, spilling out like water from a
broken vessel, faster than she could catch him back...and
she knew that it was because he wasn't her key. If they'd
had that connection, she'd be able to buffer him from the
magic and share his burden, sparing him this.

"It is too late!" Robin cried from near her ear. "The
crown was too much for him to take up! He cannot survive
this."

Tadra would not accept it. She refused to lose him now.
He was her closest friend and greatest love. He was her
trust and her compass direction, he completed her

emotionally and physically and mentally, in every way that she could imagine.

He wasn't only *meant* to be her key.

He *was* her key.

Deep within her, something fell into place, like a wandering song finding its melody.

He was her key.

Tadra wasn't later sure if she somehow tore the key connection away from Cerad to return it to where it was meant to be, or if she wrought some completely new wild magic with her absolute certainty that she and Ansel were meant to be. She only knew that she could not let the crown destroy him, and that she would hold him here with her forever if that's what it took.

"Ansel! You are here!" she told him. "You are here with me now in *this* place and I love you!"

It was strange to hear her own voice out loud again after so long, and it seemed to dampen the crackling fire that was consuming Ansel.

"Tadra…" he croaked. "Tadra...my heart…there is so much...I am everything..."

"You are my key!" she told him. "You are my heart! You are *my* everything!"

He raised his hand slowly and ripped the crown from his head, letting it slip from his fingers to the ground, where all of its fire extinguished.

The earth went still beneath them and Ansel collapsed in Tadra's embrace. "Ansel," she pleaded, balancing him upright. "Ansel?"

Ansel coughed as if he'd forgotten how to breathe, then croaked, "You sound exactly like I'd always imagined."

She kissed him then, and they would have fallen together if Henrik hadn't caught her by the arm as Rez appeared at Ansel's far side to keep him standing.

"Hound-keeper. Ansel." Trey was there, too, sweeping all of them into his arms in an expression of support and affection.

"People...in this world...don't...hug...all the time..." Ansel gasped.

"I feel that this is a remarkable occasion," Rez said firmly.

Heather added wryly, "What with the whole rebuilding of faeryland and everything."

Then, at last, Tadra could look around and see what Ansel had wrought.

Through the flickering portals, her world stretched out in its full glory again. The taint of darkness that had faded it for so long had been rolled away, replaced with life and beauty like Tadra had never imagined would be possible again. It was the stuff of Robin's tales, the color plates in the human faery tale books, and most of all, it was Ansel's vision, pure and full of magic again.

The earth was still again, but far away, Tadra could hear car alarms screaming.

"It is...unbroken."

Tadra wasn't sure if Robin was referring to the crown, or to faery, fueled again by the magic that Ansel had unlocked and unleashed.

Robin was standing at their true size again and Tadra had to blink to look at them, because she seemed to see the fable with a hundred kinds of wings, and a hundred different faces, all at once in a dizzy overlay.

"I couldn't image it whole again," they said quietly.

Gracefully, with entirely too many arms and eyes, Robin reached out and picked up the crown that lay, inert, at their feet. It was a crown in truth now, with graceful clear points of faceted crystal in a circlet. Robin raised it to their own head and settled it in its rightful place.

When the shieldmates had released Ansel to stand unsteadily on his own feet, one hand in Tadra's, Robin strode forward and took his face in both their hands, tipping their forehead to touch his. If the crown burned his brow, Ansel didn't flinch.

"Cerad," Ansel said, when Robin released him.

Cerad was still kneeling where Ansel had left him, holding his head.

Robin glided to him and knelt at his side.

"I...remember," Cerad said. "I remember it *all.*"

"Your memories are part of who you are," Robin said regretfully. "You cannot separate a man from his *meaning.*"

Cerad looked at his own spread hands. "What do I do now? Who am I after all of that?"

Robin tipped forward and put their forehead against Cerad's, cradling his face in their hands. "You are my friend and you may choose your own life from here. Come back to our world and be my companion again. Or stay in this world, if you mean it no harm now. You choose your own destiny."

Cerad looked with aching longing through the open portals. "I could go home?" he said, his voice full of yearning. "After all that I did?"

"It is undone," Robin said simply. Tadra had to blink to focus on them.

"It will be remembered," Cerad said with regret.

"Then we will make new memories, and in time, the old ones will lose their power to control."

Cerad bowed his head. "I will return to our world. I have no memories here that I wish to keep close, and there is much I can atone for there."

He made a swift circle of the knights. "I owe you an apology," he said generally. "I used you without mercy and would have done worse."

The knights all murmured acceptance, but Tadra drew herself up as Cerad came to where she stood with Ansel.

"You, most of all," Cerad said. "I took something that wasn't mine to have."

Her key bond with Ansel.

Ansel's arm around her shoulder squeezed, but he didn't offer to speak for her.

Tadra only smiled at him. "A hard-won prize is more valued than a careless gift," she said, looking aside to Ansel. "We made what was not given to us and I would not trade what we have for any spell."

Ansel, whose face had been a masterpiece of conflicted emotion, softened into a tender smile.

I love you, she signed at him with her free hand. *You are my key.*

You are my heart, he signed back.

Cerad looked from one of them to the other and his smile was full of pain and understanding. He bowed to them and turned back to the nearest portal. Rainbow-colored grass was bending in a sweet breeze to a horizon of crimson hills. Tadra did not realize how deep it was until Cerad waded out into it and disappeared from sight.

The warehouse itself had been demolished, not just flattened to rubble, but replaced with a grove of living evergreen trees.

The humans who had been freed of evil influence were milling about in confusion, starting to shiver in shock and chill. The knights and their keys went to round them up and set them on the path back to their lives, the comfortable enchantment of faery forgetfulness already filling in the gaps of logic. Tadra suspected that they would carry vague memories of a very wild party for the rest of their lives.

That left her standing alone with Ansel and Robin, the

winter night brightly lit by the glory of faery through the portals.

"The magic," Ansel said, rubbing his head. "It's all back in faery now?"

"Yes," Robin said simply. "You returned it to where it had come from, as we will."

Tadra looked at them in alarm. "You intend us to go back with you?"

Robin looked like they had considered no other outcome. "Your firebird cannot exist in this world with all of its magic in faery. Would you relinquish that to remain?"

Ansel's hand in Tadra's tightened, and she looked at him to find that he was frowning at her in worry. "You could return," he said. "You are a protector of the crown and your kingdom is restored. I would come with you."

For one split second, Tadra was divided. Her duty in the world she'd come from was once the only thing she'd known, and there was her loyalty to Robin and her shield-mates, and all the possibilities of the revitalized faery. And on the other side, there was a cold, curious human world with Ansel. Dear, brave Ansel, who loved her in ways she'd never dreamed. Ansel, who loved this world. She could not ask him to leave everything here.

The moment was gone as quickly as it had come. *I stay here with you,* she said, and she signed it, because she had forgotten that she could speak again. *I love you.*

Then she *couldn't* speak, because Ansel caught her up in a desperate kiss and they had no need for words at all.

"Your firebird," Ansel said achingly when there was space between their mouths. "You'll lose all of your power."

"All the knights who choose to stay here in this world will," Robin said. "They can only access the power on our side where the crown is. I will be sorrowful to leave this world behind, but I know that it will not be long for me until I see you again, if you choose to remain here."

The others had returned from herding the humans back to civilization, safely away from the faery portal that still sizzled brightly in the night.

"Our world has no need for us now," Henrik said thoughtfully.

"We are only human here, but there is no shame in being only human," Rez said firmly.

"Damn straight," Heather said, elbowing him in the side.

"This world may need defending in the future," Trey suggested. "There may be other threats."

"We could not leave it unguarded," Rez agreed.

None of them offered to cross the portal after Cerad.

"This is our home now," Trey said. "Our home with our keys. Our duty is here."

"We'll have to get you driver's licenses or something," Daniella said.

"Maybe jobs?" Gwen suggested.

"I would be happy to sling burgers," Henrik told her nobly. "If there are not occupations for knights."

"The mall *could* use some better security guards," Gwen suggested drolly.

"You have made your choice," Robin said without judgement. "We must say our farewells swiftly."

They exchanged long, meaningful embraces with each of the knights and keys, and when they put their arms around Tadra, she felt a deep sense of satisfaction and peace. Robin, her mentor, her crown. She would miss *them* more than she would miss faery.

Ansel didn't say a word about unnecessary embraces

when Robin enfolded him in their arms, and they traded a short exchange of words that Tadra couldn't hear.

The portals shimmered in warning and Robin let Ansel go, stepping back into a forest of gleaming purple vines. "I'll see you," they said…

…and all the portals crackled into nothing.

The darkness when the doorways closed was so sudden and complete that they were all blind for a moment.

"What did Robin say to you?" Tadra asked, after a moment of silence where they all adjusted to the unbroken night.

Ansel chuckled. "They said they'd probably redecorate, that I used entirely too much avocado green and was heavy-handed with the sparkle, and that the whole place smelled like my warehouse. I called them Tinker Bell for old times, and they called me Meatbag. It's kind of our thing."

Tadra had to giggle, and then shiver, because she didn't have magic to keep her warm anymore. "Did you bring an extra coat?" she asked, and he insisted on taking her leather jacket off and wrapping it around her.

"I'm used to Michigan winters," he assured her, buckling it at her neck. "And since Henrik can't do portals anymore, we'll all stay warm walking briskly home."

He staggered as they set off and Tadra wormed her way up under his arm to help him walk.

"It was a worthy battle," Trey said with satisfaction as they navigated the new forest back to the road.

"We made a great sacrifice," Henrik agreed proudly.

Gwen punched him in the arm. "You wouldn't have been happy in a world without pizza. Don't make yourself sound like a martyr."

Henrik bent to kiss her. "You are correct, my key. But

do not believe that I will not miss my gryphon half. It is...unnerving."

"Very peculiar," Rez agreed.

"I will miss flying," Trey said mournfully. "But I do not regret the choice in the slightest."

"Sure," Rez said. "Bring up the flying." But he rubbed at the center of his forehead rather self-consciously. They had arrived at the edge of the woods.

Tadra closed her eyes and folded into herself curiously. She didn't feel as empty as she'd expected and she remembered Robin's warning that her firebird had bled into the rest of her, that they were entangled too completely for her ever to be completely free.

There was still a flicker far inside of her, and when she reached for it...

She was suddenly spreading wings.

If her firebird had been diminished before, it was even moreso now, stripped of the deep magic that had fueled it. It merely had traces of magic and was the size of a hummingbird, but it was a firebird, shedding sparks that didn't burn.

She made cartwheels through the air, reveling in the flight and freedom, then circled Ansel and landed on his shoulder. She shook herself, scattering her sparks all around, and gave a bird smirk to her shieldmates, who were staring in astonishment.

"Does this mean...?" Trey started.

Henrik was already shrinking into a gryphon form the size of a mouse, his feathered wings keeping him aloft until he landed in Gwen's open hands.

"Oh my God, you are the cutest thing I've ever seen in my life," Gwen said adoringly. "Socks is either going to think you're a kitten or a snack."

A split-second later, Trey was a glimmering dragon

landing on the top of Daniella's head and preening, his green tail snaking down around her neck.

Rez gave a long-suffering sigh and turned into a unicorn, small enough to get momentarily lost in Heather's long skirt before he trotted out and stabbed Ansel in the ankle.

"Hey!" Ansel protested. "What did I do?"

Tadra turned back into a woman simply so that she could laugh out loud. "You stole all the glory!" she said, slipping an arm around Ansel. "Here we were, chosen knights and trained warriors, and you were the one with the strength and sight to save faery single-handedly. It will be a wonder if we ever forgive you this slight to our pride."

Henrik seemed to flow from Gwen's hands into his human form. "Do not tease our shieldmate," he scolded Tadra. Then he bowed to Ansel, to Tadra's delight. "Do not take her seriously now that she has her tongue, landowner Ansel, keeper of hounds and fixer of technology. We are honored by your service and awed by your actions. Your courage and strength give us much to aspire to."

"Did you just call me your shieldmate?" Ansel asked. Tadra could feel the surprise in his body.

Trey dropped from Daniella's head as Rez swelled upward and both of them knelt before Ansel in their human shapes. "You are a true knight," Rez agreed.

"A credit to our kingdom, our savior," Trey added.

Ansel looked at them in confusion and Tadra stepped back to sign to him. *You are our shieldmate. You are my heart.* Then she knelt with her shieldmates and when she looked up at Ansel, she was delighted by the expression on his face: confusion, surprise, and joy. He understood the gift they'd just given him, and she knew how much it meant to him.

"I didn't do it to be a knight," Ansel said quietly.

"Of course not," Trey said, standing again. "A true knight doesn't do things for titles or glory. Your heart is pure." He took Ansel's face in his hands and touched their foreheads together.

"Your courage is unselfish," Rez said, taking a turn to press his forehead to Ansel's.

"Your strength of spirit is impressive," Henrik added, and at the end of his forehead touch, he flung his arms around Ansel.

"We don't have to hug all the time," Ansel reminded him, but he embraced Henrik back.

Tadra took Ansel's face between her palms when Henrik released him. She didn't say a word, only rested her forehead against his and let herself love him completely.

Overhead, there were noisy bursts of fire in the sky.

CHAPTER 35

There were sirens through Wimberlette and the long walk back to Ansel's house was surreal. The damage from their battle and the reconstruction of faery had not been constrained to the warehouse, and it hadn't all been fixed when Ansel rebuilt faery. He had a moment of guilt for the collateral damage, then reminded himself that he'd just saved two worlds and maybe he didn't need to worry about being able to fix absolutely everything. He was so tired that Tadra had to support him, and the destruction seemed minimal, in the scope of things.

Roads and sidewalks were broken and tilted plates in places, and there were a few trees down. It didn't look like any structures had fallen, but there were a few people wandering around picking up fallen trash cans and shaking their heads at their neighbors.

"Did you guys feel that earthquake?" Jenny asked as they passed her house. There were fireworks going off in earnest overhead now and she had her son and daughter by the hands.

"I assure you we did," Henrik said.

"Any damage?" Ansel asked. He probably looked drunk, barely able to stand on his own two feet. It wasn't out of place, for the occasion.

"All our windows rattled! One of the plates broke!" one of her children cried.

"We got to stay up late!" the other one chortled.

"Happy New Year!" everyone said to each other.

Then they were finally home again, and the dogs were ecstatic to greet them and bark and whine and demand scratches and comfort. Even Socks made a brief appearance to let them all know about her various displeasures with the world. Nothing seemed to be damaged, though a few pictures on the wall were hanging askew, and a bowl had been knocked off the counter.

That was as likely to be from Socks as it was from their final battle.

Ansel fell onto the couch and Tadra wrapped him in an afghan, a comforting mirror of the way he'd taken care of her when she had been drained of her power.

"I feel weird," he confessed to her, while the others fed the pets and rustled up snacks in the kitchen.

"You had all the power of faery in your head for a time," Tadra reminded him, kissing his forehead. "I do not expect it was a comfortable burden."

It was amazing, hearing her voice. It was both unfamiliar and so perfectly right for her, rich and velvety. "Your firebird…"

"Will always be a small part of me," she said serenely. "If somewhat tinier than before."

"You were ready to sacrifice her to save a world you'd only known a few weeks," Ansel said, freeing a hand from the afghan to stroke her cheek. "And you must have known that you might have destroyed yourself to make it happen."

"You were ready to sacrifice yourself to save a broken world you'd never even seen."

"I could imagine it," Ansel said thoughtfully. "And I know how much you loved it."

"I love you," she said, simply. She kissed his cheek, and he turned his mouth to meet hers.

They startled apart when Trey came in with hot drinks, then sagged close back together. They didn't have to pretend any more, and that was almost as much of a relief as saving the world.

Trey winked at them as he set steaming mugs of cocoa on the coffee table and said drolly, "In case you needed any heating up."

They all stayed up for another hour or so, warming over drinks and talking quietly over all that had happened.

Kevin's—Cerad's—influence over them did not go completely unremembered, but they agreed that the memories of that time were fuzzy.

"I know what happened," Gwen explained thoughtfully. "I just don't remember why I thought that everything was okay."

"It was like being swaddled in cotton," Henrik agreed. "But very pleasant cotton."

The conversation moved to their plans for the fresh new year.

"I would like to secure a job," Trey said. "It feels unseemly to continue to depend on the charity of our host."

"I'd like to open a costume shop," Heather said wistfully.

"I'm thinking about starting a Tang Soo Do studio,"

Gwen confessed. "I'd have to get some certification, but there's no martial arts available locally that's not just for grown-ups, and I miss training kids."

"I like children," Henrik said thoughtfully, and the moment turned into something with unintended depth as they looked at each other in surprise and Gwen's cheeks went pink.

Rez nodded. "I should like to travel and see some of the places that Heather has mentioned, such as DizzyKingdom and FishWorld."

"I'd like to see more of this world, too," Tadra said. "Perhaps a year of travel would be stimulating?"

"I might sleep for a year," Ansel confessed, yawning.

That was their cue to disperse to their individual beds, leaving their tea and cocoa mugs where they were. The last of the fireworks had died away to nothing, and the sirens had long since gone silent.

Ansel felt like he'd found a second wind, but he didn't protest when Tadra helped him up the stairs. He turned in her embrace to kiss her as soon as they were inside his room, and she eagerly kissed him back.

"I have been dying for one thing," he confessed, kissing her neck and holding her close.

"What is it?" she whispered, her breath ragged and dear.

"I want to *hear* you," Ansel said, letting his tongue lap her ear briefly before he put his lips against hers. "I want to make you cry out my name."

He felt her smile against his mouth. "I might be very noisy," she warned him. "You have very clever...hands."

Ansel kicked the door shut behind them and wrestled her to the bed as they tore off their clothing and fell onto the rumpled comforter.

Her noises were everything that he thought they might be, and they had no fear of being caught, or any care for Socks, who shortly found the closed door and voiced her ire at it.

It was dark in the room and when Ansel went rummaging for a condom, he turned on the light with a quick flick of his wrist, not realizing what he'd done until Tadra gasped.

A handful of floating globes illuminated the room, soft silvery light making every curve of her naked body look like art.

Ansel looked at Tadra, then at the faery lights. "I didn't even think about it," he said in wonder. "I just…"

"The deep magic will always be a part of you," Tadra said, reaching one hand to touch the cool light closest to her. "Like my firebird will be a part of me. It won't be much, compared to faery itself."

Ansel looked at his hand, then, as a test, waved it at the lights. They obediently bobbed and swirled, then distributed about the room again, floating serenely into the places he willed them and changing colors.

"What else can I do?" he wondered out loud.

"You can come and make love to me," Tadra said impatiently. She seemed unimpressed, but then, she'd grown up in faery, with a firebird of deep magic sharing her soul.

Ansel found the condom and went to join her on the bed again. "Say my name," he begged, taking her into his arms.

"Ansel," Tadra breathed near his ear as she wound her arms around his neck. "Ansel! Ansel, my heart, my key, my love…"

Ansel was divided between wanting to smother her

words with kisses and dying a little in joy at the sound of her voice as he made love to her beautiful body and brought her to high planes of pleasure. "Tadra," he begged. They didn't have to be quiet, but in the end, out of habit or need, they were making silent signs against each other: *I love you, my heart, good, better, best, I **love** you...*

EPILOGUE

At the end of that year, none of them were anywhere near where they'd imagined they would be, Tadra least of all.

Gwen was hugely pregnant, and she waded through the snow up the little slope from the road where they had parked to the site where the warehouse had been destroyed, huffing and protesting. Henrik hovered over her with a mix of pride and anxiousness. Daniella was laughing with Trey over the gift they'd brought, a CD of her first album as a professional singer.

"We don't even know if they have CD players in faery," she pointed out, not for the first time.

"I'm sure Robin will contrive a way to play it," Trey said proudly.

Heather, wearing one of the dresses from her new line, was carrying a squirming Vesta, and Fabio was dancing around their feet, spraying snow everywhere and playing with Trucker, Ansel and Tadra's big-pawed husky puppy.

The conversion of the warehouse from a commercial lot to a full-grown forest overnight had gotten a lot of brief attention, but since no one could explain it in a satisfactory way, it was generally just ignored and swept under the rug. Tadra suspected that some lingering faery magic diminished the memory of the event. The site sometimes got supernatural investigators, but there was no real evidence that it had ever been anything but a simple empty lot with some trees. The rubble from the structure itself was mostly overgrown with moss now, and covered in deep December snow.

Tadra's heart was in her throat.

Ansel's faery lights lit their way through the densely-growing trees, but none of them had the kind of power necessary to open a portal. She couldn't know what had happened in faery, or how long it had been for them. Cerad might have betrayed Robin again, or stolen the deep magic, or perhaps Ansel had not fully purged out a pocket of the darkness and it had grown again and swallowed the world. The portal would have to be opened from the other side, and if something had happened to Robin...

Ansel's hand in hers tightened as he sensed her nervousness. *Okay?* he signed, his face making it a question.

Okay, she agreed firmly.

There was no reason to borrow trouble before it found her.

She was wearing jeans and a quilted jacket, a knitted hat that she'd made herself (with Heather's patient tutelage) over her ears. This world didn't need firebird knights, but she had found a place she belonged running Ansel's re-opened secondhand store (in a new building downtown) and she was taking business classes at the local college.

She loved the work, and her job made a lot more sense when she realized that Ansel often bought some things at a higher price than he could charge in order to help people in a bind while saving them the dignity of asking for help. She was getting skilled at computers and was working on a webpage for the store. Being a merchant unexpectedly suited her skills, and she never had to worry about hiring security.

Faery seemed far away and long ago, and when they reached the grove in the center of the lot, Tadra looked up at the clear, star-dotted sky through the trees. Ansel put his arms around her and she realized she was shivering.

"Everything will be fine," he promised. "They'll come."

Tadra leaned into his embrace. She didn't have enough faery magic to keep her warm, but she had love, and that was even better.

There was a rip of sound, just before a flash of light announced the portal, and Tadra caught her breath and squinted into the brilliance. Bells of celebration rang and she could hear golden voices on the other side, long before she could see over.

"Robin!" She left her shieldmates scrambling through the snow behind her as she sprinted to meet the fable, throwing her arms around them before she could remind herself that they were the crown and it was perhaps not exactly appropriate behavior of a protector of the kingdom.

But she was not a knight any longer, and Robin was her mentor and her friend before he was her crown. They met her, forehead to forehead, smiling and laughing as the summer spilled out of the portal and melted away all of the cold and dark in a rush of flowers and fragrant air. Robin wore gold and white, folds of shimmering feathers and silk, and the crown on their head glimmered like ice.

Then her shieldmates were there, and there were more dizzying embraces as everyone tried to cram an entire year of information into a few moments of greeting.

Tadra wasn't the only one who was attending a school;

Rez was studying to be a psychiatrist, glad to have some way of pursuing his healing with human skills. Heather was selling her fashions online. Henrik and Gwen had postponed their plans to open a studio for a few years to have children. Daniella and Trey were touring for her album which, while self-produced, was performing well.

Robin absorbed it all with enthusiasm, though it could not have been a full year for them; everything looked just as it had when they said farewell to it, an endless, beginningless season of beauty.

Tadra drew back. Behind Robin's court of honor, Cerad was standing, his arms crossed. He wore red and raven black. Her eyes were used to the glory of the world now, and she could see that he looked wistful, hanging back in the shadows of the flowering trees.

She went cautiously to greet him, leaving Ansel with their shieldmates.

"Kevin," she said when she stepped into the dappled shadows with him.

"I go by Cerad again," he said. Then he knelt and offered his palms up. "I know it has been longer for you than it has for me, but I will owe you compensation until faery itself crumbles of age."

He'd stolen the key bond she'd been meant to have with Ansel.

He'd destroyed her world and dethroned Robin.

He was the reason that her firebird was barely the size of a moth.

Tadra slowly smiled, because none of that mattered now.

"You were not yourself," she said, drawing him back up to his feet. "And if you had been, I would never have been a knight, would never have been entrusted with the firebird magic, would never have found the love of my life in another world. Ansel told me what it was that he gave you that brought you back to who you are, and I believe that you have suffered more than I have by now."

Cerad bowed his head, and Tadra impulsively took his face in hers and put her forehead to his. "Use your new heart to love this world while I am away," she charged him. "That will be your atonement forever."

"It is done," he agreed. Then he looked over her shoulder and winced. "But your consort may not agree with your forgiveness."

Ansel's hand slipped into her own. "Kevin," he said cautiously. "Cerad."

Fabio did a frenzied lap of them all, Trucker at his tail, and they were pursued by the crown sighthounds, prancing and playing.

"Your work was well done," Cerad told Ansel with a bow when the dogs had returned to frolic with the main party. "Our world has never been so alive. It has more now than it ever did, new imagination and vision. There are parts that we still haven't fully explored: gardens of memories ripe for picking, deep caves of crystal inspiration, hills where sunlight casts no color."

"Magic has its own life. I just got it started," Ansel said humbly, but he looked pleased, and he shook Cerad's hand when it was offered. "Robin said they have something for us," he told Tadra. "They wanted all the knights to come."

"Hurry, Tadra!" Trey called. "We are all waiting on you. Again!" The other knights sometimes liked to tease her for the time they'd spent looking for her ornament.

Tadra hastened with Ansel back to where Robin stood near the portal, summer on their side, winter still dark on the other. Cerad came behind them, more slowly. They were met by an honor guard of dogs; Vesta was holding her own with the larger canines, even the winged ones.

Her shieldmates were standing in a semi-circle before Robin and Tadra fell into the final open place, Ansel dropping back with Daniella, Heather, and Gwen. Robin gestured Ansel forward. "This will be for you, also."

Ansel stepped forward to stand at Tadra's side, glancing at her curiously. She shrugged. *I don't know.*

They often still spoke in their secret language that wasn't quite sign. It gave them an excuse to gaze at each other, and say things they might not in front of other people. *I love you,* she signed, though by now, everyone knew that one.

Robin cleared their throat and Tadra dutifully turned her attention forward again.

"You were each ready to sacrifice yourself to save a world you'd known only a short time," they observed. "There is no payment I can make to you that is equal measure. But while you are here…"

Robin spread their fingers and Tadra felt the magic of faery surge up into her, familiar and fond.

Tadra realized at once what they were doing and she spread her wings in delight, making Ansel duck in surprise because she was not her hummingbird size at all, but her firebird in full glory and power. She streaked up into the sky like a comet, spilling sparks behind her and opening her beak to cry out in joy.

She did a tumbling roll, then returned to backwing into her place before Robin, who looked patiently amused.

They turned next to Rez. "I know that you have always wanted wings," they said simply, and then Rez was unfolding great blueish wings from his sides as he tried to prance in place and look back to see them, all at the same time. He nickered and tossed his head, his golden horn flashing.

"We'll have to teach you how to use those," Henrik

teased him, stepping back from an awkward wingstroke that threatened to knock him over. He had to dodge a kick and turned it into a leap into the air in his gryphon shape, his full size like Tadra's.

Trey barreled after them with a powerful leap into the air, and his wings blocked out the golden sunlight for a moment.

Ansel was watching all of this with amusement, still clearly unsure of his role in this pageant. Tadra had a sudden guess and settled beside him to face Robin with her beak clacking.

"Ansel, crown-for-a-time, you served us better than any of us had any right to ask you to. You were ready to sacrifice the only form you knew for a world you could only imagine. You were able to do what none of the rest of us could."

Tadra shivered back into her human shape solely so that she could clap her hands with glee as she realized what was happening.

Ansel could see that the knights were happy to have—for this short time anyway—their full power back. None of them ever said a word of complaint, but it was a hard fall from mythical hero to mostly human...even if they could still take a tiny, diminished version of their magical shape.

He should know.

Ansel sometimes wistfully remembered the power that had surged through him, and what he'd been for that time. He'd been something greater than human, had a scope of vision and an understanding of all the things that comprised life and reality. Everything had been greater and grander and more glorious.

He wasn't sorry to be human now, but he knew that he'd never be the same again. It was like remembering a few bars of a beautiful song, compared to sitting before a swelling orchestra. It was having the perfect meal and never being able to recreate the mix of spices for it again. The tiny magic he had now was a faint echo of the real thing, and the memory itself was bittersweet.

Ansel bowed his head to Robin. "I was glad to do it."

"For a time, you had all the magic of my world inside you, and that isn't the kind of thing that leaves you untouched," Robin observed. "Like the deep magic left an impression in each of my knights, you have an imprint in your soul."

"I can make faery lights," Ansel said. "But I can't do portals or scrying or change into a magical creature."

"That is because you didn't recognize your magical creature," Robin explained and Ansel had a little thrill of hope.

What would he be? he wondered. A dragon? There already was a dragon. What was left? He felt like he was waiting to be picked for a sports team, and all the best roles were already taken.

The magic settled into him like it was coming home, not the burning rush of trying to control too much, but a measured wave of pleasant power. Ansel realized he'd been bracing himself for pain and let out a breath he'd been holding.

He felt different.

"What am I?" he asked. He didn't appear to be changed in form, but he could feel it, crackling all around him like a friendly campfire. Was he a phoenix? A firebird like Tadra? He craned his head to look behind him and found a confusion of wings.

Tadra was grinning at him, ear-to-ear, with delight and joy.

He still had hands, if slightly *glowy* hands, and legs and, when he tested by touch, he seemed to have his own face.

Fable, Tadra signed at him when he looked at her with all the questions in his face. *You are a fable!*

"It was my power that you took up to save our worlds," Robin said, "and I am afraid that at the time you suffered all of its troubles and enjoyed none of its pleasures."

It wasn't like it had been before, seeing too much, feeling everything without buffer or meter. Ansel could see all the filmy layers of reality, but wasn't overwhelmed by the maddening amount of information. It was the difference between being tumbled to pieces in a vicious ocean curl and floating on a gentle swell of surf.

A fable.

Which meant… "How do I fly?" he asked, after he'd turned in a circle trying to make sense of his wings. Were they feathered? Stained glass? He couldn't tell; they teased at the edges of his vision.

"I'll show you," Tadra said. She leaped into the air and spread sparking wings.

Ansel laughed and followed her without thinking, climbing into the air behind her as easily as if he'd been doing it all his life.

It wasn't like he'd imagined flying as a child, arms outspread until they ached. It was more like running, breakneck, down a hill: thrilling and a little out of control.

The other knights joined them after a few cartwheels and swooping arcs through buttery clouds, even Rez, who had taken to his new wings with the same kind of ease that Ansel had once he trusted them.

The five of them did lazy chase-and-laugh games for a

time, then went separate ways, Tadra's shieldmates returning
to their keys as Tadra and Ansel went to explore what they
could of the renewed faery world that Ansel had built. They
spent some time in the vast canopy of a golden jungle, and
walked over crystal mountaintops that overlooked valleys of
rainbow patchwork, landing at last in a forest grove next to a
floral-scented pool of water floating with glowing orbs.

Beautiful, Tadra signed, when she shifted back to
human form. *You have the eye.*

They made love there, in a carpet of soft, musical
moss, and the very best sound was Tadra's voice, saying his
name with passion.

They drowsed together for a short time before Ansel
began to feel anxious to get back.

"We could stay here," he offered, as he had before. He
traced the long lines of Tadra's body with one hand where
she stretched happily in the moss. It was hard to imagine
returning to mundane life after wonders like this. He sat up
to pluck a bud from the tree beside them, and made it
bloom and change color and chime like bells before he
placed it in Tadra's hair, where it started to purr.

"What is power without purpose?" Tadra said,
sounding perfectly content. "I would be bored with perfec-
tion and ease. I was chosen as a knight because I love challenge and there is none left here."

"My world, on the other hand..." Ansel started wryly.

"*Our* world," Tadra insisted, sitting up. The flower in
her hair grew wings and fluttered away. "We are entangled.
I would love it because you love it, but I have come to see
all of its beauty through your eyes. It is a world worth the
labor."

Ansel leaned in and kissed her. "My friend James thinks
I should run for office."

"Office?" Tadra said in confusion.

"Local assembly or something," Ansel said. "Nothing fancy. It's...just a place to start doing some real good."

"You are good at systems, at solving problems," Tadra agreed, nodding. "And you are already working to change the world. You *should* have a title for your efforts."

"Assemblyman Ansel?" Ansel chuckled. "It's alliterative."

Tadra squinted at him. "Maybe Lord Mayor Ansel," she suggested. "Or Governor."

"I don't know about that," Ansel said. "That's probably setting the bar too high."

"You are the savior of two worlds," Tadra said with a laugh. "You are a shieldmate of the crown! You are a fable! Your ambitions are too humble!"

"You save the faery world just *once*, and all of sudden there are *all* these expectations," Ansel complained in jest. "Anyway, I'm sure that an opponent would have no trouble dredging up bad press about the eccentric Norwegian hippy commune that I run."

They laughed together and plotted a future as the light overhead turned golden and then violet. The song from the moss turned to a musical bass murmur.

"We should go back," Tadra said with a sigh. "The portal will close soon."

"Will you miss it?" Ansel asked anxiously, as they got to their feet. He sometimes worried that Tadra was giving up too much to stay with him, that she would regret leaving faery for a dingy human world.

She put her arms around his neck and kissed him. "No," she said firmly, drawing back. "*You* are my world. You are my key. You are my everything."

Her key, Ansel thought with a jolt of utter contentment. Who needed a title, or a faery world, or fable wings, when he had Tadra in his heart?

I love you, he signed in the small of her back because his mouth was busy.

I love you, she signed back against his shoulders.

They returned to the party again in a flash of fable intention through an instant portal. Ansel had no regrets leaving the power behind as all of them went back through the portal to their own world and let the veil shut again across cries of farewell and promises for the next year.

It was cold and dark, very suddenly, and fireworks exploded overhead as the old year turned into a new one.

Trucker, at Tadra's feet, whined and tucked his tail in. Ansel bent to ruffle his ears. It was slightly weird not to have wings, but he would get used to it again.

"Let's go home," he said, and he walked back to the cars with one hand in Tadra's, a single faery light leading their way.

A THANK YOU FROM ZOE

Thank you for reading! I really loved writing about Tadra and Ansel, and I hope you enjoyed their story.

If you'd like to be emailed when I release my next book, please visit my webpage and join my mailing list, where I have a complete book list by series, or find me on Facebook or Twitter. You are also invited to join my VIP Readers Group on Facebook, where I show off new covers first, and you can get sneak previews and ask questions.

These covers (and the bookmark above) were done by Ellen Million. The ornament on the cover was commissioned specifically for this book from A Touch of Glass. Their webpage is: glass4gifts.com.

I always love to know what you thought – I would love to read your review at Amazon or Goodreads or Bookbub, or email me at zoechantebooks@gmail.com. I love to hear from my readers!

Readers like you are why I write, and I am so grateful for all of your support.

~Zoe

OTHER WORK BY ZOE CHANT

The Royal Dragons of Alaska (writing as Elva Birch): A fascinating alternate world where Alaska is ruled by secret dragon shifters. Adventure, romance, and humor! Reluctant royalty, relentless enemies…dogs, camping, and magic! Start with The Dragon Prince of Alaska.

Shifting Sands Resort (writing as Zoe Chant): A complete ten book series - plus two collections of shorts. This is a thrilling shifter romance set at a tropical island resort. Each book stands alone but connects into a great mystery with a thrilling conclusion. Start with Tropical Tiger Spy or dive in to the Omnibus edition, with all of the novels, short stories, and novellas in my preferred reading order!

A Day Care for Shifters (writing as Elva Birch): A hot new full-length series about adorable shifter kids and their struggling single parents in a town full of mystery and surprise. Start the series with Wolf's Instinct, when Addison comes to Nickel City to take a job at a very special day care and finds a family to belong to. A gentle ice-cream-straight-from-the-container escape. Sweet and sizzling!

Green Valley Shifters (writing as Zoe Chant): A sweet, small town series with single dads, secret shifters, sweet kids, and spinsters. Low-peril and steamy! Standalone books where you can revisit your favorite characters. Start with Dancing Barefoot!

Suddenly Shifters (writing as Elva Birch): A hilarious series of novellas, serials, and shorts set in the small town of Anders Canyon, where something (in the water?) is making ordinary citizens turn into shifters. Start with Something in the Water!

Birch Hearts (writing as Elva Birch): An enchanting collection of short stories and novellas. Unconstrained by theme or setting, each short read has romance, magic, and heart, with a satisfying conclusion. And always, the impossible and irresistible. Start with a sampler plate in Prompted 2 for fourteen pieces of sweet-to-sizzling flash fiction, or dive in with the novella, Better Half. Breakup is a free story!

Made in United States
North Haven, CT
07 November 2021

10922759R10154